Left of the]

CW00587868

by

Monica Tracey

The past isn't dead –
It's not even past.
Wm Faulkner

To my friend, Pauline.
With best wishes,
Monica Tracy (Perry)

Circaidy Gregory Press
Independent Books for Independent Readers

Copyright Information

Printed in the UK
by Berforts Group Ltd

ISBN 978-1-906451-35-6

Published by Circaidy Gregory Press
Creative Media Centre,
45 Robertson St, Hastings,
Sussex TN34 1HL
www.circaidygregory.co.uk

Cover Art
Mediterranean Moon by Catherine Edmunds

Catherine Edmunds is a busy portrait artist and illustrator who has provided cover art for several Earlyworks Press and Circaidy Press publications, including her own poetry collection *wormwood, earth and honey* and her novel *Small Poisons*. Her most recent illustrations can be seen in Daniel Abelman's *ALLAKAZZAM!* and *The A-Z of Punishment and Torture* (BeWrite Books). The cover art for *Left of the Moon* takes its inspiration from the works of Vincent Van Gogh.

You can see more of her work at
www.freewebs.com/catherineedmunds

Monica Tracey writes with sympathy, warmth and wisdom. Her gentle, assured storytelling will please a wide readership, and her composed and confident prose is a joy. She writes about the big and universal themes, love and loss, war and a kind of conditional peace, bringing to these topics two qualities that rarely go together: a depth of experience, and a keen appreciation of life's pleasures and possibilities.

Hilary Mantel, July 2011

Thanks

To my daughter Christine Racciatti for help with research in Abruzzo and in Rome.

To my friend W. for her vivid account of surviving the tornado in the Venetian Lagoon in September 1970. (I have transposed the story to 1943).

To Fred Cooper and his son Pat for use of Fred's memoir "Maybe it's Because" and his citation.

To the War Graves Commission for information on the British Miliary Cemetery on the Sangro.

To Kay, my peerless editor, for tireless help and wise guidance.

Monica Tracey

For Richard and my children

And in memory of
Frederick Douglas Cooper M.M. B.E.M.
1919 - 2007

Prologue

Carrickfergus

When I was small my father and I often walked along the shore between Whitehead and Carrickfergus. We always stopped at a haven that was hidden by rocks from passers by and sheltered from winds off the Lough. He said this was where he found me, a tiny baby wrapped in swans down. Wise-eyed seals with the faces of old men had watched over me and shrieking gulls kept me safe from harm.

We'd sit at the very spot and I'd listen once again to the tale of the tragedy that darkened the life of King Lir whose beloved wife, Niamh, died giving birth to a baby girl. After weeks of mourning, Lir married his wife's sister. At first she loved the king's children but as time went by and she had no children of her own, she grew jealous of the love their father had for them and the poisoned arrow of hatred lodged in her heart. One day she took the children to the shore of the Sea of Moyle where she turned them into swans, condemned to sail for three hundred years on that stormy passage between Ireland and Scotland before regaining their human form. The swans, who still had the power of speech, sang as they sailed the troubled waters of Moyle and the music of their singing was so sweet that those who heard it never desired any other happiness. Even the angels in heaven stopped playing their harps and bent down to listen. After months of searching in every corner of the five kingdoms of Ireland, Lir found his children and learned what their step mother had done to them.

Each time my father told the story of the children of Lir, I waited, wide-eyed, for him to add, "Not everybody knows that there was a fourth swan, even more beautiful than the other three. She was the youngest, no more than a baby, and the most dearly loved of all Lir's children. The poor, distracted man begged his wife to release his children from the spell. This, she said, was not within her power. When the king threatened to kill her, she agreed to release the baby,

1

but on one condition. The tiny swan had to leave her sister and brothers and sail down the coast to..."

"Carrickfergus, Daddy," I would shout, "right here where you found me and you wrapped me in your coat and brought me to Kenmara."

"I did indeed and it was the happiest day of my life. You were the loveliest wee child I ever clapped eyes on. Your hair was spun gold and your eyes as blue as the sky on the day I found you. I called you Isabella, which means beautiful, and I brought you home to live as my wee girl."

He thought the gift of a daughter would make his wife happy.

I did not make her happy and I never dared to ask why.

Chapter One

Kenmara

Time has overtaken me at a gallop. Part of me is still stuck in Monday after the dash from airport to hospital. A head-on collision, they said. Liam was a lousy driver in a hired car. Now it's Thursday. The funeral's been dealt with and my grief and rage at Liam for dying have subsided. I wanted to stay for a while at the cemetery to memorise the position of his grave and say goodbye to him on my own, but my family considered that duty had been done and I was obliged to obey their wishes.

My brother Hugh is driving me, his wife Linda and his daughter Una to Kenmara, the home where I grew up. It is seven years since I was last here. We go down the winding drive to the house, which is hidden from the main road by pines, oaks and elms and arrive at a double-fronted nineteenth century villa, covered with ivy and Virginia creeper. Red and yellow roses are already in bloom in beds below the stained glass windows on either side of the front door. Kenmara is a warm- looking house, substantial and friendly. A home where I should have been happy.

Rose, the senior sister-in-law and wife to my brother John, had decreed that the whole family should assemble, once the main business of the day was dealt with. Our family, the McGlades. Not Liam's. Ma could not be expected to entertain a crowd of common people in her grand house. Ma's world divides into 'people like us' and 'common people' and it was a source of fury and amazement to her that Hugh and I chose our life partners from 'no go' areas of the city. We will be a small gathering: Ma, my two brothers and their wives, me and Una. Hugh's older children, who were press-ganged into coming to the church for the funeral Mass, found urgent reasons to disappear as soon as the service ended

I walk round the house to where the garden slopes towards the Lough, trying to get my head round the fact that Liam, the funny,

3

clever man I married eight years ago, is dead and that all hopes of reconciliation have died with him. There should have been an explosion of grief at his death as there was for Princess Diana, but Liam will be mourned only by his family, by me, and by his girlfriend when she finds out about the accident. Liam was a rabid republican. If he knew I was thinking about him in the same breath as Diana, he'd turn in the grave he has so recently occupied.

At the service the priest urged the congregation to remember Liam's family and his widow in their prayers. Liam's widow! That threw me. Then I thought, my God, could that be me, already dressed for the part in a black suit borrowed from Linda? But widows are elderly women like my mother who embraced widowhood with outstretched arms. Not twenty-seven-year-olds.

The Lough and the Down coast are wrapped in haze and it's as if I'm peering through misted glass at a blurred, though familiar, scene. Today the damp leaves of chestnut, oak and beech trees screen the estate below the garden, giving the illusion that the grounds of Kenmara sweep down to the estuary. A plane from City Airport glides through the grey sky. I wish I was on it and on my way back to London. I'd wanted to leave after Liam's life support was switched off, but in Ireland the rituals of death must be observed. Had I left immediately, his family and mine would have lost face, for a married man's funeral without the presence of the widow would create nearly as much gossip and bad feeling as a wedding without the bride.

Footsteps on the gravel, coming close. I turn. Good God, it's Ma. Under her own steam. No gun pointed at her head. No hand prodding her in the back. She's going to tell me off for insulting her by staying last night with her housekeeper, rather than with her at Kenmara. I should go towards her but my feet have taken root in the soft ground and I'm a six-year-old child waiting for the lash of her tongue. She stands beside me, a frail woman in expensive black. She's aged since I last saw her, still beautiful despite her slowed movements and a new crop of wrinkles that must have cost her hours of anguish and a fortune in beauty treatment.

"Isabel," she says, "I'm sorry about your husband. You didn't have long together."

"Nine years since we met. Nine up and down years." I'm talking to myself rather than sharing my thoughts. "More down than up."

4

I want to ask her to call Liam by his name. Just once, but she has taken my hand. What's come over her? Is she really sorry for me? Is she trying to make up? Whatever the reason, my mother and I are standing close together. My hand has relaxed in hers. Her bony fingers are warming mine, which are meshed through hers. It feels good, though neither of us can find a word to say. I could ask her if she misses Daddy. No. She'd think I'm winding her up.

"That's Cultra over there, if we could see it. Do you know what Cultra means?" I turn to look at Ma. "It means, 'We've got more money than you have.'"

Did Ma and I ever laugh together before? If we did, surely I'd remember.

Rose's shout slices through our laughter.

"Isabel, what do you think you're doing keeping your mother out in the cold? She'll get her death. Come on in at once."

Like guilty lovers Ma and I spring apart and Rose bustles back to the house. Rose is the sort of woman who bustles even when she's sitting still. After seven years I can't help noticing how everyone has aged. Rose's wedding photographs show a handsome, dark-haired woman, almost as tall as John. After her marriage she gave up practising as a solicitor and concentrated on being a perfect mother and a perfect housewife. Flesh has fallen from her face and the hollows under her eyes have darkened. Once inside the house, she pours sherry into five glasses and asks John to propose a toast.

A toast? We've been to my husband's funeral, not a wedding.

I have learned never to question Rose. Who will we drink to? Absent friends? Our dear departed? To Liam's untimely, or timely, death?

"To the family," John says.

We drink without reference to the dead, or to his and Rose's three children in London or Hugh's three, who are anywhere other than Kenmara. My father's absence pervades the house. I expect to hear his booming voice, the sound of his laughter, to hear him cry out, "Isabel, what kept you so long?" I expect him to fill his big armchair, to order John to fill our glasses to the top and say he'll have neat whiskey. I expect him and Ma to find something to bicker about. Anything.

But it is as if he, like Liam, had never existed.

5

Kenmara is a bright house of many windows. On warm days, sunlight dances through most of the rooms but never penetrates the dark brown chill of the dining room or the whiskery shapes in the walnut wood of the sideboard that used to terrify me when I was small.

"Isabel, you have the seat of honour." Rose shows me to the spot she has designated as the head of our round table.

"And I have the honour of sitting beside my beautiful mother." John holds Ma's chair for her to sit. Every ounce of John radiates prosperity, from his graying hair, the jowls of his handsome face to the extra pounds round his middle.

"My mammy says you're adopted. Your big brother's your real daddy," Orla Dolan often said to me.

She was my best friend at primary school. We were both seven years old. I didn't scratch her face or kick her shins. I hoped she was right and John and Rose were my real parents.

"I'd like to propose another toast," John refills the sherry glasses. "To Isabel, to my wee sister. Good to have you at home in your own family."

Ma, Linda and Una say, "To Isabel," and Hugh adds, "To my wee sister."

All eyes are focused on me in that head-nodding, long-faced way that is reserved for the bereaved or the dying. I am no longer an outsider, but a fully paid-up member of the McGlade family. A prodigal daughter, I sit at my mother's table from which Liam had always been happy to absent himself. I smile at everyone, though I feel disorientated. I need to absorb the suddenness and the finality of Liam's accident, his death and burial. But there is no time. Though technically the chief mourner, I have been spurned by my husband's sisters, who wanted me to be excluded from the wake and funeral services, and tolerated by his parents and brother because they had no option but to accept John's offer to pay the funeral expenses.

When I return the smile that softens my mother's stern face I'm telling her how much I need her to love me, to laugh with me, to cherish me like a real mother. I smile at Hugh, whose phone call told me about Liam's accident and who met me at City airport and took me to the hospital. At John, who wrapped his arms around me after Liam was pronounced dead and drove me in pre-dawn drizzle through streets emptied of inhabitants to his home in the suburbs.

6

And I smile my thanks to Rose for welcoming me as she had always done when I was small, for trying to tempt me with lasagna and trifle and for leaving me to pretend I was sleeping. A warm glow spreads through me. The heart of my family is a good place to be.

In my honour we're having an Ulster fry – bacon and egg, black pudding, mushrooms, tomato, fried soda farls and potato bread.

Before being dispatched by Rose to the kitchen, Linda asks, "Would you like one egg or two, Mrs McGlade?" Her husky voice is low and easy on the ear, despite what Ma calls her back-street accent. Ma plays a game of yo-yo with her daughters-in-law. For the moment, Linda seems to be in the ascendant.

"Just give her everything, except the black pudding and she can leave what she doesn't want. Bring John's plate in next. Hugh isn't the only one who needs to work," Rose says.

"I'd really like some black pudding, Linda. It's ages since I tasted it. My father used to have black pudding every Saturday and Sunday."

"Shame about Liam," John says. "Such a waste. A first class brain and a brilliant future."

"He was a nice fellah. Enjoyed a pint and a laugh," from Hugh.

Having paid tribute to their sister's dead husband, my brothers begin to argue. Hugh loses his temper. He tells John he's not in court and he should stop being a bloody know-all. He starts eating from the plate which Linda places before him. Ma assumes her wounded Madonna expression and says he should wait till everyone is served. There are two eggs on her plate, one a picture of milky perfection, the other an overcooked effort fringed with greasy, brown lace.

How long did Liam have, before metal telescoped through metal, glass through glass? The scraping. The din. The car a total wreck and his face unmarked. I had nagged at him to learn to drive. Like my brothers I had a driving licence at seventeen. Where Liam grew up young lads learned to drive by joy-riding.

A telephone shrills close by in the hall.

"I'll get it," Rose carols. "I'll tell whoever it is that it's an inconvenient time."

Rose is a fine woman who belongs to the 'when I open my mouth, let no dog bark,' school of discussion. Her views on politics, religion and the evils of working mothers are stated with the conviction of a Papal dogma. I like and respect her, but always after a short time alone with her I have an urge to cover my head with something thick enough to shield me from the sound of her voice.

Holding the telephone aloft, she comes into the dining room. "It's Grace. I told her we're just going to eat and the men have to get to work."

"Does she know about Isabel's husband?" Ma half-rises and stretches her hand to take the phone.

Before I can say I spoke to Grace yesterday when I was at Minnie's, Rose interrupts, "It's not for you, Rita, love. She wants to speak to Isabel."

As I rise to my feet, a fog of disapproval clots the air around the table. Ma has turned into a Sphinx. Rose tut-tuts. John's mouth flops open. Hugh helps himself to toast, which Linda has buttered for him. Una smiles the eager smile of a young girl trying to please everybody.

I take the phone and go into the hall to speak to my cousin. Grace is the only child of Ma's elder sister, and is usually taken for my mother. She was a rock to me when I was a student in Sussex, especially after my baby died and when Liam left me.

"Isabel, I've been warned not to speak for long," she says. "I can't get Liam's death out of my head. He was a fine man in many ways and very likeable. How are you? How are you coping?"

I tell her about the funeral and the meal to which I must return.

"I'm going to ask you to do something for me. I'm going to Italy on Tuesday and I'd love you to come with me. You'd be doing me a favour. I wasn't looking forward to going on my own and my boys wouldn't be interested. Mamma and I planned this holiday years before she died." She pauses, waiting for me to speak. "Isabel, you don't have to make up your mind now. I'm not putting pressure on you, though I'd love you to come."

I think about my empty house and its memories of Liam. I think about adjusting to a life from which he has gone forever. I think for about five seconds and say, "I'd love to go. Thanks for asking me. Call me tonight in London with the details. Sorry, Grace, I must go back. Everybody's waiting."

8

I return to a table of expectant faces.

"How is Grace?" Ma asks. "Did she know about your husband?"

"She did. I phoned her yesterday from Minnie's." I look at the faces of my family. "She's going to Italy next Tuesday. She's asked me to go with her."

The temperature of the dining room plummets. Ma's knife and fork slip from her hands and clatter on the milky egg on her plate. The yolk busts and spatters the tablecloth.

"Can you get away from work just like that at the drop of a hat? You have had time off already, haven't you?" Disapproval is etched between the furrowed lines on Rose's forehead.

"I think you should go with Grace," offers Linda. "You're great friends with each other and it will help to take you mind off –" she hesitates. She searches the ceiling for words to finish the sentence, "off things."

"Linda's right," says Hugh. "The sun will put the bloom back in your cheeks and all that pasta will fatten you up."

"You don't think it's a bit soon….after Liam, you know, to be going off on holiday? I know you weren't really a couple like John and me but it won't look too good, will it?"

John interrupts before I can reply. "So, Isabel, our cousin wants you to go on holiday to Italy with her. Does she indeed? Maybe Rose has a point. It is rather soon after Liam's death, don't you think? I know Italy well. Wonderful country! I've been to Tuscany, to Rome, Florence, Bologna and Venice and to Sorrento and the Amalfi coast and Sardinia and Sicily, of course."

"Of course! Is there any place you haven't been to, John?" Hugh asks.

"I work hard, I earn my keep and I play hard, Hugh. Maybe you should take a leaf out of my book." John turns to me, ice in his voice. "Does that mean you'll not be staying for a few days with our elderly mother, who would appreciate some time with her daughter?"

Our elderly mother, passive as a statue, is staring at her hands with the surprised concentration of someone who has just discovered an extra finger.

"I'm getting the seven o'clock plane. I'll have to get in touch with the office first thing. I've some leave built up. And I'll have to get ready for the trip." I'm shaking, stammering my defence. I search the blank screen of Ma's face. Our truce is in tatters. "I'll come over and

9

stay a while when I get back from Italy. I'd really like to do that, Ma."

"And where exactly is Grace intending to take you on this jaunt? Is it Tuscany, Umbria or the Venetian Riviera? Perhaps you'd care to enlighten us." John sounds like those lawyers on American television, who know how to tie the accused into knots and trick them into admitting anything. And he's succeeding.

"I...I don't know. She didn't say and I didn't ask. I don't care. I want to get away..." My voice is a mouse squeak. A dying mouse squeak. I look round the table for support. Out of the corner of my eye, I see Ma twisting her napkin, twisting, twisting as though she's programmed to tear it to shreds.

"That sounds great, Isabel," says Linda. "Like those mystery tours we used to go on. Do you remember, Hugh, we all got..."

"My sister is no longer a child, Linda, and as far as we know, she's not embarking on a treasure hunt, as you put it."

Linda winces under the full force of John's glare. Linda is a capable wife and mother. She does the accounts at Hugh's garage and, in emergencies. She puts on overalls and helps with repairs. Feeding times with the McGlades can reduce her to a shuddering pulp.

John takes a deep breath. "Am I expected to believe, Isabel, that you, an educated woman, genuinely don't know where you're going? Surely you asked."

Hugh jumps to his feet. "Don't you shout at Isabel like that, or at Linda."

The insides of my lips are raw and my arms are rigid pokers. I look round the table at my brothers, both ready for a punch up, at Linda cowering beside Hugh, at Rose quivering in disbelief, at Ma, straight-backed and full of hell, who is making her way towards the sitting room. Even Una has stopped smiling.

A fairly normal mealtime at Kenmara. The greater the occasion, the greater the potential for disaster. Birthday parties. Ma's sixtieth.

Her fury when John carried in the cake. She was not a child and did not need any reminder of her age. A shocked ten-year-old, I watched her turn her back on six flickering candles and on the 'Happy Birthday' Minnie's wavering hand had written in pink icing that oozed from a specially bought icing bag.

10

Disaster was stamped in capital letters over family Christmases. The Christmas before I went to university. The giblet Christmas.

The hall, dining room and sitting room were decorated with holly and streamers. Christmas card chains hung across each room on lengths of string. The tree was heavy with lights and chocolate baubles. Piles of presents almost eclipsed the crib beneath it. My brothers, their wives, my parents, their seven grand-children, and I were seated at the extended dining room table. The children had been forbidden by Ma to pull their crackers until the plum pudding had been doused in brandy and flamed. The turkey with its two kinds of stuffing had been allotted – brown and white meat for the men, breast for the females. Daddy dispensed the gravy. Making the Christmas gravy was his annual contribution to cooking for the household – a task which involved many implements, a running commentary, much supping of wine and chaos in the kitchen.

Everyone dutifully said how wonderful the gravy tasted.

Except Ma.

"It tastes of nothing. You left out the giblet stock," she said, damming the flow of gravy from the rest of her meal.

"You've always got to find fault. You saw me simmering the giblets. You complained about the steam."

"Simmering is one thing. Adding the stock's another," Ma jabbed her fork across the table at him.

She left the dining room and returned bearing a saucepan in which boiled giblets lay in a dark brown sludge. Blind to the storm brewing on Jack's scarlet face and the veins bulging on his neck and temples, she held it under his nose. "You didn't add the giblet stock, did you? Go on admit it. Be a man and admit you forgot."

Hugh and the boys got on with their food. Una started to cry.

"Can we go home, Mammy? Can we go home?" Linda's elder daughter whined.

"For God's sake give it a rest, Ma," John shouted. "Who gives a damn about the bloody giblets?"

Stunned for a second, Ma ordered John to apologise for his language. Rose spluttered her shock and disapproval.

"That should stop you complaining." Jack snatched the saucepan *and poured its contents into the gravy boat, splashing the table cloth, Ma's snow-white cuffs and Rose's new-for-Christmas striped dress.*

Ma stormed into the sitting room and settled down for an afternoon's public sulk. Daddy settled down to getting drunk. Before my brothers and their families left, they asked me to accompany them. Ma said no. I would spend Christmas in my own home.

I leave the table.

"I'm going upstairs to change," I announce.

I fetch my hold all from Hugh's car.

As you stand outside a familiar room, about to turn the door handle, you already have a picture in your mind of what you will find inside: furniture in its allotted place, well-known pictures and ornaments. Your fingers feel the fabric of curtains you have closed and opened over the years. You remember smells and sounds – spilled makeup, joss sticks, a creaking floorboard, gulls screeching.

I open the door and my hands shoot to my face. I could have walked into a hotel bedroom. All traces of the years I slept, sulked, studied and gossiped here with friends have been removed. No books or discs, no albums crammed with snaps charting my life in Kenmara. Framed photographs of Daddy and me after my First Communion and on my first day at Infant School have disappeared. My mind's eye sees Ma stripping my room in a fit of temper because I left without saying goodbye to her after Daddy's funeral.

Grow up, Izzy, I tell myself. A woman with her own home has no right to expect her mother to keep a shrine to her adult daughter.

And this is the moment – not after Liam died, not when confronted by the hostility of his sisters, not standing at his graveside – when something inside me snaps. My sense of being drugged vanishes, together with my guilt for upsetting my mother. Choking back sobs rising from the depths of my stomach and wiping an imagined slap from my face, I pull back my shoulders, stand up to my full height and stride from the room.

Liam often reminded me that in my cosseted existence I had never known hunger or cold. I had never known what it was to have a brick or a petrol bomb lobbed through the window. I had never lived with the fear that my home would be burned to the ground.

Agonizing about a mother's indifference was a luxury only the indulged middle classes could afford.

Outside Ma's bedroom I hover, my hand on the door handle, plucking up courage to enter the place forbidden to every member of the family, especially her husband. Sometimes when Minnie was cleaning and when Ma was out, I would creep in and open the wardrobe letting my hands brush against the rough texture of tweed, the softness of wool, the cool rustle of cotton and silk. I would sit at her dressing-table and move the two side mirrors, until my face reflected my face, reflected my face, reflected my face in never ending mirrors. Blood pounds in my ears as I creep into the room, which still smells of Ma's *Je Reviens* and her face powder. A stair creaks. Footsteps stop. I freeze where I sit looking into the mirrors, where glowering reflections of my brother John in the doorway, stare back at me, stare back at me, stare back at me, stare back at me…

"What are you doing here? You know nobody is allowed to go into Mother's room."

"Nothing, just having a look," I mumble and skulk into the passage.

He closes the door. "Don't you think the least you could do is to go down and speak to your mother before you dash off on your foreign adventure?" He turns and waits for me to follow.

All memories of his generosity and kindness fly out the window. One shove in the back would send him hurtling down the stairs, but it would make me miss my flight. I follow meekly behind him.

I can't wait to get away from all this emotion, the anger always on the verge of erupting. Grace is calm. She does not sit in judgment. She is not prone to moods. She is like a sister, the best friend I've ever had.

While we wait for Una to tell Ma that everyone is leaving, the minute hand of the grandfather clock in the wide hall moves from five past, to ten past, to a quarter past. Long enough for other Christmas scenes to slide into my mind.

Christmas mornings. One of my brother's football socks stretched the width of my single bed, big and flexible enough to contain all sorts of odd shaped things. In the toe, always, a fifty pence piece, a Clementine and a packet of gold wrapped chocolate coins. Everything else was wrapped and sealed with sellotape. The excitement of tearing off Christmas paper, my fingers guessing, or trying to guess, the contents that have become a jumble of items which changed over the years. Colouring books, novels, pencils, crayons, sachets of shampoo, card games, hair bands, slides, curly wurlies, a diary or calendar, notelets and best of all, each year a small doll in national costume. An Irish colleen in green dress and red shawl, Scottish and Welsh dolls, a Flamenco dancer, a white-faced Japanese girl in red kimono, a cream fan clutched in her hand, a pair of Austrian dolls, the boy wearing leather trousers and a Tyrolean hat, the girl in a leather skirt and white blouse and plaits that reached her waist. Ma said they were flaxen-coloured.

Long after I stopped believing in Santa Claus, I used to stay awake waiting for my parents to tiptoe into my room, my father hardly able to hide his excitement and Ma ordering him to get out before he wakened the child. I waited still as a statue, eyes closed, heart pounding till she came and stood at the top of my bed. I waited for the light touch of her hand stoking my hair, before she bent over and kissed my cheek. Not the lips-sealed-tight graze on my skin of her perfunctory Christmas morning greeting, but the warm lingering of a mother's lips and her whispered, "Happy Christmas, little Isabel."

Another three or four minutes pass. Long enough for us to pace up and down; to look at watches; to worry about missing a plane, being late for an appointment; getting caught up in rush hour traffic. Long enough for me to think about going to my nearly seventy-eight-year-old mother to say goodbye as a daughter should. I do not go, lest her aloneness and her unspoken blackmail force me to abandon my holiday with Grace. Just now I need to escape the engulfing memories of Kenmara and Liam. Grace is calm, She listens and is not judgmental. She faces the future with hope, whereas Ma's head is turned towards an unforgivable past.

I kiss the air on either side of Ma's face and mutter something about seeing her soon. Hugh promises to return, after he closes the garage, to put a washer on the kitchen tap and replace the hall light bulb.

14

John's Jaguar purrs down the drive. Ma waves a limp wrist as the rest of us climb into Hugh's Ford. She pauses for a moment in the doorway, goes back into the house and closes the door.

Chapter Two

I went with Hugh, Linda and Una in his clapped-out car, which he admitted was a poor advertisement for a garage owner. He took the road from Carlisle Circus to the Lower Falls. There were empty spaces where rows of grey houses used to huddle. Low rise homes had sprung up, their flowering gardens looking ill at ease in their drab surroundings. The graffiti had been updated and the sky was still grey.

"How did you think Ma looked?" Hugh asked. "You'll have seen a big change in her."

"She's become an old woman since I last saw her, and even more moody. I couldn't make her out. One minute she seemed really pleased to see me. The next minute she'd closed up like a clam and couldn't wait to see the back of me."

"I don't think that had anything to do with you. She's told me a few times she hates Rose bossing her about in her own house," Linda turned round to look at me. "John should have a word with her."

Hugh slowed down at traffic lights. "Linda, you know as well as I do that John's not remotely interested in poor old Rosie. He's got better fish to fry."

I leaned forward, annoyance at Ma instantly put on hold.

"That's nothing but talk and you shouldn't spread gossip about your brother," Linda said.

"You know what they say about no smoke without a fire." A grin spread across Hugh's face. He stopped the car at his garage and got out.

"Does Ma know about this?"

"Of course she doesn't. Besides, she wouldn't hear a word against John."

"Or against either of her sons." Linda slid into the driver's seat. "After we drop Isabel at the airport I'll take Una home and come straight back here and see what needs to be done."

"She's coming back to keep an eye on me, to make sure I'm not at the bookies." Hugh kissed his wife's head and said to me. "Keep in touch with us, Isabel, there's a good girl." He half turned to go, then he said, "Don't worry about Ma. I call in three or four times a week to fix a fuse or whatever's bothering her. She gets into a panic if something stops working. She misses Daddy. She's lost without him."

"But ...but they didn't get on. They were always arguing about something."

"That's what kept them going. They rubbed along together all right, especially after you left. They'd no option," Hugh laughed and said goodbye.

As Linda parked the car at the airport she said, "Rose is good to your Mammy, Isabel. She has her over every Sunday for her dinner and she cooks meals for her freezer. Your Mammy gets wee notions about people. The latest is that Rose is going to put her in a home. Next week she could have it in for me."

I passed through the baggage scan and body search and into the departure lounge where dark-suited business men, each a clone of the others, talked into mobile phones as though their lives depended on the conversations that engrossed them. Families of young children squabbled. Mothers doled out crisps and sweets and pleaded for peace. One father threatened his screaming son with a smack. A little girl sitting opposite smiled at me. A typical Irish child. Freckled face, black curly hair and blue eyes. Eight years old or nine. Maybe I was staring too intently, for the child's mother drew her daughter into the circle of her arms. A blush flooded my face and neck. I stood up and went to the snack bar.

I had left this airport many times without a backward glance. Until today I never felt the loneliness my friends described each time they left Ireland. Loneliness for what? For a place I called home, where I grew up, where I didn't have to explain who I was, where I spoke with the accent of all around me. But now, with Liam and my father gone, I'd lost my bearings and the ties that grounded me to this city had broken loose, leaving me adrift.

Liam and my father are buried here, Liam in the overgrown cemetery at Milltown where knee high weeds and grasses colonised pathways, where the feet of mourners squelched over dense green or tripped on hidden gravestones, where inscriptions carved on granite and marble headstones can no longer be read. If I ever visit Milltown again, I could search in vain half way down the hill on the right for Liam's grave The encroaching wilderness will have swallowed it together with the graves of all those interred around him. And no visible memory will remain of the murder and mayhem the place has witnessed.

My father lies in Carnmoney in the double plot he bought for himself and Ma. John took me there yesterday, before we went to Minnie's house, to see the headstone erected in memory of John McGlade, who died on the ninth of April 1997, and the blank space for Ma's relevant details.

I had gone with Daddy years ago to visit the plot shortly after he bought it.

"It's near the entrance so your mother can see what's going on and she'll be able to keep an eye on everybody." He laughed and added, "Mind you, she doesn't allow me to share her bed, so she's bound to kick up a hell of a fuss when she finds out she's going in there beside me."

So what was I lonely for? A sense of belonging? The low hills around the Lough, the love Minnie showered on me last night when I stayed with her, or was it the dread of returning to a house to which Liam would never return? An end to hoping we might get back together, an end to aching for his touch that used to send desire coursing along every nerve of my body?

Liam, who said life should be lived as though we were immortal, had been cruelly cheated. Death happened to old people, to drug addicts, to smokers whose lungs were kippered in cigarette smoke, to drunks with poisoned livers, not to a fit, athletic man of thirty-three, a man full of promise. Liam was fire and passion, a thundering presence. A man like him should not have been closed down in stages, silently as a pebble dropping into an ocean. He should have died as he lived: noisily, on his feet, taking on the world.

The figure I saw last night in his parents' front room was a waxwork model of the man I married. New grey suit, white shirt, blue tie. Patent shoes with polished soles. Wild hair gelled and lifeless as a wig. I memorised his sharp features, lips pursed and purple and thought I should have held on to the memory of his head and my head on the same pillow in the thrumming silence of the Royal Victoria Hospital. Mourners streamed into the airless room,

18

paid their respects and left. Rims of cups and glasses on the china cabinet. Pollen from the bowed stem of a lily staining a white tray-cloth. Icicles growing on candles. Pools of wax in saucers. The raw grief of his sisters. His mother staring into her son's coffin. Her cough hacking through the drowsy rhythms of the Rosary. Her hand damp and limp in mine. The scent of lilies mingling with the smells of beer, cigarettes, stewed tea and the sweat of tightly-packed bodies.

What had he been thinking about before the crash? The trip he'd been planning to the Glens and the Giant's Causeway to banish his father's fears that his son had grown away from his roots and his family? An outing for his mother and sisters? The presents he would buy for them?

I was a second year student at Sussex University and pulling pints in the East Slope bar when Liam blazed into my life. I saw him scythe through welcoming hands and join a group of lecturers. He was about my size, dark-haired, low-browed and crumpled-faced. No oil painting, as Ma would say later. His movements were quicksilver, darting to where someone called him, hand outstretched, head thrown back when he laughed, livening each group where he stopped, downing pints as if he hadn't had a drink for a month.

He ordered a round at the bar and when I repeated the order, he asked, "What's a nice Ulster girl like you doing in a place like this?"

He told me he was from the Ardoyne in Belfast and was lecturing in twentieth century history. His eyes widened when he heard I lived on the Antrim Road. He said he wouldn't hold that against me. We talked till my boss tapped my shoulder and pointed to the crowd clamouring for attention.

"Can I walk you home?" Liam asked and we both laughed at the familiar, old-fashioned request. We took the long way to Bright Helm, the residence I shared with five students, and arranged to walk in the woods close to the campus the following day after his two o'clock lecture.

Those early months with Liam were the happiest I had ever known. What would have separated us in our home city drew us together in Sussex. It was as if I had been half asleep all my life and Liam wakened me into joyous living, as if I had been shallow breathing before I met him and suddenly my lungs filled to brimming with the sea air of Sussex. Liam grabbed at life. He had mapped out where he was going and I floated beside him, carried along by his love and his enthusiasm. He said I made the sun shine brighter. He said I lightened his soul and, best of all, I made him feel six feet tall. There never was such an autumn. The scent of crushed grass and the mushroom smell of our love-making. Liam's sinewy body, his weight light on me, leaves crackling beneath us. A squirrel tall on hind legs, paws clutching acorns. Shafts of sunlight through a russet and brown ceiling. Running into the sea at Brighton, brushing sand from shivery skin. Kissing the salt taste from each other's lips. Wonder-filled days. The fun of it. The devil-take-tomorrow joy of it. Springtime coves, long grass under a starry sky, the scent of summer in the air. Tramping over the Downs and along the shore. The warmth of my single bed.

There is a fragile time when the needs and affection of lovers are evenly balanced. In the early weeks, Liam was consumed with me and grudged the time I spent apart from him, but as time passed I became 'the more loving one'. By summer the scales had tipped and the love I thought would last forever had become a burden to him. If I had not been pregnant, our affair would have burned itself out and we would have drifted apart. Liam would have taken a post at City University and I would have moved with my friends into a house in Lewes Road, a short walk through the Level to the pubs and shops in Brighton. Instead, we got married in Catford in South London with my friend Marie and one of Liam's colleagues as witnesses. Ma's comment on our union was, "Marry in haste, repent at leisure."

And morning sickness, varicose veins and a swollen belly turned the lively girl Liam met in October into a self-pitying heap. Liam's bearings were fixed. He had mapped out each phase of his life. His plans and ambitions had not included a dead baby and a wife off her head on Prozac. If he wanted to bring me to my senses he would say, "You know your problem, Isabel. You're just a pretty face," or "There's less to you than meets the eye."

A cloud fell on me as I boarded the plane to Gatwick. The last time I flew into City Airport was on the day I learned that Daddy had been in hospital for two weeks. He'd had a stroke and was in a coma. My grief at the thought of not being in time to say goodbye to my father was poisoned by anger at my mother. Her timing had been as deadly as it was effective. She had waited until Daddy lost consciousness before letting me know he was in hospital.

John was waiting for me. He put his arms around me and stepped back when I laid into him like a fury, or a ten-year-old brat.

"Why did nobody tell me Daddy was in hospital? He won't know I came to see him. He'll think I didn't care. Daddy loved me and I loved him. You could have phoned. Hugh could have told me, You…"

"Shut up, will you, and grow up. This isn't about you, Isabel. It's about the family." John choked back sobs that racked his body "Daddy died two hours ago. We were all with him. He didn't regain consciousness after the stroke." His voice broke as he put his hands on my shoulders. His tone was gentler when he said, "I've lost my father as well. So has Hugh, and Ma's lost her husband. You needn't curl your lip like that. They'd been married for forty-five years and now she's alone. She's the one we have to think about. Don't you forget that."

John took my hand when we went to view my father's body. Ma had surrounded herself with a wall of silence and I didn't dare ask why she had not let me know that Daddy was in hospital. It suited me to think it was her revenge for all the times Daddy refused to toe the line and for the united front which he and I had often presented to her.

I had passed the eleven plus and assumed I would go to the local convent with my friends from junior school. The fourth of September approached and all my friends' mothers had already bought the green uniform of our new school. The day before term started, Daddy agreed to confront Ma.

"I would like to see how Isabel looks in her new uniform," he announced.

"Since when have you been concerned with what Isabel wears? You'd be better off mending the fence at the road and mowing the lawn than interfering in my business. I don't need you telling me my duty. Or her."

We both knew Ma was methodical. She would have bought the uniform but was not prepared to discuss the matter with him.

Discuss!

Insults were batted back and forth between them. Daddy should remember whose name was on the deeds of the house. He was no more than a lodger and if he didn't stop using filthy language he would find himself on the street. He said marriage to her was like being handcuffed to the devil. He swore he would kill her if he stayed another moment in the house and stormed off in his car.

Game, set and match to Ma.

She woke me very early next morning and told me to put on a grey and white striped blouse, a grey skirt, royal blue jumper and grey socks. A label with my name had been sewn on each article and on all the clothes already packed in a suitcase.

"You are going to go to the school I went to when I was your age. I know you will like it," she said as she buttoned the blouse.

Too sleepy to think and surprised by Ma's friendly and confidential manner, I did as I was told. Hugh drove Ma and me to a convent on the Antrim coast where I was deposited. That night, in a cubicle in a dormitory with about twenty girls, I cried myself to sleep. Sister Kevin, a very small nun who supervised the first years, told me it was not unusual to feel lonely on leaving home for the first time. She gave me a medal of the Sacred Heart and said I would soon make friends and settle down to life as a boarder. What I remember of my brief time at boarding school is bewilderment and desolation. Was this building on the edge of the Atlantic an orphanage where I was to be locked up forever because I was a sinner? Would I never see my Daddy and my brothers and friends again? Had my mother, like the wicked stepmother in 'The Children of Lir' found the perfect way to banish me from her sight and from my father?

Two weeks later I was summoned from class to the headmistress' office. Though Sister Paula never raised her voice, her paper-thin presence in a long white tunic and black veil cast a chill over the assembly hall and any classroom she entered. Was I going to be punished for talking during lessons or slouching in chapel, or had something terrible happened to Daddy?

My knees stopped knocking when I saw him sitting in Sister Paula's office. He got to his feet and threw his arms around me "Isabel, Isabel, my own wee girl," he said and I blushed to see him wipe his eyes with a crumpled handkerchief.

22

"Sit beside your father, Isabel. He has driven up from Belfast because he is lonely without you and wants to take you home with him." Sister Paula bared her teeth in a brisk, let's-get-this-over-and-done-with smile. "We will be sorry to lose you as I have good reports of you, but I cannot go against a father's wishes."

Before I had time to absorb Sister Paula's words, Daddy spoke in a quavering voice, which I knew he was putting on to impress.

"As you can see, Sister, I am an old man, maybe far too old to have a child as young as Isabel. Not a day goes by that I don't thank God for my beautiful daughter. But I have to ask you, Sister, how many years do I have left to enjoy her company before God calls me?" His charm could melt a glacier and he knew it. He paused to study the effect he was having on the headmistress. She could have been a statue carved from ice. "You, of all people, will understand why I cannot bear to be parted from Isabel."

Part of me wanted a hole in the floor to open up and swallow me and the other part noticed the slight quivering of Sister Paula's transparent nose.

In the dormitory I threw my belongings into my suitcase and hurried down the stairs, terrified Daddy would have left without me. We had steak and chips, followed by chocolate and vanilla ice cream in a restaurant on the sea front. He was delighted with his performance at the convent and I hadn't the heart to tell him I had wanted to curl up and die.

As we approached Belfast, my mind turned to Ma and my heart to putty. What would she do when she saw me? Would she return me to boarding school like a parcel delivered to the wrong address and what would she do to Daddy?

He took a long slug from his hip flask, passed me a bag of eclairs and said, "Leave your mother to me. I'm your father and I decide where you live. Have a handful of sweets and forget about her."

Outside Kenmara, he emptied the flask in one gurgling swallow, took my hand and led me into the house Ma greeted our appearance in the sitting room with stunned amazement, followed by a shouted tirade. Who did he think he was to countermand her decision concerning my education? He was to turn around, deliver me straight back to the convent and take himself off wherever the hell he wanted, for he was not welcome in her home.

Daddy poured himself a tumbler of whiskey, motioned me to sit beside him on the sofa and forestalled Ma as she geared up for her next attack.

"I'll tell you who I am. I am your husband and Isabel's father and if anyone leaves this house it will be you, for you are an unfit mother for my child." I was used to my parents' screaming matches, none of which Daddy seemed to win. But this time, his voice, loud but calm, drowned Ma's reply. "Against my better judgement, I agreed to marry you and many a time I've regretted that decision and I've wanted to clear out and never catch sight of you again for as long as I live. In fairness, you gave me three fine children any father could be proud of and I am grateful for them." He talked on through Ma's splutterings and fury. "But I will never forget coming home on Minnie's day off to find you had strapped my eighteen-month-old daughter in her cot so that you could drink tea and play cards in the garden with your cronies." He paused and continued to speak more quietly, but with nail-hitting emphasis, "You tied down a helpless child, your own daughter, no more than a baby, and left her crying and scared out of her wits." He had brought up that incident on other occasions, never with a passion that sounded completely genuine. "Let me tell you this straight, Missus, I would not have it on my conscience to leave Isabel in your care without me to protect and look out for her."

Daddy had a way with words but I didn't think he was capable of stringing so many together before Ma shouted him down. I saw she was winded and her weakness made me strong. Her subsequent ranting and abuse passed over my head. I moved a fraction closer to Daddy. He squeezed my hand. This was one fight Ma had lost.

That night I heard Daddy stop outside my door. He knew I was crying, though I wasn't making a sound.

"What's wrong, Isabel?" He wiped away my tears with the corner of a sheet. "Don't cry, child. You're home again. Safe and sound. Can I get you anything?" he whispered.

"I want my mammy," I sobbed. "I want my mammy."

"Your mammy's downstairs, Isabel. Will I get her for you?"

"I don't want her, I want my real mammy. I want my real mammy."

"Oh, Isabel, my little child, I'm sorry."

I pressed a dry edge of the sheet into his hand.

The plane left the runway and flew down Belfast Lough. My eyes searched for Kenmara but low cloud had blotted out the upper slopes of land that rises from the shore. I remembered how Liam had summed up my parents after his first visit to Kenmara. Ma had been in full mistress-of-the-manor mode and Liam's Ardoyne accent had got thicker by the minute.

"Your Da's a good sort, one of the best, but your Ma," he shook his head, "she's a right bad-tempered old witch and she really thinks she's a cut above the rest of us." After pondering for a minute or two, he said, "Mind you, Isabel, it can't be easy for her with you and Jack all lovey-dovey together and ganging up on her."

When I protested, he patted my knee and said, "Think about it. An outsider can see things you don't want to see."

The day of Liam's burial was not about my mother. It was about his parents clinging to each other in Milltown cemetery, where their family and the McGlades had faced each other across their son's open grave like armies about to engage in battle. His father wore a navy suit and crumpled white shirt, his mother a shapeless black coat and a hat that hid her face. Before Liam's doctorate was conferred, he had sent money to his parents to buy new clothes for the ceremony.

"Don't get no more degrees, son, or you won't want nothing to do with us," his father said to him when we met up with Liam in the university grounds, while his mother lit a cigarette and inhaled smoke into her one remaining lung as if she was breathing oxygen.

The day of Liam's burial was about the stricken faces of his sisters, who blamed me for taking their brother from them and who had turned their backs when I tried to speak to them before the church service. It was about their tears running through black mascara and a thin, cold rain dampening the soil their brother Kevin had cast on the coffin. It was about the words of the burial service that were muffled by the sound of an engine left running in one of the funeral cars. It was about the family returning home to the finality of their loss.

But try as hard as I could to dislodge her, Ma stuck like an ache in the front of my head and would not be dislodged. Our short-lived closeness after the funeral. Her swift reversal to the unreachable woman I grew up with.

Sometimes we can trace an event that changed our lives back to a precise time and say, "That's it. That's when it happened." Like that Wednesday at half-past four outside Charing Cross Station when Liam and I bumped into a colleague of his called Annie, a petite, dark and rather intense woman who greeted me politely, while all the time her eyes flicked to some unseen presence over my shoulder. No warning bells rang out. No sixth sense told me to beware. But when, months later, Liam said he was moving in with Annie, I conjured up in vivid Technicolor every detail of our meeting. A hot July afternoon, a scarlet-faced taxi driver, his two passengers wearing vivid green and red saris. A group of noisy teenagers in Arsenal shirts pushing past. A thin, young man selling *The Big Issue*, sweat flowing into a matted beard And my replacement, bright brown eyes, cropped hair, mobile lips, her skin pale and flawless, neat in a blue and white striped shirt and white jeans. Three minutes shop talk between her and Liam before her 4.45 appointment.

Grace's phone call! Was that such a moment?

Until I said I was going to Italy with Grace, John had fussed over me as if I was the lost sheep returned to the fold. And he could not have been more generous. Even Ma had visibly thawed. I replayed the scene, shot by shot.

I burst in to the dining room, excited by the prospect of a holiday with Grace. Sledgehammer silence. Ma clutching her heart. Her cutlery bouncing from plate to floor. Pretending not to be involved and all the time twisting her napkin into knots. Rose's predictable whine. John interrogating me as if I was a criminal and he was God Almighty. Me stumbling and stuttering like an idiot. Ma stomping off clutching her chest and nobody giving a damn about her. Me so pissed off, I hardly said goodbye to her.

Weeks would elapse before I found out the reasons for my family's reactions; before I learned how our time in Italy would alter both Grace's life and mine, or the effect it would have on Ma, on my brothers and their families.

26

"We will shortly be landing at Gatwick. Please make sure all seat belts are fastened."

Only five days, four whole days before I would go to Italy, where I would put the sadness of Liam's death behind me and enjoy whatever Grace had lined up for us. I would phone my friend Marie as soon as I got home. She had known Liam for almost as long as I had. She would listen and advise me. She had sat beside me at our first lecture at university and told me her grandparents were Irish, Indian, Jamaican and Mexican.

"I can't believe I'm a student at Sussex University and I'm sitting in a lecture theatre. A lecture theatre," she repeated and as she rolled each syllable over her tongue her lovely face glowed with wonder. "Nobody in my family went to a grammar school before me. I heard some of the girls in my class talking about going to university. I was eleven. I'd no idea what a university was but I decided, that if that was where my classmates wanted to go, so did I. And here I am, in a room like a cinema. In Sussex University. Can you believe it?" Marie's wide brown eyes questioned me. Her small hand clutched my arm.

My parents and I had assumed that I would go to university. Fees would not be a problem.

"You see," Marie said, "If you have clear aims in life, you're half-way to achieving them."

She left Sussex with a first in English. She loves her job as head of English in a City Academy and adores her two small daughters. I left when I was six months pregnant with nothing.

As the plane touched down I made a mental list of what I wanted from life:

1. Children
2. A man to father them.
3. To finish my M.B.A. in the autumn and get a more demanding and better paid job.
4. To have a good relationship with my mother.

I arrived at Brockley to a scarlet-streaked sky and to the warmth of a London evening in June.

"A'right Izzy, where you been?" shouted Junior from across the road, while he danced to music blasting from his car. "Betty said you was away."

"I've been to Ireland, Junior. Say hello to your mum for me."

"You oughta say where you was going. She was worried when she didn't see you."

When you live on your own, no one clears the mess you leave behind. Crumbs and scraps of bread lie stale and undisturbed on the breadboard; unwashed plates and cups wait in the sink.

Flowers withered in smelly vases; letters lay scattered over the mat in the hall and dust had been falling steadily for days. My answer machine showed six messages. I'd listen to them in the morning. Just then I needed to enjoy the peace of my house, the peonies and early roses in the garden, the sound of an invisible train in the cut.

There's something insistent about a telephone cutting through silence.

"Izzy, where were you? You never told me you were going away. I was worried sick about you." Glynnis, my next door neighbour, banged an accompaniment on the wall as she spoke. "Where were you? I've no milk. Haven't had a cuppa since morning."

"I'll get you some from Cost Cutters, Glynnis. I need some myself. Won't be long."

Carton in hand, I rang her bell and announced myself to the white shape bobbling behind frosted glass. I waited for the safety chain to slide from its sheath and the door to open. Glynnis, in a white satin housecoat, pulled me inside, doubled-locked the door and led me into her kitchen. Though she had become more hunched since Liam and I came to Brockley six years previously, she was still a pretty woman whose unlined face showed little sign of the poverty and hardship of her childhood in Merthyr, or the ill-treatment she had suffered from her late husband.

"He wasn't up to much, that husband of yours." Her voice rose in my defence when I told her about Liam's death. "Too full of himself by far. You were too good for him, Izzy. Far too good. Our mam said Ted wasn't fit to lick the dirt off my shoes and she was right."

Then she told me about finding her Ted lying dead beside her, still warm and twice as ugly.

28

"I nearly did myself a mischief forcing the bugger's arms and legs into clean pyjamas. Then I changed the pillow cases, couldn't manage clean sheets with him sprawled all over the place, and I had to vacuum through before I called the doctor. Wasn't going to have people talking about me, was I now?"

As I was leaving she said, "You're like a daughter to me, Izzy. You must always tell me if you're going away. A young girl on her own like you could be murdered in this city and nobody would know for months."

She kissed me and watched till I was safely inside.

"Why can't we go back to when we were happy, before Grania died?" I used to ask Liam.

"Because you can't wipe out what's happened. You and I are poison to each other. You'll only be happy when I'm dead."

Clinging to the edge of the double bed I had shared with him, I added another item to the list I made on the plane.

Someone to hold me, to ease me into sleep.

Chapter Three

Kenmara – Rita

I wave goodbye to the two cars disappearing up the drive and go back inside. The dishwasher churns and putters and my empty house settles into its quiet rhythms after the noise and turmoil of my family's reunion. Una offered to stay the night with me but I don't want to inflict my worries and bad temper on her. There's nothing the matter with me. Lots of people years younger than me are more forgetful. I'm in perfect health, mentally and physically, and I'm not having anybody saying otherwise. The family like to exaggerate the turn I had last year and they talk as if I'm about to peg out any minute. Well, I won't give them the satisfaction. I take my pills every day and I'm as fit as any one of them. I don't want to think about what happened to me this morning before John picked me up. I was flustered. That's the only explanation I can give, plus the fact that I most definitely did not want to go that funeral, but John insisted. To show family solidarity, he said. In recent years I find it easier to give in to him than have a row that he's guaranteed to win.

I might as well admit what's really bothering me, that is apart from Grace asking Isabel to go to Italy instead of me. I've been trying to put the stupid incident out of my head all day, telling myself it was just a blip that could happen to anyone. That's all very well, but how many times have you heard about a perfectly sane woman finding a teabag in her sleeve? I should have stuck with loose tea instead of the floor-sweepings they stick into bags. It's Rose's fault. She said teabags would be easier for me and she put a packet in the cupboard. I find it always helps to blame somebody else!

This morning after breakfast, sitting in this very chair, that's what I found in my sleeve. A teabag. A dry teabag. My hands shook as I fumbled to put it in the tin marked TEA and take a tissue from the box marked TISSUES. Maybe finding a teabag in your sleeve is no big deal and I should forget about it. The thing is, I've always had a great memory. Whenever there's an argument about the past, I'm always right. I can recite every line of *The Highwayman, Horatius, Lord Ullin's Daughter* and all the miracles in the New Testament. I know the dates of the Tudor and Stuart monarchs, the towns of all the counties of Ireland and England and I can sing by heart songs that I learned sixty-five years ago. So why can't I remember putting a teabag in my sleeve?

If I'm not careful, I'll talk myself into my dotage. It's much safer to focus on Isabel and Grace. Anger gives me a chance to blow off steam, whereas worry is like a knife tearing at my insides. Many would say my daughter was right to shake the dust of Kenmara from her feet. Still, she shouldn't have humiliated me by staying with Minnie Burns at a time when families are supposed to present a united front. Maybe I didn't need to tell Isabel when I saw her outside the church that she looked as if she was in the last stages of consumption. Did I want to punish her? To make her feel bad? I don't know. There are no back doors in me. I pride myself on saying what I think, though there are those that don't like to hear the truth about themselves. Besides, a mother should be able to say what she likes to her own daughter. That doesn't hold in my case. Considering the way I've treated Isabel, I'm lucky she bothered to come here today. Why don't I admit that I had hoped, even planned, to have a few days with her to explain why I treated her so badly? To ask her forgiveness.

I look out at the dreary day. When Jack was alive I'd see him pottering about, pruning, cutting, dead-heading. Always busy. His day full. I resented his busyness. His hands full of muddy onions, buckets of potatoes, flowers for all seasons.

I go to the front door. The drive is empty. It will stay empty till Hugh comes this evening. Everyone says how lucky I am to be shielded from the hum of parents taking children to school, from the squealing and revving of traffic on the Antrim Road. Shielded from life. When you're old, privacy can be a prison. A slow and a lonely death. The truth is I miss Jack. I miss finding fault with him. I miss the rows I provoked without reason. The laughs we had, usually at his expense. I miss him mending fuses, stopping the overflow, doing the hundred and one jobs I took for granted. I miss the space of his big feet. His muddy boots. His smell of the earth and ripe tomatoes. Him reading out bits of the Irish News to me. I complained about that as well. Jack was a man born to be happy. That was hard for a woman with my nature to bear. Right now I'd give a lot to hear him clumping into the kitchen, to yell at him for leaving the back door open, for trailing dirt over the floor. I'd give a lot to start over again.

Everything was going well today. We were a family at last, me and my three children, till Grace phoned. John refused to believe Isabel didn't know what part of Italy she was going to. I believed her. Isabel's headstrong. She acts first and thinks later, like the way she broke Jack's heart plunging into marriage with a man she hardly knew. That husband of hers may have been a Doctor of Philosophy, but I'll say this and I'll say no more, "You can take a man out of the slum, but you can't take the slum out of the man."

I was angry with Grace and I still am. She has had everything life could offer and she chose Isabel, my own daughter, to go to Italy with her instead of me. She owes me. I welcomed my sister, Kate, her English husband and Grace to Kenmara every summer when they came to see our Ma and Pa. Kate wasn't slow to criticise the way I looked after them and tell me what to do. I had them year in, year out, Pa wetting himself, the police finding Ma in her nightdress wandering down the Antrim Road like a demented bat. Give Jack his due, he did a lot for Pa, playing cards with him, taking him for walks and to the pub, but a man couldn't be expected to clean the mess in his father-in-law's trousers. Now, could he?

Minnie used to bake cakes and make special roast dinners for Kate and her husband at a time when meat was still rationed in England and they left with joints of beef and lamb, sausages, fruit-cakes and soda bread. A fat lot of thanks I got. It never occurred to Grace, or her mother, to invite me on the trip they had been planning to Italy, the one that was cancelled when Kate had her first stroke. When they first mentioned it I was sure I was included, if only to thank me for all I'd done for them. If only to give me a break. I assumed she would take me after Kate died. Just another slap in the face from my selfish family. As for Isabel, when all is said and done I'm still her mother, as John reminded her.

I really envied my sister's closeness to Grace. More like friends than mother and daughter. It was easy for Kate. A hard-working husband who thought the world of her and their daughter, instead of the sponge I'd been lumbered with. Kate was very secretive, kept her private life close to her vest. For all I know, she and her husband could have been fighting like polecats behind closed doors. I shouldn't laugh, though I'd like to think her marriage wasn't as perfect as she would have us believe.

The trouble is I'm a nasty, jealous, old woman, expecting everybody to dance attendance on me and taking the huff when I'm ignored. John's always gadding off to play golf in Florida, or in South Africa and places I've never heard of and it never occurred to Linda or Hugh to take me with them to Majorca last year.

My only trip abroad was a pilgrimage to Lourdes fifteen years ago, where I had to share a room with a holy Mary from the Falls Road. Her breath was poison and she'd a tongue that could cut corn. When she wasn't tearing the other pilgrims apart, she was muttering the Rosary and there was no rest from her at night. The stuff she came out with shocked me at first. Then it entertained me. It was more like sharing a room with a low-life prostitute than the deputy head of a big school. I used to watch helpers hauling her into the healing water of the grotto and it wouldn't have bothered me if they had let her drown and I could have a good night's sleep. You're probably thinking that the pilgrimage didn't do me much good and you'd be right.

I go into the garden. A breath of air might stop me brooding. No wonder I forget things. My brain is too crowded, too anxious. A plane rises across the Lough and soars into the sky. Before long, another plane will take my daughter out past Whitehead, Carrickfergus and the villages along the estuary. I wonder if she'll cast a glance at Kenmara or will she be glad to turn her back on it and on me. I love this view at every hour of the day and in all weathers. Sometimes in the morning the Lough is a river of gold. Quiet days when the water and skies are still. The sound of waves crashing in a storm, hurling pebbles on the shore and the walkway.

Neither of my daughters-in-law is fit to be mistress of Kenmara. I'd rather the house burned down or fell into the sea than think of Rose adding pine extensions, conservatories with Velox windows and blinds; turning the lawns into concrete parking space. As for Linda, she's fine in her semi-detached in Andersonstown with her trashy ornaments and framed photos of that huge family of hers. Don't get me wrong. Linda's all right and she would follow my written instructions to the letter, but the very thought of her brothers and sisters and all their brood rampaging through Kenmara gives me palpitations.

It's Rose who worries me. I know her game. Convince everybody, including me, that I'm past it, not fit to be on my own. Then she'll move into Kenmara to look after the doddering mother-in-law, and before I can turn round, I'll be shipped off to some nursing home. I've seen those places. I know what they're like, the stink of urine and boiled slops. Old folk pushing trolleys like dolls' prams along corridors and they're the lucky ones. Two weeks in a circle of dribbling, peeing, half-dead old women and a few old fellows too shaky to feed themselves, but still trying to feel up the nurses, and I'd be as bad as them. It's not going to happen. I'd sooner take arsenic. I'll have a talk with Hugh when he comes.

I stand on the edge of the garden. Jack terraced the slope and planted shrubs and low trees to stop erosion. The white flowers in January were called... I'll remember the name in a minute. It's on the back of my tongue. You know the ones I mean. White, not very exciting, but white. It will come to me. Forsythia and Daphne in early spring and the whites, reds and pinks of flowering cherry. And apple and pear blossom in May. And the red and white shrubs that turned purple over the years, growing old gracefully like me. They've got a girl's name too, I think. Daphne. No. I said Daphne before. They are in flower till the pink, blue and white hydrangeas bloom. Jack never lost an opportunity to show off the gardens to visitors and to milk praise for his labours. I wasn't slow to remind him who was the sole owner of Kenmara. Jack remembered the name of all the plants in the garden right up to the end. So what? I have more important things on my mind. Still, I wish he was here. I'd like him to know how much I miss him, how sorry I am for treating him like dirt. It's a sad thing that my life is full only of regrets for the way I behaved.

Damp is seeping into my bones and the wind from the Lough whips what's left of my hair over my face. I hurry indoors and sit gazing out; seeing nothing. Thinking about Isabel. And all the while anger, rancid as week-old soup, simmers inside me.

It wasn't my fault. I was out of my mind with worry. Pregnant at forty nine. I didn't think I could be. Thought it was the menopause. I'd done my duty. Two grown sons. My own bedroom, till Jack burst in, drunk and slobbery. How would any woman feel? On *Woman's Hour* and in the English papers it's called rape in marriage. Over here we knew all about a husband's conjugal rights but the notion of women's rights hadn't reached Ireland in 1975. I dreaded the handicapped child I'd probably be stuck with for the rest of my life. Suppose what was growing inside me turned out to be female. I'd been lucky twice, but luck has a habit of running out. Three months bedrest before the birth. Two days labour before they cut the baby out of me. Was it any wonder I hated that red, squawking infant? Hated it for being alive, for the mess it had made of my body. I wouldn't look at her; wouldn't even give her a name. Jack wanted her to be christened Isabella. I had to remind him that we weren't foreign. I'd have given her up for adoption if Jack hadn't put his foot down. Doctors and nurses pleaded. They coaxed. They scolded. I couldn't tell them why I must not be allowed to care for a female child, not after what I had done to the two wee girls I was trusted to look after. You've got to understand, I'm not a bad person. It's just that life has been hard on me. Very hard.

No living person knows about the wee girls, or the terrible part I played in their lives. For decades I tried to bury them in the farthest corners of my mind. For decades I tried to wipe my memory clean of them but Daisy's stubby fingers and her moon face and little Bridget's crinkly smile and navy eyes are as vivid today as the faces of my own sons.

This is no time to think about Daisy or Bridget. I'm respected in the city, a woman of property. A woman without stain or blemish.

"It's not unusual for someone your age to feel resentful, especially after the labour you've had. Once you begin to feel better you'll just love your wee baby."

"Dislike of a newborn infant is a classic symptom of post-natal depression and Mrs McGlade has had a very hard time," I heard a junior doctor tell a student nurse.

"She's a selfish woman."

"Life's been too good to her. That's her problem."

"Should be ashamed of herself. She has a gorgeous wee baby and all she can think about is her figure."

Such was the verdict of the coven of new mothers who stank of the milk that dripped through their nightdresses, who tried to make me touch the baby the nurses had put in a cot beside my bed, to breast feed it! The infant hadn't suffered. Minnie Burns looked after her better than most mothers would and Jack was a besotted father, when the spirit moved him and he wasn't off on one of his jaunts, pleased as Punch with himself for having fathered a child in his sixties. They told him I was suffering from post-natal depression. Maybe I was. I had good reason.

When I came home from hospital, I'd often slip unbeknownst to anybody into the room where Isabel slept. She was the most beautiful baby and the loveliest child any mother ever had and I did not deserve her. My fingers ached to touch her, to feel the softness of her skin, to touch her curling hair, to see it coil around my finger, and my arms longed to hold her. With all my heart I wanted to tell her how much I loved her, but I didn't dare. I didn't dare watch Minnie bathe my plump baby or echo the cooing sound she made. I saw Isabel grow up to look like me when I was young and I prayed she would stay innocent and not live under the shadow that blighted my life.

If Isabel became ill when Jack was away, I had no choice but to care for her after Minnie went home. I cherished those times as much as I dreaded them. I was a real mother, looking after my child, giving her goat's milk when she had chickenpox, wrapping a bandage soaked in vinegar round her neck to ease the pain in her throat, coaxing her to gargle with warm water and a teaspoon of vinegar. I'd sit by her bed during the night checking that she had survived my care. That she hadn't died like Daisy.

Only once did I act on impulse. Her screams stopped my heart. I ran outside, buried her face in my skirt to hide the sight of her cat, Mitzi, steamrollered by the post van. I pressed her to me and promised she would have a new cat that same day. Two hours later, the pet shop van arrived with a fluffy kitten. Isabel's tearstained face glowed with joy. "What will I call her?" she asked. I suggested Molly because she was round and cuddlesome. Isabel hugged the kitten and she hugged me. "Thank you, Ma. Thank you for Molly."

I dare not show her love but at least I'd given her something to love.

How I wish I could have allowed myself more moments of closeness.

A key turns in the front door. Hugh? Already? I'll ask him to fix the towel rail in the bathroom and change the bulb on the landing. Maybe he'll stay a while. It would be good to have time with him on my own. I never cease to wonder why my son, who had all the

36

advantages money could buy, ended up a manual worker and how Liam Brogan from the slums of the Ardoyne managed to become a senior lecturer in history. Jack and I assumed Hugh would have a profession in medicine or in law like his brother. His hands and his backside were constantly welted with beatings from his father and the so-called Christian Brothers. None of us had heard of dyslexia when Hugh was a child and the belt and the cane were the only remedies for laziness. Dyslexia or not, I never thought a son of mine would go to the secondary modern school for rejects any more than I thought I'd have a daughter-in-law from Ballymurphy with a name like Linda. Common as muck, was my verdict when Hugh first brought her home. I refused point blank to go to their wedding and did my best to stop Jack from attending the event in the company of gunmen and jailbirds. Typical of Jack, he said it was the best wedding he'd been to, especially when the British army burst in on the reception and arrested two of the bride's brothers for possession of firearms and ammunition.

Out of nowhere, or maybe because I'm remembering my reaction to Linda, a faded image flits across my eyes, the image of a lad I knew when I was sixteen or seventeen and thought I was in love with. His family were labourers. Mine had delusions of grandeur and high hopes for me. It would never have been allowed. It might not have worked. Who knows, for the wisdom of winter is madness in spring.

Rose appears in the doorway. My heart misses a beat. She's changed from her Sunday suit into a jumper and trousers that do her hips and her beam end no favours.

"Hello, Rita."

She towers above me, a hawk about to swoop.

"I thought you looked a bit under the weather earlier. Maybe it was all too much for you, so I decided to pop in to check that you were all right. We'll have a cup of tea and a chat. The traffic was a nightmare, nose to tail, but here I am. "

No. No more chats about my health, about Rose and John moving to Kenmara to keep an eye on me. I'm not frail. The daily walk up Castle Hill that Dr McVeigh ordered keeps me straight and supple. I'm fitter and more active than before the heart attack.

"I didn't know you had a key to my home. I don't remember giving you one." My heart's racing out of control. My bottle of pills is in a drawer on the other side of the room.

"Now don't be like that, Rita. We're friends, we're family. John and I only want what's best for you. I'll get that tea. I'm gasping."

"Is it John's key you have?"

Stupid question! Rose always manages to make me seem fumbling, stupid and nasty, an old woman losing her mind.

"I had one cut for myself." My son's wife pauses and in a voice, syrupy with patience and resignation, she adds, "in case anything happens to you. You're too old to be left on your own." She smiles that gummy grin of hers, eyes glazed like a fish on a slab. "Maybe it's time you carried a panic button round your neck that would ring me if you fell or had an accident."

A gadget round my neck, as if I'm a latchkey child or a soldier carrying identification.

Rose puts two cups on the table beside my chair. I slide a coaster under each of them.

"There you are, Rita. There aren't any biscuits in the tin. Did you forget to order any? Next time I'll bring you some, or a wee cake, one you can keep in the fridge."

The air crackles with silence. Not like Rose to be lost for words. Maybe I've been too hard on her. Maybe I should stop seeing her as an enemy. She's John's wife and she brought up his children well. Even so, I'm frightened of her. Scared she'll weasel her way into my home, scared she'll make John take power of attorney over me. Martha Phillips' son did just that and the poor soul didn't last a month in Saint Luke's. Martha was ninety-one, years older than me, when her daughter-in-law and her son started tearing her home apart. Poor Martha, she was a bit forgetful. Still there was no need to put her in a ward where an attendant had to tap a code on the wall before anyone was let in or out. As if she was in prison or a lunatic asylum.

Please God, don't let them do that to me. I'd rather be dead than think of Rose ensconced here.

"Rita, I came here on my own to ask you about something I heard a while ago. It's something that concerns you and your family." She searches my face for a reaction. "Something that's been on my mind ever since. I didn't believe a word of it. I still don't, but I thought the best thing was to ask you to your face." She pauses, expecting to be questioned. "You know what people round here are like for a bit of gossip. It's meat and drink to them. I hate gossip but it's been nagging at me since I heard it."

Another pause. If she's waiting for me to speak, she'll have a long wait. My face is a mask. My face is a mask, but my stomach's writhing and my heart's been wrenched from its moorings. It bats at the walls of my chest the way a trapped bird crashes against a window. If only Hugh would come. If only I could take a couple of pills. I won't let Rose see what she's doing to me. I'll sit still and dumb if it kills me. What am I afraid of? Maybe it's nothing to do with me. Maybe it's another malicious rumour about John, spread by trash that are jealous of his achievements. Yes that's what it is. I won't listen to a word about him.

Rose leans forward. In a conspirator's voice she starts, shakily at first, then gaining momentum. Though she sprinkles her words with "I don't believe it for one minute" and "Nobody would even think such a thing about you" and "I'm sure it's a load of rubbish" her tale is quickly told. The story of Bridget. An outline, raw-edged with a blank space at its centre. Her expression is one of shock and disbelief, but I know she's enjoying every minute. What else does she know about Bridget? What poison will she filter into my ears and spread round the city? No. Rose is only fishing, hoping to catch me off guard.

For decades, I dreaded this moment and often wondered who the accuser would be. As my own generation died, I had relaxed. I never imagined I would be the subject of gossip by someone who hadn't even been born when the events she referred to took place.

I make myself walk over to the window, dragging each step as if I've a ball and chain attached to my ankle. Evening mist has lifted and the coast on the opposite side of the Lough is emerging clear and enclosing. Rose has stopped talking. A corner of my eye registers her rigid form perched on the edge of her seat, the mouth half-open as if she wants to speak but doesn't dare.

"Are you all right, Rita? You look terrible. Let me get you a glass of water and a couple of your heart pills."

Eyes fixed on the sea, I ask, "What do you intend to do with this piece of lying gossip?"

"Nothing. Nothing," Rose stammers, stutters and says, "I don't know. You know me. You can rest assured. I wouldn't breathe a word of it. I just…I just thought it best…"

I turn towards my son's wife and enunciate each syllable as if I'm speaking to a backward child, "If you repeat this gossip to anyone. Anyone. I will have Peter Kavanagh draw up a new will and neither John nor any of your children will inherit one penny from me. Now give me the keys to my home and leave."

My heart slows down soon after I swallow the pills, but the sour bile of panic rises into my throat. White-knuckled, I clutch the upholstered arms of the green chair my father bought after John was born. My eyes wander over a sepia photograph of my parents, stern-faced on their wedding day. Pa's arm is clamped on Ma's shoulder. A potted palm grows out of her straw hat. The Chinese hearth-rug, now faded by years of sunlight. Jack's wedding present to me. Hollows in the sofa where my boys used to hurl themselves into the corners. Three china mice, a mother and two babies attached by a gilt chain, a present from Hugh when he was eight. He told me they cost seven and six. I want to gather them in my arms and cling to them, my precious belongings, my anchor in a world that is shifting out my control.

I consider my next move. Nothing can absolve me from the guilt I have lived with for most of my life. Its weight has settled on my shoulders. It has become as much a part of me as my right or my left hand and I don't think I can live without it. The beginning of an idea takes root in my mind, an idea I must mull over before doing anything.

First thing in the morning I will ring Peter Kavanagh's office and make an appointment. After Jack's death, John assumed he would handle my affairs. Thank God, I didn't allow him to bully me.

Isabel won't have arrived at her home yet. Though I haven't telephoned her since Jack died, I know her number by heart. When the answer machine instructs me to leave a message, I read out the words I had written, crossed out and rewritten so often I'm no longer sure of what I want to say.

Today I missed my chance to start building a bridge between me and Isabel. I hope I'm not too late.

40

Chapter Four

I dreamt again last night that I was a baby swan searching for my sister. Not a dull-coated cygnet, but a miniature of the swans I loved to watch on the Lagan and the Bann. Their graceful gliding. How they rise, necks thrust out like bowsprits; how they beat the water until webbed feet appear in a pitter-patter run. Then whoosh, with a beating of wings they lift off, singing in an angry bass voice, "Why? Why? Why?" as they fly above rivers and trees.

I was swimming from Carrickfergus to the Sea of Moyle, where my sister and my two brothers were condemned to sail until they were released from the spell cast by our stepmother. My legs were weary from paddling along the coast and I was buffeted by giant waves that threatened to hurl me against rocky cliffs or into the mouths of creatures risen from the depths. In the far distance I could hear the voices of Lir's children singing their lament for our father, for their home and for their baby sister who disappeared under the dark waters of Moyle shortly after their banishment. I paddled faster until their singing, sweeter than any music ever heard, filled the air around me. The stately shape of my sister swam into my vision; the shape I had come to know as well as I knew my own. She called me by my name and I was within a wing's beat from her when the dream dissolved, as it always did.

Liam said I was simply reliving the story my father used to tell me. He lived in the present and found the interpreting of dreams a waste of time, indulged in by foolish women. Marie said I was looking for Grania and the other children I might have had, not for a character from Irish mythology. I have had this dream since I was small, usually at some time of crisis, and each time it fills me with a sense of loss and desolation.

I switched on the answer machine. Three messages from colleagues and friends from work telling me to keep in touch and ring if I needed anything. Elaine, my boss, saying I was entitled to three weeks' holiday plus compassionate leave. Half listening, I drew circles in the dust that furred every surface in my house and it struck me that it wouldn't matter to anyone if I disappeared under a blanket of dust.

Grace's voice, "Welcome back, Isabel. I hate to think of you on your own. Come down here once you've sorted yourself out. Give me a ring and we'll make arrangements for travelling to Italy. Thanks for saying you'll come with me. I'm really looking forward to spending time with you."

I stopped doodling and sat bolt upright at the next message. Ma! Stilted and precise.

"Isabel, after you left I spent a long time thinking about you and the family. I have decided to have a birthday party." A pause, then as if reading from a prepared script, "I would very much like you to be here. I want to have all my family around me. Grace said you would not spend longer than a fortnight in Italy. I hope you can come."

I thought the message was finished, when she spoke again. The studied correctness had gone. Words tripped over each other as if she was cramming in as much as she could before being cut off. "Please come, Isabel, please come. If you can make it a couple of days beforehand, I'd be very happy. Please try to come, to come early. I need to talk to you. There's something I have to tell you. Something important."

Something important! Was that what she was going to tell me when Rose interrupted us? I replayed her message. Ma never pleaded. Never asked favours. She achieved her ends by other more calculating means. When was her birthday? July, somewhere near the beginning or the middle of the month. Grace would know. Waves of shame washed over me. What sort of daughter had no idea of her mother's birthday? I pictured Ma, ramrod-straight in the wide hall of Kenmara, a skin and bone figure, taking stock of herself in the gilt-rimmed mirror above the telephone table, readusting her hair, admiring the lines of her nose and cheeks, checking her face for surplus powder. My annoyance subsided. A sad, old woman still clinging to a long-vanished image of herself.

But why should Ma, who had been too vain to acknowledge her sixtieth or seventieth birthdays, decide to celebrate at seventy-eight? Perhaps she feared she wouldn't reach eighty and wanted to put her house in order. And what could she possibly have to say to a daughter she'd ignored for over twenty-seven years? Maybe she was in the early stages of dementia. That would account for her confusion and dropping her knife and fork yesterday, for the words she couldn't remember, for her leaving the table during the meal. Ma prided herself on her appearance but inside her well-maintained and expensively-groomed body, bits must be crumbling and breaking down. She could be afraid she was dying and wanted to be reconciled with me. My poor, lonely mother; I was too hard on her. I knew about loneliness, but I was young enough to make a new life.

"Why does she not like me? Why is she so horrible?" I used to ask Minnie.

"Your mammy was far too old to have a baby. Having you nearly killed her. Give her time and everything will be fine."

Nearly killing a parent was a serious crime for a three-year-old to come to terms with. That didn't stop me praying that Ma would die and Daddy would marry Minnie.

Sometimes, on Minnie's day off, Ma had to take me along to one of her afternoon bridge parties.

"My ball and chain," she would say to explain my presence to her hostess.

I hated Ma and I hated her friends with all the loathing and anger I could muster. I hated the way they took out compacts, bared their teeth and painted red gashes over their mouths after tea and sherry. I hated them for snarling at each other and blaming their partners when they lost a game; for the grudging way they fished in special bridge purses and counted out pennies as if they were all that remained between them and starvation.

I dearly loved my father. When I was small he cared for me in an absent-minded, grandfatherly way and we became good friends once I was no longer a pestering child. I was proud to go with him to Mass on Sundays, to walk up at the front of the church while he greeted everyone he passed as if he was royalty. If anyone asked if he was my grandfather, I would take his hand, glare and say, "No. He's my daddy." My poor father, doomed to stay married to a woman who scoffed and despised him.

Though I knew he loved me, I was amazed when he left me twenty thousand pounds in his will for a down payment on a house. Ma had been shocked to learn that her husband, whom she referred to as a layabout and a sponge, had saved that amount of money without her knowing. Liam and I had already decided to make an offer for the house in Brockley. He disapproved of inherited wealth and the idea of living in a home that had been partly paid for by his wife's father offended his principles. He said he felt like a guest rather than the man of the house. Maybe it was easier for a guest, rather than a husband, to walk out.

Sunlight poured through the sitting room window over the furniture we had picked up in second-hand shops and sales – a chintz sofa and armchair, wicker chairs, a low table and book cases, the Indian rug Marie gave us when we moved in. The chattels Liam no longer needed.

Memories of my father had helped to distance me from Ma, but I hadn't shaken her off completely. "Please come, Isabel. Please come. I've something important to tell you. Something very important."

Yesterday, after the funeral, she had come of her own free will to stand beside me. She had taken my hand and I had relaxed in the unexpected closeness of the moment. I held her hand, which warmed my fingers as it warmed my heart. We stood together, at ease in each other's presence, a normal mother showing concern for her daughter's loss. We had even laughed and Ma didn't hold with laughing. I once heard her tell Minnie she couldn't stand Daddy's family because they laughed too much. Whatever. I was no nearer to understanding the unknowable woman I called my mother. I dialled her number to say I would go to her party. The phone rang unanswered.

"Rita's birthday's on the eleventh of July," Grace confirmed. "She telephoned yesterday evening to invite me to the family reunion. Will you go, Isabel?"

"Yes, of course I will. Now, tell me about our Italian trip."

"The flight leaves Stansted at eight in the morning. I'd hoped to drive up to your place on Monday evening but I'll have to leave it till Tuesday morning. The roads will be clear so I should be with you about half four. Thanks again for coming with me."

"I'll be glad to get away. Too many memories here. I'll ring the office and book some time off."

Upstairs in the box room I switched on my computer and clicked email. One message stood out. From Liam, dated the day before he had left for Belfast.

Hi

Going home for about a week. Dad not well and Kevin's worried about him. I'll hire a car and take him out somewhere every day. Been promising this for years. Spoke to Crystal and Warren today. Should have the decree absolute the week after next. We'll both be relieved to make a clean break and get on with our lives. Will be in touch when I get back. We'll have to meet and talk over practicalities and I'll collect the remains of my stuff from your place. If you'd rather not see me just throw everything in the bin.
Take care.
Love
Liam.

Thousands of dust motes danced in a sunbeam. My arm sliced through them. Nothing changed. I shifted out of their range. A car stopped outside. Footsteps. A door banging. The corpses of two flies lay on the windowsill. Not squashed. Perfect, apart from being dead. I wiped layers of dust off the monitor. Minnie would have removed the spots and stains with a chamois leather. I didn't have a chamois leather The message remained. Starker. More defined.

It was as though Liam's death had merely been a rehearsal for the finality of this moment. Arms clamped across my chest to keep myself from falling apart, I stared at the computer. His email had laid waste the dream I had wanted to cling to. The dream of him and me abandoning divorce proceedings and making a fresh start. It had ripped a lump out of the place that stored my memories and my hopes. The empty space ached as it had after Grania died, when I used to hug my arms tight across my belly to close up the hollow where she had grown.

I went to the bedroom I had shared with him. Nothing had changed since last night, yet it echoed hollow and booming, a space empty of him. I threw open a wardrobe where the clothes he hadn't bothered to take drooped on wire hangers, spindly and forlorn as headless ghosts. I stuffed them into bin liners, inhaling his night-time smell, his morning taste of toothpaste and sleep. 'Sling everything. Get on with the rest of my life,' as he put it. The grey suit bought under protest for graduation processions, the shape of a stain imprinted on the left knee. The denim shirt he got for our first visit to the cemeteries of Northern France and Flanders. *Shut your eyes, grope in the dark, stop your fingers recognising each item. Drop everything into the bin bag.*

I re-read the email and deleted it. Click. Gone. Nothing. Perhaps I should have printed it, just in case. In case of what? I closed the door firmly behind me.

I swiped Liam's CDs from a shelf, together with his books on photography and diving. His face looked out from two silver-framed photographs: one of him in the grounds of Queen's University after receiving his doctorate, smiling for the sake of his parents. The other on a beach near Carnac. Water on slippery skin. The sea-salt taste of him. His head and shoulders ploughing through waves till he disappeared from sight.

Into the open mouth of a bin bag I dropped my life with Liam to the gratifying sound of metal against glass.

I had grown deaf to the sounds of passing trains but, since Liam's message, every sound set my teeth on edge. And the drone of planes had magnified to such a pitch, I might have been living under the flight path of every airport round London. The fridge contained only a few scraps of cheese, celery, olives, and ham curling at the edges. I stopped myself from pouring a second glass of wine. I had been down that path too often.

I shouldn't have thrown out the photographs! That was wrong! Destroying Liam's likeness was like walking on his face, killing him over again. In Kenmara we kept all our photographs in overflowing boxes in a cupboard which was rarely opened. Even snaps of people nobody knew. Just in case, Ma said. I fished the photos out of the bin liner, took them from their frames and stuck them into one of boxes in the built in cupboard beside the fireplace.

I stood at the kitchen window surveying my overgrown garden. A butterfly flew in through the open door. I watched its agitated flight as it knocked again and again against the window. "Look, the door's open," I told it. "It's not far away." It paid no heed. I tried to shoo it from the window, but it went on battering against the pane. I tried to redirect its path with a cookery book It flew over my head and returned, intent on flinging itself against the window. Worn out by its efforts, it collapsed on the sill. I was loath to touch it. I'd been told when I was small that butterflies lose their special dust and die if they're touched. It would probably die anyhow if it didn't find its way out. Scared of damaging its fragile wings I cupped the tremulous creature in my palms and for a few seconds I felt its feeble fluttering until I opened my hands. It paused, unsure, then rose in the air, flew down the garden and over the apple tree.

My mind empty of everything but the brown and orange butterfly I had held in my hands, I weeded overgrown and tangled flower-beds, hacked at shrubs which had encroached on an already crowded and limited space and set about shearing the grass that had grown too high for mowing. Though the muscles in my arms and my back screamed, I urged myself forward, developing a rhythm which eased the effort until what had once been called a lawn emerged, coarse and tufted.

I stretched my arms towards the sky and in a vivid flash I realised that Liam's email had liberated me. For years I had been hunkered in darkness at the bottom of a well, not wanting to see that there was blue sky above. Now, I was free to climb out, free to move my limbs, to let the air of early summer fill my lungs. The man I'd been mourning was not my husband who had been absent for the past six years. He was the rose-tinted and silver-framed memory of a young man who had swept me off my feet in the autumn of 1995. He was my twenty-five-year-old lover, as yet untouched by the loss of his child, and not yet out of love with a second-year student from his native city.

I went upstairs and emailed my brothers to thank them for taking care of me before and after Liam's death. I closed down the computer and left the door to the box room wide open.

The phone rang. I hesitated. It was Marie, not Ma. She was coming to see me tomorrow about ten. We would have breakfast together and go shopping in the West End.

Next morning, the usual pile of junk mail lay at the hall door. I could buy cashmere at fifty per cent discount; send money to Oxfam and Cancer Relief; arrange to have new windows fitted, order pills to cure arthritis, the effects of ageing and impotence. I slit open a typed envelope.

Isabel,
Do not go to Italy. You will live to regret it if you do.

That was all. No sender's address. No date. No signature.

Goose-bumps pimpled my arms. The postmark was unreadable. Who could have sent it? Ma. It had to be her. An unsigned and anonymous one-liner with an undercurrent of threat. Yes. That was Ma's style, but Ma couldn't type. None of her friends owned a computer. She could have asked one of her grandchildren. Too risky. Besides, Ma didn't act on impulse. She brooded, plotted, worked out every eventuality before putting her schemes into action. Why should she want to stop me going for a holiday with Grace? It wasn't as if she expected me to spend time with her. She couldn't wait to get rid of me. It had to be John or Rose. They had both put pressure on me to stay at Kenmara. John's sudden change from concern to blame. His creepy appearance outside Ma's bedroom. But my brother really cared for me. Rose! Yes, it could only be my long-suffering sister-in-law.

My heart was still thumping when Marie arrived with croissants, chocolates and champagne.

"Tell me everything when I've made the coffee. I'm starving," she said, filling the kettle and two glasses. "How are you?"

I said I was fine, which was more or less true.

Marie, who has the body of a model and the appetite of an elephant, put croissants under the grill and suggested we eat on the patio.

"Now," she said, when we were settled, "tell me how you really are."

"I'm not sure. I thought I had done all my crying over Liam, but after he died a black cloud descended on me, one that I couldn't escape from. And I had that dream again. The one I've told you about."

As if she was comforting one of her children who had fallen and hurt her knee, Marie stroked my hand. I studied her face, trying to read the thoughts forming behind her smooth brow.

48

"You're in mourning, Izzy. It's to be expected. You loved the guy. You were married to him. You had a child with him and you've been clinging to those memories." She switched off the grill, spread butter and raspberry jam on the croissants in silence as if she was sifting her thoughts before putting them into words. "We're programmed by nature to remember happiness rather than misery. It's a survival mechanism. My dad used to beat the crap out of my mum at least twice a week and he put her in hospital with a broken nose and cracked ribs. I was gob-smacked when she cried on and on for weeks when she heard he was dead." She shook her head as if she couldn't believe what she was telling me. "To hear the way she talks about him you'd think she'd been married to Nelson Mandela." Marie bit into the croissant and wiped crumbs from her mouth. "And it didn't stop her marrying another bastard. As for that recurring dream of yours, we've talked about it before. I'm sure that's part of grieving. Part of loss. It's about yearning, yearning for the children you and Liam should have had. A space that needs to be filled."

After a glass of champagne, she said, "Steve's taking the girls swimming and they're going to his mum's for lunch. I'm free for the rest of the day. We'll go up the West End, and get you stuff for your holidays." She topped up our glasses. "Then, because you're off to Italy, I'm taking you to an Italian restaurant for the best meal you've had in your whole life. What part are you going to?"

"No idea. Grace didn't say and I didn't ask."

"Well, wherever it is, here's to a great holiday." Marie and I clinked glasses. "And here's to us."

It was as good a moment as any to tell her about the email from Liam and the sense of relief I had when I came to terms with it.

"That's good, Izzy. Since Liam left you've been carrying a placard with 'not available' written on it in capital letters. It's time you started to live."

I said I looked forward to making up for lost time, passed the anonymous letter across the table to her and asked what I should do about it.

She read it and grimaced. "It's from some crank with a grudge or someone who's jealous of you. It doesn't have to be from your family. It could be anyone from work who's jealous of your last promotion. It could be from me, because I don't see why you should be swanning off to Italy when I have to teach every day and look after two kids when I come home." Then, as if she had a divine revelation, she said, "It could be from that guy, you know the one you went out with, the one you dumped when he wanted to move in with you. Remember, he turned nasty and stalked you for ages."

"Pete? I don't think so, but I suppose he's a possibility? How would he know?"

"How did I know? Grapevine, whatever you like to call it. All our friends knew about Liam's accident and they knew you asked for leave to go on holiday." Marie stood up and slid the sheet of paper across the table. "Put that in the bin and forget it. You and I have serious shopping and eating to do."

Marie's trained eyes scanned the rails of clothes in a boutique in Bond Street. She handed me a floaty dress in shades of blue. "This is you, Izzy, the new you. You're bound to pull in this."

"I'd like to think so, but don't forget I'm going on holiday with my sixty-one-year-old cousin." I twirled in front of the changing room mirror. "All the same, if I'm going to pull, this is the frock."

"You're going with Grace, not some old woman on a zimmer. She's not going to stop you going out on the town. You got to live, Izzy. Stand your ground."

"I've missed you. God, but I've missed you. You've always been there for me in good times and bad." I hugged Marie. It was good to laugh, to feel free and reckless. Like a student again.

"It's two-way traffic, you know. You babysat my kids every night when Steve was in hospital and you stopped me cutting his balls off when I thought he was playing away." She burst out laughing. "If you hadn't, I'd never have had Melissa."

The food we had in an Italian restaurant off the Strand lived up to Marie's description. We ate in reverent silence, savouring every mouthful of scallops, prawns and lobster in a thick creamy sauce. *Lasagna Marinara*, a dish to look forward to if I ever get to heaven.

Marie was right too about the anonymous letter. I put it out of my mind and went to sleep dreaming about gliding in a gondola under the Rialto Bridge and along the Grand Canal where a pair of elegant swans paddled beside me.

50

Chapter Five

Newbury Road is a place of speeding cars, music blasting from taxis, the hurrying feet of early morning travellers on their way to the station, their slower steps on the homeward journey. At half-past four in the morning the only sound was the drone of a plane flying low in the sky, its tail-light blinking like a following star. Our early start meant that Grace and I missed the morning bottlenecks in South London and avoided delays on the motorway. The Blackwall Tunnel route from London to Stansted is not inspiring at the best of times, but on the first day of our holiday, not even the gloom of early morning drizzle or the implied warning in the anonymous letter could dampen my hopes and my high spirits. Liam and I disliked this road carved out of nowhere without any connection to those whose lives it had interrupted. The wide skies of East Anglia unnerved me and filled me with longing for the near horizons of my childhood. Cave Hill, the Black Mountain, Castlereagh Hills, soft against a low sky. I conjured up a map of Italy, the great bulk of snow-covered Alps to the north and the backbone of the Apennines down the middle. Bays and rugged inlets. Mountain streams. If any plains existed, there was no sign of them on my map.

Apart from lorries beetling along the inside and middle lanes, traffic on the motorway was light. Grace drove in preoccupied silence. Despite the big age difference, Grace and I were very close. Though I thought of her as a big sister, I was always pleased to be taken for her daughter. We were both tall and fair and looked like photos of our mothers when they were young. She had stayed with me during the sleepless days and nights of hoping against hope that Grania would live. She sat with me by the incubator where my too-soon-born baby lay at the centre of a spider's web of tubes and wires, where we willed her to get a hold on life, to breathe on her own, to be strong enough to be touched with bare hands. Grace was with me too when Liam found refuge from my weeping and my misery in work and in the company of others, when he accused me of drowning him in my sea of grief, of trying to pull him under with me.

A mishmash of hurtling memories, thoughts, regrets and plans cut through my excitement – Liam, my family and their reaction to my holiday with Grace, Ma's birthday party, lasagna marinara, the anonymous letter, my new frock, words and phrases from the disc *Italian for Beginners*. And Liam.

We left the M11 and followed the sign to Long Term Parking. Each time I drove with Liam to Stansted the approach terrified me. The sudden appearance of signs taking us away from the airport along a winding road to a limbo of car parks. Instructions to go a certain zone. Driving up and down rows of closely parked cars, eyes peeled for a space and Liam half-asleep beside me.

In the queue for the check-in desk for Pescara, we talked about Ma's birthday party.

"Rita knows she's treated you badly. She wants the whole family, especially you, to be with her." She seemed to be weighing the situation as we grew nearer to the check-in desk. "I know it's important to her, but nobody one could blame you if you decide not to go."

"Not half, they couldn't."

We were still laughing when we placed our luggage beside a desk where a young woman with white claws for fingernails gave me a one-way ticket to Pescara.

Pescara. I rolled the name over my tongue. Pescara. I liked its softness, its sibilance, its mystery. Somewhere Odysseus might have stopped on his wanderings; where the men who fished with Christ might have settled after the Crucifixion.

"Where's Pescara and why a one-way ticket? Are you thinking of leaving me there, or are we not coming back?"

"It's almost directly opposite Rome, on the Adriatic. A single ticket means we're free to leave whenever we like. Maybe we'll go to Rome or down to Sorrento and see Pompeii or if you like, we can go to Venice, as long as I'm back for your Mum's birthday. Why are we going to Pescara?" Grace paused and looked over the heads of travellers milling past us. An elegant figure in a cream trouser suit and brown top, she suddenly seemed ill at ease, as if she was unsure of, or had forgotten, the reason for our journey. She bent to pick up the boarding card that had slipped from her passport. A strut marking the route to passport control bisected her face and I noticed, as I did on rare occasions, that the two sides of her face didn't match, that the left side was broader and heavier-jawed than the right. I'd first remarked it when I saw her through the frame of a bookcase at her desk in the library at Hastings, and again at her mother's funeral. She stood up and the difference was barely perceptible. "Why are we going to Pescara?" she repeated. "Because my father's buried near there."

"Your father!" I swallowed hard. "What did you say?"

"My father is buried near Pescara," Grace inched along the queue for passport control.

Grace's father! Uncle Harry, the quiet English doctor married to Aunt Kate, was Grace's father. She spoke in the same measured way as he did; she had inherited his low-key approach to life, shared his interest in books, in local history and geology. His remains lay beside her mother's under a marble tombstone in a double plot in Hastings cemetery. I had seen him buried, watched yellow clay fall on his coffin. I had helped serve food and drinks to mourners at the family home. There had never been any mention in the family of an Italian.

"Do you mean that Uncle Harry wasn't your real dad?"

"That's right."

"My God! When did you find out?"

"When I was about sixteen or seventeen and needed a passport, Mamma decided I should know. Later Papa helped me with research, though he wasn't keen at first. I think he was afraid it would distance me from him." She added as an afterthought, "As if anything would! After he died, Mamma and I meant to make this trip together, but it wasn't to be." Her words were spoken with a finality that dammed the stream of questions straining to pour over my tongue.

Well, that was a turn up for the book! Aunt Kate had had a fling with, or maybe married, an Italian without anyone in Ireland knowing or letting on. The Aunt Kate I remembered was one of those strait-laced women you see in churches, their heads permanently tilted at a pious angle. A reverend mother in civvies. It was hard to think that any man in his right mind would want to go to bed with her. I couldn't see her taking off her nurse's uniform that was as stiff and starchy as she was. But I hadn't known her when she was young. I'd always pictured her as frosty and untouchable, an older version of my own mother. Minnie, who used to meet Kate, her husband and Grace each year when they came to Kenmara, said they were a happy family, content in each other's company.

Daddy often told me that Ma's upbringing had made her a bit odd. Her parents had kept her under lock and key, with only the pair of them for company until her father decided that Jack McGlade might be a suitable son-in-law. He had fallen in love with her beauty – Ma would have said with her money – though he was certain she had agreed to marry him to escape from her parents. If Ma had had a secret lover, the joy of falling in love and being loved might have softened her. She would have held the memory of that closeness deep inside her like a precious liquid, which might have over-brimmed into care for her husband and love of her children. Poor Ma, enclosed like a nun in her parents' pub way back in those far-off days, in a country where sex was as grievous a sin as murder, where secrets were ferreted out and broadcast in satisfied whispers round the community; she would have had more opportunities to murder her mother and father, than to fall in love.

A screen above us indicated that our flight was now boarding. I bought two cards and wrote to Ma,

Thanks for inviting me to your birthday party. I'll see you there. About to get the plane to Italy. I'll try to come a couple of days earlier. Isabel.

I also wrote a card to my neighbour, Glynnis, apologising for not telling her I would be away for a while. I would post them as soon as we arrived at Pescara airport.

Saying she needed to sleep, Grace closed her eyes and shut out the questions she knew I was itching to ask. Why had she waited so long to visit her father's grave and why had he abandoned Kate and his daughter to go and live in Italy? Maybe when she woke up she would tell me more about him, where he had met her mother, how long they lived together. Grace was born in 1943. Her birth father could have been living in England and been injured in the Blitz. It wasn't unusual for men to fall in love with their nurses. Kate might have refused to go with him to Italy after the war. The book I had brought to read on the flight lay unopened on my lap as various scenarios flitted through my brain. I shook my head to offers of drinks, sandwiches, alcohol and scent as questions stacked up in my head. It

54

was hard to believe that Ma, or someone in her tight-lipped, busy-body community, didn't know about Grace's real father.

Why do you live with your granny and granddad? Have you no mammy and daddy?

For many years I believed the elderly couple I lived with were my grandparents, or a couple chosen to look after me till my real parents came to claim me. I looked forward to the day when my mother and father, young and active like my friends' parents, would take me to live with them and their other children. I told my friends their reasons for leaving me. They had been seriously wounded excavating lost cities in South America; they were held as spies in a Siberian prison; they had lost their lives in an African jungle. I was convinced that unborn spirits hung around in space till they were given bodies to inhabit, like children in an orphanage waiting to be adopted. I had been the result of a glitch in the system that was designed to pair children with parents, a tangling of wires, which had delayed my birth by over twenty years and thrust me on an unsuspecting couple on the brink of old age. Before I realised that such questions upset him, I used to ask my father who I would have been if I hadn't been me, Isabel McGlade.

"That's a tom-fool question. If you hadn't been born, you would have been nothing. You wouldn't have existed," he answered. "I've told you that a dozen times. Now, can we close the subject, once and for all?"

His reply was unthinkable. Never to have been born would have meant I had been rejected. An orphan spirit, condemned to float loose in the heavens. An ugly duckling of a spirit, restless and wanted by nobody. Stuck in a time-warp, until Jack McGlade forced my existence on his nearly fifty-year-old wife. I had only to look in the mirror to see how I resembled my mother, though in my case her almost perfect beauty had been well watered down by my father's homely features.

I sometimes forget that having old parents had its advantages. My brothers loved me. They tried to give me a normal family life in their homes and their children were like brothers and sisters to me. Minnie's daughters, who were older than me, treated me like a doll. They plaited my hair, dressed me in clothes they had outgrown and took me on outings with their friends. Was it any wonder I became self-obsessed, the centre of my own universe?

I saw from looking at the flight path on the monitor in front of my seat that we were crossing the Apennines and would soon be landing at Pescara.

Grace yawned and said she had slept well. As we stepped from the plane she showed more interest in the heat rising from the runway, the luminous quality of the light and the sight of fully-armed soldiers than in discussing her birth father. Not being a seasoned air passenger, my heart was racing with the magic carpet effect of being transported from the damp cool of early morning England to the blazing sunshine of an unknown place on the coast of an unknown country. I floated six inches above the ground as if the magic carpet had not quite landed. And the soldiers were all film-star handsome. Dark hair, tanned skin and slim and, despite their weapons, relaxed and chatting with each other. While Grace was at the car hire office I looked into shops selling jewellery, local honey, olives and peppercorns and I studied the notices for properties in an estate agent's windows. All written in English.

We left the cool of the air-conditioned airport and went through automatic doors to find a Fiat Punto somewhere among dozens of parked vehicles. A blast of scorching air hit us as if an oven door had been opened and heat fell out of the sky. It burned through the soles of our shoes and dazzled our eyes. It had roasted car seats, controls and dashboard.

A few miles after leaving the airport, Grace eased the Fiat on to the motorway where banks of crimson, pale pink and white flowers lined the verges, bloomed in the central reservation and climbed slopes in waterfalls of colour.

"It's wonderful, like driving through a never-ending garden," I said, "Do you know what those flowers are?"

"I don't know what they are called, but this is the Autostrada dei Fiore. The Motorway of Flowers. Look out for Val di Sangro. That's where we turn off."

Unlike the M11, the motorway had cut through people's lives. It bordered vineyards, farms and blocks of apartments. Bridges supported on enormous columns connected deep valleys to the left and tyres thudded over sections of the bridges with the rhythmic sound of a slow train. The Adriatic was on our left, and on the right the foothills of the Apennines. One large mountain dominated the others. Grace said it must be the Maiella, the second highest of the range. To me it was paradise. Like my brother John and Marie, I thought we would go to one of the well known tourist areas. I'd imagined crowded beaches, beautiful architecture, music, famous ruins, meals in busy restaurants, chatting and making friends with interesting people in cafés, not this uncrowded region and not on a search for the spot where Grace's unknown father was buried. Had I known, I might have thought twice. I had seen enough graveyards recently.

It was twelve o'clock when we reached a sign in English and Italian 'British Military Cemetery.' Grace drove up an unmade road through dappled greenery that arched across the track. She parked under a fig tree. We put on hats and emerged into the searing heat. I followed her as she made her way towards the Visitors' Centre with the sureness of someone who had been here before and was already familiar with the layout. In the shade of the atrium we looked over the names of the dead. Two thousand, five hundred and forty-four men were interred here; soldiers from the United Kingdom, Ireland, Canada, Australia, New Zealand, South Africa and India, including prisoners of war who escaped and died while trying to reach the British lines.

Oblivious of me, Grace walked out into the heat, stopping to read the names on headstones. I lingered, unwilling to intrude into her private search. She moved with urgency, as if trying to make up for the times this visit had been postponed

The cemetery formed a wide arc on a south-facing slope. Immediately behind, the ground fell sharply from a scrub-covered cliff to the valley of the Sangro River. When Liam was preparing his doctorate papers on the Ulster divisions at the Battle of the Somme, I had gone several times with him to cemeteries in France and Belgium. There, I had seen acres of white headstones, rows upon serried rows, like an army arrayed for battle. Maybe, because I was much younger and absorbed with the insecurities of my marriage, I had thought of the thousands of men who were buried there as statistics of war, not as human beings with parents, wives and children. There was an intimacy in the curved rows of headstones of the Sangro Cemetery, a sense that the men buried here were with mates they had known, had lived, bickered and joked with, men with whom they had fought in other campaigns and seen the horrors my generation knew only from war films.

I stopped to read an inscription to a nineteen- year-old soldier:

To the world you were only one.
To us you were the whole world

Another message to a son, aged seventeen, from Mum and Dad:

You gave your young unfinished life for us
May we be worthy of your sacrifice.

Many of these soldiers were the same age as the first year lads in my classes at university, who behaved like kids, flicking papers at girls, farting and sending crude messages during lectures, whose idea of a good time was getting drunk or stoned. Wars, if we ever thought about them, happened in far-off countries in places we had never heard of. John and Rose constantly complained that their sons, who were perennial students, only got in touch when they wanted money.

I walked past neat plots, past mounds where roses, lilies and geraniums bloomed among other bright-coloured flowers. I read messages from wives, children and parents and wondered about the headstones that bore only the name, number, regiment and the date of the soldier's death. Lulled by silence and heat, I continued through the scent of flowers and shrubs. Swarms of butterflies flitted by, clouds of white against a cloudless sky. They landed on flowering plants, wings folded and almost invisible till, as if on a signal, they resumed their fluttering way. Liam taught me the names of butterflies in our garden. He said that the ancient Greeks were so impressed by the fragile beauty of the butterfly they named it Psyche, a word that means the human spirit.

In an area reserved for troops from India, many headstones were marked with the inscription.

A soldier of the Indian Army is buried here.

No name or date of his death.

Another tombstone marked the resting place of the youngest soldier in the cemetery:

58

Gulab Khan, 13th Frontier Force Rifles.
17th November 1943. Age 15.

A fifteen-year-old dying in a war in a country that meant nothing to him and among men whose language and customs he didn't understand. Perhaps he had lied about his age when he set out on an adventure he hoped to remember and talk about when he was an old man.

As I read the names and ages on each tombstone I realised with shame how trivial my problems were, set beside the shortened lives of the men buried here, almost all of them years younger than Liam was when he died.

I bent down and scooped up a handful of soil. I held it in my palm, opened my fingers and the remains of these soldiers, and the children they would have fathered, their children and their children's children, trickled back to the earth. And I thought of each soldier leaving for war with the hope of coming back to a wife, to children, a girlfriend, to parents, brothers and sisters. The months, maybe years, before those they had loved, those who had composed the inscriptions of the tombstones in this peaceful place received the telegram that put an end to their hoping. Then, as if I was scattering seeds on newly tilled ground, I blew the grains that lay in the hollow of my hand to whatever winds might fan the summer heat on the Sangro.

Shielding my eyes from the sun I looked across the cemetery. A shimmering haze blurred the scene and created a sense of distance. I felt detached, as if I was watching a film set in a foreign country. A woman, whose head was bowed, was kneeling, one hand resting on a headstone. As I struggled to focus, two men, one very old, the other much younger, came into the picture. They paused at several graves where the old man placed something, stood to attention, saluted and moved on. The younger man cupped his companion's elbow and led him to a bench where they sat looking over the wide sweep of the cemetery. The woman at the grave did not move.

I rubbed the film from my eyes and went towards the spot where Grace knelt. On the headstone an inscription read:

Anthony O'Brien. Age 23.
No 6847564, London Irish Fusiliers.
21 November 1943
R. I. P.

No message from his parents or Aunt Kate, no record of his place of birth. Perhaps he had no family. Perhaps they knew nothing of their son's death, merely that he had vanished as many had during the war years.

Grace's mother, my Aunt Kate, had known.

An Irish surname. A regiment, I supposed, for emigrants or men with Irish ancestry. It could have been the Irish connection that attracted Anthony O'Brien to my Aunt Kate. 1943. Poor woman, her baby was born in the spring of the year her father died.

"He's a long way from home but he could hardly be in a more beautiful place than this. Just look around, Isabel," Grace said without taking her eyes from the inscription.

To the east, the Adriatic reflected the blue sky. Beyond the cemetery the land was covered in low trees and scrub and the only sounds were the hum of insects and the flow of a river below the escarpment.

We left the graveside and walked towards the two men. The older man, who had the bearing of a soldier, took off his hat and stood to attention. Patches of brown spattered the pale skin under wisps of white hair and sweat ran down his face. He was in his eighties and was shorter than his companion who was fresh-faced and dark-haired. He could have been forty or forty-five.

"Good afternoon, ladies. I'm Fred Cooper and this is my son, Pat."

Grace took Fred's hands in both of hers. "I'm Grace Sheridan and this is my cousin, Isabel. We are very pleased to meet you."

To my surprise, my cousin, who is the most reticent of women, said she had seen him place poppies on certain graves and asked if he had fought in Italy during the war.

"I fought here on the Sangro in 1943. I left many good comrades behind." Faded blue eyes swept the cemetery. "I come back with one of my sons whenever I can to pay my respects to them."

His son interrupted with a smile, "Dad, you keep coming back because you love the place and because the local people treat you like a hero."

"I saw you kneeling at a grave," Fred Cooper said. "Was he a member of your family? Maybe somebody I knew?"

"He was my father. Anthony O'Brien. The London Irish Fusiliers."

"London Irish Fusiliers, I knew many of them. Good lads. They loved a fight." He smiled to himself as his wet eyes ranged once more over rows of tombstones.

Like a child who has just heard the beginning of a story and is afraid the narrator is going to stop, Grace squeezed his hands. "Maybe you knew him, my father. You see, I never did."

The old man's brow wrinkled. "I may have done, but it was over sixty years ago and I'm ashamed to tell you we called all the Irish lads Paddy, same as we called the Scots Jock and the Welsh Taffy. It was no disrespect, just the way it was." When he saw Grace's disappointment, he asked," Do you mind if I come with you to look at your father's headstone? Something may come back to me."

"Put your hat on, Dad, you've been too long in the sun," his son said. "I'll be in trouble back home if I let him get sunstroke."

Grace cupped Fred's elbow as she had seen his son do and we made our way to the second row of headstones.

"18th December. I remember it well." Fred shook his head. We stood for a moment in silence. I imagined him reliving the events of the battle that had cost Anthony O'Brien his life. "We lost a lot of men that day, including some good friends of mine."

"Don't stay more than a minute, Dad." Pat said.

As I walked with him toward the shade of the atrium, Pat told me his father bought poppies each November to put on the graves of his comrades.

I remembered how pleased I had been when Liam trusted me to proof-read his thesis. Though I checked each page several times for missing words, spelling mistakes and typing errors, I got little sense of what he had written about a battle in the First World War. And until now, I had never met anyone who had taken part in a war, which was as remote to me as the battle of Waterloo or the Crusades.

I was born when the Troubles were at their height. Liam and Linda's families grew up with the constant fear of rioting and random killings. But for me, the Troubles were items on news bulletins, headlines in newspapers and blazing rows between my father and his sons. John is a member of the liberal Alliance party. Hugh is a passionate republican and my father's political ideas blew with the wind. As for the Second World War, I knew that Belfast had been bombed and that my grandfather had made his fortune from serving drinks to rich American soldiers

I eased the collar of my shirt from my neck. "I'm roasted. We're not used to this heat in England. Your father and Grace need to hurry out of the sun and we have to find a hotel or a guest house."

"We stay in a family hotel about ten miles south of the Sangro. It's a lovely place. The owners are really friendly and they make a real fuss of Dad. It's home from home."

"It sounds great. How do you communicate? Do you speak Italian?"

"No, no. Only a few words like *vino* and *grazie*. The wife of one of their sons speaks English. She drove us here, the first time Dad and I came to Abruzzo. Ah, here they come at last," he said, as Grace and his father approached. "I'd better get the air conditioning running or Dad will be suffocated."

Chapter Six

Kenmara

Another day stretches ahead, same as yesterday, same as every day. Bursts of sunlight through the windows are swallowed by a rush of grey. I've seen days when, around eleven o'clock, the sun shines from an almost cloudless sky; its rays bathe every south-facing room in an orange glow so intense you'd think brilliant lights had been switched on inside. What would I not give for such a morning? The *Irish News* lies unopened on the coffee table beside me. I should have cancelled it after Jack died – but I need to read the obituaries. At my age, I have to know who to cross off my Christmas card list, which family will need a Mass card and who has joined the ranks of widows or widowers. My friends are dropping off like wasps in autumn. Some of them would be better off dead. A mercy to themselves and to everybody else.

I glance through the window to where a P&O liner sails into the harbour. I jump to my feet and can't believe what I see. A stream of sunlight is pouring down through a small opening in the cloud cover and it looks as if handfuls of diamonds have fallen from heaven and are twinkling on the surface of the Lough. Since I came to live at Kenmara in 1952, I have never seen such a play of light and water. It's like an oasis of diamonds glittering on a grey desert and I daren't tear my eyes away, in case the waves of the Lough close forever over all that sparkling. Long after the sun has disappeared under dense clouds, I cling to the image of dancing light as if it's a secret revealed only to me. I feel privileged to have caught a glimpse of beauty, which I know I may never see again in my lifetime. In recent times I find myself clutching at memories like these. I'm not daft and I'm not trying to bring back the past. Believe me, that's the last thing I'd want to do. What's past is gone and done with, thank God.

Maybe I'll never see snow drifting in the garden the way it used to in those freezing winters when John and Hugh were wee lads. Jack used to help them make great big snowmen, each one with its own special scarf and hat. I'll never forget their excitement every morning when they saw them rock solid, like frozen sentinels, guarding the house, or the brutal way they kicked their shrunken remains over the grass.

Jack was close to nature and loved watching the changes of scene from the garden. Clear days when Galloway and the coast of Scotland seemed near enough to touch. October nights and a harvest moon casting yellow shafts across the Lough. How he would have loved the circle of diamonds dancing on water.

He gave up trying to include me in his excitement at cloud formations, at the first cyclamens or snowdrops. He said that I mocked his delight in nature and closed my eyes and ears to the first flowers on the forsythia and to the colours and sounds of woodpeckers and thrushes and of ducks and geese that stop here on their flights from Canada and the Artic. I didn't bother to tell him how in early spring I loved watching pairs of thrushes on the fence leapfrogging each other in a courtship dance, or robins pecking in freshly turned earth. And I still think magpies are beautiful birds in spite of Jack's loathing of them. It's true I did more than my share of belittling him and wasting my energy in anger, in resentment and in wanting the impossible. And it's too late to tell him I'm sorry.

He wasn't meant to die. He was strong as an ox. Never ill. So, he had to pee an awful lot. It happens when you get old. We didn't really exist below the neck in Ireland in my day. The closest we came to mentioning certain areas of the body was 'private parts' or 'down below' and I wasn't going to bring up the subject. After John made him see the doctor, he was taken into the Mater Hospital for investigations. I didn't ask what they might be and I most certainly did not want to be told. He was the life and soul of the ward. There was always a crowd round his bed. They soon scattered when I went in to visit him. I hate to admit it but my arrival was like a cloud blotting out the sun.

We had been rubbing along fine after Isabel left, though I know he pined for her. He was like a herring on hot coals listening for her call every Sunday evening. He'd rush to pick up the phone. I'd hear him asking when she was coming home, and he'd count the days till she came. He gave up boasting about her achievements to anyone

64

who would listen. I often told him his expectations of Isabel had been too high, that he had put too great a burden on her.

The letterbox rattles. I dash into the hall, my heart in my throat. A letter and a postcard from Isabel, of Tower Bridge by night.

Grace and I are at Stansted, about to catch the plane to Italy. I'll come to your birthday party. I'll arrive around the 9th if that's all right with you. Isabel.

Isabel's coming and she's coming early! I had almost given up hope. I clutch the card to my heart, which is thumping twenty to the dozen. I'll have time alone with her. Two days, maybe three, to explain. To hope against hope that she'll forgive me, or at least that she'll understand.

I read her message again, *...about to catch the plane to Italy –* And jealousy, sharp as toothache, stabs through my joy. I should have been on that plane instead of Isabel. I have more right. Grace and her mother owed me, but debts are easily forgotten.

Not by me, they're not.

What a wicked old woman I am! Never content. Always on the lookout for slights. I won't waste any more time resenting Grace for not asking me to go with her to Italy. I have two fine sons. They're concerned about me in a dutiful way, though Hugh is wrapped up in his family and in his work. As for John, he's wrapped up in himself. I used to be able to bend my family to my will without them knowing, and it's been hard to feel that power slipping from me.

My fingers tremble as I open the letter from Rose. What new gossip and half-truths from my daughter-in-law are about to shatter this peaceful morning? I'll put it in a drawer till I feel stronger. I wish there was somebody I could turn to, somebody to advise me, to calm me down. The sad truth is that I am nearly seventy-eight years old and I haven't a friend or a relative I can trust. And I've brought my loneliness on myself.

I put a pill on my tongue and have to drink a full glass of water before my throat opens to swallow it.

Dear Rita,

I can't tell you how sorry I am for upsetting you. I was stupid and insensitive and showed no regard for your feelings. I had no right to disturb you with malicious gossip. You behaved with great dignity though I could tell that you were very upset and angry with me.

You are very important and dear to me. Since the boys left home, I have come to need you to give my life some purpose. I know my fussing gets on your nerves and if it is your wish, I will not bother you any more. However, my dearest hope is that you will forgive me and take me back into the family.

Your loving daughter-in-law and friend,

Rose

I read the letter twice. For well over twenty years Rose has never admitted to being sorry for anything. I know I've been hard on her, never thought her good enough for my son – the woman wasn't born who would have been good enough for him. I've always looked for ulterior motives in Rose's efforts to help me. Maybe I'll have a word with John and tell him to start treating his wife with respect and encourage her to get a paid job. A woman with too much time on her hands is her own worst enemy. Too much time to think and scheme. That's my problem, but scheming only works when you still have a future you are able to control. Brooding and regretting start when all you have is the past. Women of my age have few topics of conversation – their past lives, their children's and their grandchildren's achievements, and their own ailments.

I share my past with no one. Not a living soul.

This coming birthday is the time to put my house in order, to face up to what happened to Bridget; to tell Isabel why I ignored her throughout her childhood; to explain that I wanted her to stay at boarding school for her own safety. I had already lost one daughter. My greatest fear was of losing another.

And I will tell her about Daisy! The whole story. I stand by the window, seeing nothing. Remembering. Remembering what I have tried for a lifetime to forget. October the twentieth 1937. A

Wednesday. The date is carved into my mind and will be till the day I die.

People might say Angela and I were children and didn't know what we were doing. We both knew full well. Though only eleven years old, we had the minds and the cunning of adults. I hear myself say 'we' and 'both', because I desperately need Angela to take her share of the blame. How many times did she say it had nothing to do with her? She just happened to be there.

I'd known Daisy for all of her five years. She lived in Bangor, about fifteen miles from my parents' public house on Limestone Road. About once a fortnight her daddy brought her to stay with her grandparents, the Corrigans, our next door neighbours. Some people said Daisy was stupid. A bit soft in the head. Mammy said she was one of life's innocents.

I really liked her, especially when she was small and she loved me. I liked the way her face lit up when she saw me. Besides, there was always a roasting fire in Mrs Corrigan's grate, whereas our house was freezing until Mammy came upstairs at five o'clock. Whenever I went to play with Daisy I got cake and lemonade. Fruit cake or Madeira or my favourite, Battenberg. Four squares in each slice. Pink and yellow. A cushion of red jam between and marzipan that peeled off in a yellow coil.

When I had finished eating and drinking and was bored with Daisy's easy jigsaws and baby books, I would pretend I had to go home to start the tea or do my homework. Daisy would cling to me and say in a whining voice, "Don't go, Rita. Please don't go. Tell me another story."

And her Granny would say, "Tell her Goldilocks while I get her Granda's tea ready.

That was the trouble with Daisy and her Granny. Never content. Always wanting more.

I'd tell the story quickly, but if I was really fed up with Daisy I'd change the ending.

She would look up at me, eyes wet, bottom lip trembling. "No, Rita, that's not right. The daddy bear didn't eat Goldilocks up. Say he didn't. Please say he didn't."

I blame Angela for many things. I can't blame her for the silent tears on Daisy's cheeks.

On that October, I was setting out to meet Angela to go to the park. Our mothers were sisters. We had both been born in the City Hospital, Angela two days before me, and we had been best friends since then. No sooner had I appeared in the street than Daisy and Mrs Corrigan arrived at their front door, like cuckoos popping out of a clock.

"Go with Rita," Daisy said, running towards me. "Go with Rita."

"Rita, love, Daisy's Granda's not well the day. Could you take her with you for a wee bit There's nobody I would trust but you, Rita, with our precious wee girl," Mrs Corrigan said, glad to get shot of Daisy's endless racket for ten minutes.

Before I could say I was meeting Angela and didn't want a runny-nosed kid trailing along with me, Mrs Corrigan was bundling Daisy into her red pixie hat, coat, mittens and muffler and slipping a sixpenny piece into my hand.

"What's she doing here?" asked Angela, glaring at Daisy.

"I'm looking after her for her granny. She paid me sixpence."

"Well, she didn't pay me," Angela said, all huffy.

I've always hated autumn. People raved about its lovely colours, but for me it was a time of withered flowers and withered leaves that were slimy and treacherous underfoot. It was the fog and drizzle of November, the month of the dead. Statues and crosses in churches wrapped in black and all the mumbled prayers for the Holy Souls.

The warm summer of 1937 had lasted through September into October. As we walked under an arch of russet, yellow and brown colours, I remember thinking it was like fairyland, like the scenery on the stage of the big school where we sometimes went for concerts.

Daisy pulled on my hand. "Rita, look up Rita, butterflies, millions and millions of butterflies!"

Yellow, orange, golden and brown leaves floated above us. They hung and hovered in the slight breeze. Until that moment I had only ever seen leaves slanting down in a whoosh of wind and racing along the ground. For minutes I stared up into the trees and watched with Daisy as leaves, like swarms of butterflies, danced above and drifted slowly around us.

"Daisy, you clever wee girl. You clever wee girl. Isn't she brilliant, Angela?" I hugged her to me and then Angela and I took Daisy's hands and ran with her for a while, sweeping her up off the ground.

68

We were walking up a slight incline out of the shelter of trees when a sudden wind cleared the path and a rush of sycamore leaves jumped and bobbed helter-skelter past us, barely touching the ground.

"Look, look. More butterflies racing over the path," I said.

A frown puckered Daisy's forehead. After a few seconds she said, "They're not butterflies, Rita. They're too big. They're birds that can't fly."

Angela started to laugh. "Daisy, you're brilliant and Rita's stupid. Some birds can't fly and those are birds that can't fly, not floating butterflies. Come on and we'll play 'Daisy, Daisy.' "

We joined hands and danced, singing:

"Daisy, Daisy, give me your answer do.
I'm half crazy all for the love of you
It won't be a stylish marriage..."

I was going through the motions, though my heart wasn't in the game. Daisy had no business showing me up in front of Angela.

"More, more," Daisy shouted, her face red with the effort. "All turn round. Start again." We soon got bored with her, so we raced to the big chestnut tree, leaving Daisy whinging behind us. That was when I discovered I had dropped one of the new gloves Mammy had knitted for me. I hunted all over through piles of leaves, scared of the telling-off and the slap I'd get. Angela wouldn't help and I knew Daisy would be worse than useless.

"Rita, there's your glove," she called out and there it was, to the right of the path in front of her.

"Pick it up and bring it to me. At once, good girl."

"Yes, Rita. Yes." Her face glowed as she bustled forward to hand me the glove.

"Thank you, slave. Daisy will do anything for me," I boasted to Angela. "Anything." I threw the glove as far as I could. "Go on, boy, fetch."

"She's not your slave. Her granny pays you to look after her," Angela said with a smirk.

I have played the next ten minutes over and over so many times, each second is imprinted on my mind. How I threw sticks and ordered five-year-old Daisy to fetch them back between her teeth. How I made her lie, face buried in leaves, while I counted to twenty, my foot on the small of her back. All to impress Angela.

"...See, know-all, she'll do anything I command."

"I bet you a shilling to her Granny's sixpence, you couldn't make her drink that water." Angela pointed at what must have been a birdbath, a circular slab of concrete on a pedestal. About two inches of scummy water had gathered in the hollow that had been scooped out of its slimy surface.

I raised my foot from Daisy's back. She scrambled to her feet, wiping dust from her eyes and nose and stood beside me. There were bits of twigs, coiled up insects and bird droppings in the water. Daisy's trusting face gazed up at me. Angela sensed my hesitation.

"See, you can't make her because she's not your slave. You're her slave."

She started to laugh, great chortles of triumphant laughter. She held out her hand for the sixpence. From that moment, what happened was between Angela and me and had nothing to do with Daisy.

"Daisy couldn't reach the water. She's small for her age," I said, preparing to walk away.

"You could pick her up if you really wanted to. She's not heavy."

I thought of all the things Angela's shilling would help me buy. A better pencil case than hers, one with a ruler and a compass. A china ornament for Mammy's birthday. A pearl necklace from Woolworth's. I didn't look at Daisy. I grabbed her and held her head over the water.

"Put your mouth down and drink, Daisy," I said, coaxing, but she kept her lips shut tight. She wriggled and squirmed till my arms were aching. Then she started blubbering.

"Some slave," Angela spat the words with contempt.

That's when I pushed Daisy's face into the water, shouting, "Drink, go on drink, stupid."

Angela glanced down at her coolly as if she was looking at a goldfish in a bowl. "She's not drinking," she announced, stretching out her hand for the sixpence.

"I'm going to hold you here till you drink the water. Do you hear me, Daisy? I'll hold you till you drown."

70

I placed my hand on her head and shoved. Her lips moved below the surface. I put her down. She stood shivering beside me, water running over her face and a sticky stream flowing from her nose.

"Stop crying. It was only a game. You're not hurt, are you? It was our game, so you won't tell your Granny." I waited till she nodded her head. "Now take off your pixie and wipe your face."

She was useless at cleaning herself. In the end, I had to wipe the dirt out of her eyebrows and rub her snotty nose with the pixie.

"There's your shilling," Angela stuck the silver coin under my nose.

"Keep it. I don't want it. I'm taking her home." I turned to walk to the gates.

"Oh no, you don't. I know you. I'm not having you telling everybody I don't pay my debts. You won it. You take it."

The shilling dropped into my pocket to lie beside Mrs Corrigan's sixpence.

I went with Daisy to the sweet shop, the image of her supping filthy water stinging my eyes. I felt like Judas when I kissed her and bought her a packet of sherbet and a box of Smarties.

"You're far too good to her, Rita," Mrs Corrigan said, smiling at Daisy's yellow mouth and sticky hands. "She's a lucky girl to have a friend like you."

I couldn't look her in the eye.
Or Daisy.

I sit down, relieved. After all these year I have faced up to the Daisy story and can lay it to rest. I'll have a cup of tea and a chocolate biscuit. Maybe try to arrange a game of bridge or ask Una to spend the night with me. No need to think about Daisy again.

I have no problem with telling lies. The catechism teaches "No lie can be lawful or innocent and no motive, however good can excuse a lie, for a lie is always sinful and bad in itself."

I think that is a load of rubbish. Sometimes we don't tell the whole truth. We hold back the bit that will hurt ourselves or others, especially ourselves. No one is any the wiser and no one suffers. I specialise in half-truths, not in lies. I tell myself I left Daisy in her granny's care, her face yellow and sticky with sherbet. Now I can move out of her shadow and get on with my life. Daisy loved me.

She wouldn't say a word about what I made her do. Even if she did, nobody would believe her.

So why can I not get her out of my head? I put on my walking shoes and jacket. Nothing like a bit of exercise to clear the mind, Jack used to say. After a serious shouting match with me, he would go into the garden, chop and dig for an hour and come in as right as rain. On more serious occasions he would march off and exercise his elbow raising pints and his tongue by telling stories to anyone who wanted to listen. I trudge up the drive on feet weighted with lead. It's no good. I reach the corner and the elm tree where Isabel used to hide the respectable outfits I bought for her and her put on the skimpy, trashy clothes I had forbidden her to wear. I wend my way back to my beautiful home and go into the hall if I was entering a prison.

I have not told the whole story, only the beginning.

I need time to recall what happened next, why I have blamed myself ever since, why I have buried Daisy in some shady, forgotten part of my brain. I will think about it tomorrow, or maybe the day after.

Chapter Seven

In my imagination our holiday had featured famous cities, beaches on the Bay of Naples or Capri, perhaps a journey through the rolling hills and tall cypresses of Tuscany on our way to Sienna, Florence, or one of those terracotta hilltop towns I knew from paintings and films. Such scenes still lingered in my mind as Grace followed the hired car driven by Pat. The road wound sometimes along the Adriatic, sometimes through countryside that was as yet unaffected by months of summer heat. Absorbed in what I had just learned about Grace's father, I was aware of olive groves on arid hills and of silent villages. They were so still their inhabitants might have been whisked away by some Pied Piper, or fallen into a heavy sleep which made them deaf to the rumble of lorries and of cars passing close by their windows.

Grace's calm profile gave no hint of the emotions aroused by finding her father's grave. Had her mother told her stories or shown her snaps of the man whose blood flowed through her veins? Had she described him? Said what had attracted her to him? How long they had spent together? Aunt Kate was too serious for one-night stands – or was she? In a London of air-raids and threats of raids, of death and destruction, a London where an endless tide of wounded and dying poured into every hospital, men and women must have grabbed at any chance of closeness. Of loving and forgetting.

I thought of my father and his fanciful account of finding me on the shore near Carrickfergus. I remembered how he had guided and shielded my childhood, how unbearable life would have been without him.

"We were lucky to meet Fred," Grace said, as if continuing a conversation with me. "I was impressed by his sincerity and his loyalty to his comrades." She turned to me, excitement bubbling in her voice. "Isabel, don't you think it was an amazing stroke of luck meeting somebody who fought in the same battle as Anthony O'Brien?"

"It was more than coincidence, Grace. It was fate. Pat told me his dad had insisted on going to the cemetery today in the midday sun. Seize the day. Find out all you can from Fred."

Grace glanced at me with the indulgent smile of a mother, unwilling to curb her over-enthusiastic child. "I'm wary about staying at a hotel we haven't seen. Shall we have a look before committing ourselves?"

Pat turned off the main highway on to a small road close to the beach and stopped at the Hotel Aragosta, an imposing building whose glass-fronted facade gleamed like polished silver. Giant palms in pots added to the cool of the air-conditioned foyer and from the dining room we heard the sounds of voices and the rattle of cutlery. A smiling, round-faced woman emerged, wiping her hands on a white apron. She greeted Fred and Pat in rapid Italian and called out to someone in the dining-room. Grace nodded at me. We were to follow our destiny. Through her rapid Italian, I made out the words "Signor Fred," and "Pat," and, almost instantly, a young man appeared in the foyer carrying two glasses of beer on a tray.

Pat said, "This is Signora Gina, wife of one of the owners. She trained as a chef in Geneva and speaks perfect French."

In my A level French I said "Bonjour, Madame," and told her how delighted we were to meet her. Though I knew that Grace had been attending Italian classes for the past two years, I was impressed to hear her book a room with a balcony and a sea view with gestures that helped me guess what she was saying. Gina introduced the man who came into the foyer as her husband, Claudio Cellucci, and explained in French to me that he and his brother, Tiberio, had won the top Italian prize for the cooking and presentation of fish dishes of the Abruzzo region. She pointed to a photograph on the wall which celebrated their success.

Claudio and Tiberio! The strong, aquiline features of both men could have been taken from coins of Roman emperors. Claudio welcomed Grace and me and called, "Ottavio!" As if conjured out of the air, a young lad, more cherub than Roman emperor, appeared, picked up our suitcases and showed us to a large room on the first floor. It had two windows, one looking over the entrance, the other with a wide view of the sea which was about two minutes from the hotel.

"This is wonderful," I said, throwing open the shutters. "Here we are in a lovely hotel. We have two new friends downstairs and you speak Italian like a native."

"Hardly. I can book into a hotel, buy shoes, single and return tickets and I can order a meal. That's about it." Though Grace laughed, she seemed distracted as if only half listening. "I can make myself understood but generally I get about ten percent of what I hear, and only if it's spoken really slowly. The rest I just guess at and say *si* and *non* a lot." She grinned, "I get a lot of mileage out of *prego*." She concentrated on unpacking, folding clothes and hanging skirts and a dress in the wardrobe. "I think we should shower, change and go down for lunch."

In the shower room I studied my misted reflection in the mirror. An unformed shape, not yet a recognisable person. Years of avoiding Ma, of anticipating her next move and keeping a step ahead had taught me to be a shadow, ready to disappear or merge, chameleon-like, into the background. To shrink. Not occupy too much space. Sometimes when I could no longer stand the rows at Kenmara, I would swan-dive to the bottom of the Lough to crouch on sand and pebbles, away from my parents' fury and the storms swirling the water above me. Safe in my own element.

Underwater swimming gave me the sense of a safety barrier between me and reality. Like the months on Prozac after Grania died. A half existence, not having to think, clunking along like a robot. Silence and separateness, away from the sounds of shouting, laughing and splashing. This was the life I assumed in Kenmara, putting on a cloak of semi- invisibility after shedding the guise of the laughing, ready-for-anything teenager I was with my school friends and the lads from Saint Malachi's who hung around the gates of my school.

I had gone from the house I shared with five other students, each with our lockable bedrooms, to the closeness of the marriage bed and two rooms not yet marked out as our personal territory. When we moved to Brockley, I used to observe Liam as he came up the short path to our front door. A spring to his step, lips parted in a smile that brightened his face and I'd rush to open the door before his key found the lock. Hunched shoulders, creased brow, and lips narrowed to extinction sent me dashing upstairs or into the kitchen to wait for the greeting that would set the mood for the rest of the day. And I would will the sour evening to slide into the pale light before dawn when, after half-asleep love-making, I would lie spooned into Liam. He would put his arms around me until we drifted apart in sleep. I learned the sanctity of his exclusion zone, the box room at the top of the stairs for his computer, his filing cabinet and the ordered drawers of his desk. And I welcomed the clutter of our bedroom, where the floor was the natural home for discarded shirts, socks and shorts. Experience taught me how far his private space extended. I learned when and by how much the boundaries had been moved when my attempts at conversation interrupted his thinking or made him lose the thread of an article that engrossed him. I learned to leave the newspaper folded, pages in the correct order and to realise the effect my high-heeled clacking on wooden floors had on his creativity. I learned to busy myself cooking, cleaning and fuming until my sexy, funny husband re-emerged, as he usually did.

I stood barefoot on the marble floor of the balcony looking at the sea where waves broke and spread white to the shore. Knowing Grace, she would have studied the Italian campaign and the battles in which Anthony O'Brien might have been involved. With Fred's help, she would try to retrace his movements and I would tag along, learning something about a war that ended almost 60 years ago.

When Grace emerged from the bathroom, I said, "Thanks again for asking me to come and for telling me about your father."

No reply. Perhaps the whirr of the dryer had drowned my voice. Perhaps her thoughts were with the soldier whose grave she had visited. Anthony O'Brien could have been a patient at the hospital in London where Aunt Kate worked. They might have met at some club or pub where Irish people congregated. Try as I might, I couldn't see Kate, a Pioneer-pin-wearing teetotaller, knocking back pints in a pub in the forties. Maybe I would ask Grace. Maybe I would wait until she was ready to talk.

I said Grace and I were very close. I should have said that our relationship was a one-way system. She gave and I took. In my early weeks at university, before I discovered drinking and partying, she invited me most weekends to Hastings to her house, which had a large garden and a view over the Channel. She cooked delicious meals, took me shopping and listened to my single-minded prattling.

76

Grace's husband had died of lung cancer when her elder son, David, was seven and his brother, Simon, two years younger. She had nursed both her parents through their last forgetful years. And then along I came, obsessed with each new chapter of the Liam or the Ma saga.

It was time to grow up. To look out for Grace for a change.

We were shown to a table in the dining room, which had a high ceiling and a wall of one-way glass. Salads, fruit – peaches, nectarines, grapes and cherries – and a choice of desserts and ice creams were displayed on a table in the centre.

Gina approached our table accompanied by a slim, dark-haired young man who had been taking orders from a group of noisy couples at the far side of the room. She introduced him as her son Franco. He welcomed Grace and me in halting English.

"Tomorrow comes my wife, Marilena. She is a teacher. She speaks English very good." He hesitated, spoke in Italian to his mother, then a smile covered his face as he said, "I was two years in Manchester at the restaurant of my cousin. Marilena was a student in Manchester. I don't speak English too good."

"I wish I could speak Italian as well as you speak English," I said. "Tell your wife we look forward to meeting her."

After the meal, we joined Fred and Pat where they sat on the shaded terrace.

"This is where Dad most likes to be. On winter days in Bracknell we look forward to having a beer out here, chatting to Claudio and Tiberio with Marilena's help. You'll love Marilena. She's lively and she's lovely."

His father interrupted, "And we talk about going back to Scerni. That's the village where I was stationed before and after the battle of the Sangro. I'm a lucky man. I've made many friends in Scerni. We'll take you there, if you would like, Grace. Your father will have been there too, before we crossed the Sangro." Fred turned to Pat, "I want to talk to Grace. Why don't you take Isabel for a walk along the shore?"

I was glad to leave Grace alone with Fred and go to the shore with Pat. Italians speak at a much higher pitch than the English, or even the Irish, and it was good to be quiet with Pat. When I remarked on the silence he said it was still lunch or siesta time. Hotels close to the Aragosta did not seem to have opened. Pat assured me that on summer evenings visitors came from the neighbouring town and villages to eat and the air filled with the sound of dance music. The white village below the Aragosta, which consisted of one small shop and a cluster of houses, was equally quiet.

We passed a station which Pat said was on the main line from Venice to the very south of Italy. And then we were on the beach. The long strand reminded me of empty beaches in Donegal. I stopped to breathe in the fresher sea air and to take my bearings. A slight breeze cooled the intense heat of the sun that blazed in a cloudless sky. Once more I noticed the luminous quality of the light, the intensity with which it reflected the colours of sky, sea and sand. I accepted Pat's offer of coffee at a bar built on stilts near the water's edge. It was empty apart from two old men who stared at us as if we were unidentified creatures cast up by the sea. Pat shook hands with the waiter, also a member of the Cellucci family, who brought us coffee and indicated that it was on the house. As we drank, I asked Pat about his family.

"When my mother died," he said, "I moved in with Dad. We're a close family. He was heartbroken and we didn't think he would survive on his own. He's eighty-four, you know, and getting frail. It's the thought of coming here to the Aragosta and seeing his friends in Scerni again that keeps him going."

Listening to Pat's quiet voice and watching the ebb and flow of the Adriatic reminded me of sitting by the Lough with my father, half-believing the changing versions of his past. Like him, Pat was easy to be with, a relaxed and contented man.

"It's a strange thing, Isabel. We've gone with Dad to all the places where he served in the war, Egypt, Tripoli, Normandy, Belgium and Denmark but this is where he most likes to be, here at the Lido di Casalbordino. My whole family look forward to coming here almost as much as he does."

As we strolled along the shore Pat said, "When we saw you and Grace in the cemetery, we thought you were mother and daughter."

78

"Lots of folk think that, because we look so alike. Our mothers were sisters and Grace and I have been very close, especially since I came to live in England." Then, without meaning to, and probably because Pat was a sympathetic listener and almost a stranger, I told this man, whom I had met only a few hours previously, how Grace had helped me cope after Grania died.

"Grania. It's a lovely name. I've never heard it before. Is it Irish?" he asked.

I said it was the Gaelic version of Grace and I told him Liam had died last week. "Grace has been widowed for a very long time and she didn't think either of her sons would want to come here with her. I'm very glad she asked me."

I said I knew nothing about the countries in the Balkans and asked Pat about the blue-green hills on the horizon.

"It's an optical illusion, Isabel," he said. "I think Croatia's directly opposite, but it's too far away to see from here."

It may have been no more than a reflection of light on water, but I continued to see a ridge of low hills along the length of the horizon.

"My father came from Innishmore, one of the Aran Islands off the west of Ireland. He told me about a mystical island that rises out of the Atlantic whenever there's a disaster at sea. He said it's a refuge for shipwrecked sailors and anyone in danger on the sea. It's called Hy-Brasil, the Isle of the Blest."

"And did your father ever see the island?" Pat asked, with a smile.

"I remember asking him if he'd seen Hy-Brasil. He said he had, that it was just beyond the horizon." My voice broke at the memory. I recalled the lines carved into my father's face, his mass of white hair, protection in his large hands. He loved me more than anyone in the world and I had arrived too late to say goodbye to him. I tormented myself thinking of him waiting for me to sit by his bedside. It had never occurred to me that he might have been quietly getting on with the business of dying. Pat bent to tie his shoelace. I took a deep breath. "My father said Hy-Brasil was a land of sunshine and peace, where there is neither sorrow, nor death." I turned toward Pat. "He was a great storyteller and his stories grew and blossomed with each telling. I believed everything he told me." I laughed and added, "Maybe I only pretended to believe, to keep him happy."

"You keep searching for your island, Isabel, and one day, I'm sure you'll find it."

"Anyone can see it, if they search hard enough. It's just over the horizon."

We looked to where waves foamed over rocks and over breakwaters which had been laid parallel to the shore. Pat told me that coastal erosion was a major problem along the Adriatic. When he first came to Casalbordino the beach was about three times deeper than now. The darker sand I had commented on had been brought from the seabed near Venice in an attempt to hold back the encroaching waters and the stones left in their wake. He glanced at his watch and said he should return to the hotel to make sure his father was having his afternoon rest. I kicked off my sandals and stood at the edge of the sea, watching him go as waves curled and uncurled over my feet.

Jack McGlade had had a way with words. "I thought the gift of a baby daughter would make my wife happy," he'd said to me. My mother might have a different version of my conception and of giving birth at fifty – if I had plucked up the courage to ask her.

I gazed towards the changing shapes of the hills where the sea met the sky, searching for Grania on the quiet waters. Faceless dark under a tangle of tubes and patches. Tubes taped to cheeks, protruding from nose and mouth. Was she wearing a cap, or was that another baby in another incubator, or a picture on the television? The image disappeared and I couldn't bring it back. I don't trust my memories of Grania any more. They have spilled through my fingers and I have reshaped and fashioned them many times. She was the baby I had dreamed of. Black-haired and dark-eyed like Liam; a child to mend our marriage. Her unborn movements had thrilled me. Slight, almost imperceptible at first. Later, I felt her miniature limbs dancing, boxing, the rhythm of her heartbeat. I think her eyes were black when the slits of her lids half-opened and her skin was red and shrivelled. Liam, Grace or I sat with her for three days and nights. When I wakened in the nursery for premature babies, a nurse told me that my baby had passed away. Passed away! As if she had risen up and glided of her own will to some other place. Liam and I were asked if we wanted a photograph taken of her in her coffin. He and I belonged to the same culture. The same religion and taboos had formed us. No photographs. No foot- or hand-prints. I was not considered fit enough to accompany Liam and Grace to my daughter's cremation.

Back at the hotel, Grace was on the balcony absorbed in reading material on the Italian campaign, which she had downloaded from the internet. She sat up with a start when I came in.

"I've been thinking, Isabel. Maybe you were right and Fate led us to Fred. He's dignified and courteous, like my father." She corrected herself. "Your Uncle Harry, I mean. Before Mamma and I decided to come here, I met up with several veterans of the Adriatic campaign. They told me their experiences. They showed me their medals and answered my questions – but none of them wanted to help the way Fred does." She looked at me and said, "You're worn out, Isabel. You must get some sleep."

"Don't worry about me. I'm fine. I didn't have to drive from Hastings to Stansted in the small hours of the morning and I haven't been on a quest to find my father's grave." I put my arms around Grace and cradled her. Her stiffness ebbed from her. "Let me look after you for a change. God knows it's my turn. I don't know how I would have coped without you, especially after Grania and then when Liam left."

"That was a long time ago, love. You've a new life ahead of you and you must seize it with both hands." She kissed me and said, "We helped each other. I haven't forgotten the weekends and holidays when you looked after Mamma – and she wasn't easy, poor soul."

I nodded agreement at the memory of Kate hurling food at Grace and me, her biting me and her carers, me trying to restrain her from jumping out of the moving car.

It was Ma I had longed for when I left the hospital, after Grace went back to her family and Liam returned to work leaving me doped out of my mind. I wanted her to look after me, as only a mother could, as she had one day, long ago.

Images, bleary and formless, struggling to take shape through a fug of tranquillizer. Kenmara. A post office van driving away. Mitzi's striped body, splayed in front of the house like a baby tigerskin rug. My scream shattering the morning.

"Isabel, Isabel." Fear in Ma's voice. Black dark in the sheltering folds of her skirt. Arms clutching me, picking me up, squeezing me to her. Her fast breath on my neck.

"Don't cry, my baby. Mitzi didn't feel anything. I'll get you another cat today. I promise. Don't cry."

Molly, my fluffy, white-pawed kitten, in a wicker basket.

I wasn't allowed the other babies my body cried out for. There was always an excuse. I was unstable. In no fit state. Liam's new post in London. His studies.

Never the real reason.

Ma didn't come to see me after Grania died. She had a chest infection. She had never travelled by plane. She couldn't face the boat journey to Liverpool and the train to Euston.

On a day packed with events and revelations, I was surprised that the memory of my father had stuck in my head. I dreamed about foggy days when the Lough would disappear under a grey blanket and mist would spread over the shore, over streets, gardens and parks. It would creep across the estate beyond our garden and slither up the terraced slopes until Kenmara and the drive were standing on an island in a sea of fog. And somewhere in the dream was my father telling me about Hy-Brasil. I was with him climbing up to the three thousand-year-fort on the cliffs of his home on Innishmore, as he had often promised we would, to search the Atlantic for the magical island.

When I woke, light chinked round the shutters. I jumped out of bed and rushed to fling open the door to the balcony. Waves were not crashing round the Aragosta or lapping under the balcony. They rolled white-edged to break with soundless splashes on the shore, exactly as they had yesterday. Light from the not-quite-risen sun blazed the sky. My fears subsided after it rose above the horizon and the sea turned to a brilliant azure, more intense than the paler blue of the sky. A single ship sailed far out from the shore. Perhaps it was carrying sand from the sea-bed to bleach on the sunny beaches of Abruzzo. I watched as it moved slowly south, a puny speck on a vast stretch of water.

Chapter Eight

Kenmara

For the next few days after I left Daisy at her Granny's I lived in dread. What if Mrs Corrigan came to our pub and told Mammy about the cruel way I had treated her wee grandchild. At first Mammy would not believe her. She would say I loved Daisy and I would not hurt anyone. It was not in my nature. Mrs Corrigan would insist, tell her exactly what had happened and say how upset Daisy still was.

Then Mammy would look me in the eye in the stern, accusing way I knew only too well and ask, "Is this true, Rita?"

I would deny everything as I always did. But this time things were different. She wasn't asking if I had eaten the last piece of cake that was meant for my Auntie's visit on Wednesday. Nor was she accusing me of taking two pennies from her purse. She could read me like a book. If I said Angela made me, that it was her idea, she had stood over me till Daisy drank the water, Mammy would clout me really hard. She would say I was a telltale as well as a wicked bully and a liar. My father would have to be told and he would decide the punishment I deserved.

There was a coolness between me and Angela. I think it was more on my side than on hers. I told myself it would blow over. We often had rows, but we always made up soon after.

Days passed. A week passed. Once October became November I started to relax. Daisy had gone back to her parents' house and forgotten about the whole stupid thing. Anyhow, it was not as if I had hurt her. There were no marks on her.

No cuts. No bruises.

About two weeks later Mr Corrigan came to our house. I knew from his sobbing and from Mammy's cry of, "Oh no, not wee Daisy" that something terrible had happened.

"She was only a wee girl, but she was a fighter. She fought for three days, three whole days..." His voice dissolved into loud, gulping sobs.

Mammy led him upstairs to an armchair in the living room. He sat on the edge, little and shrunken, tears streaming down his wrinkled face. He just sat there twisting his cloth cap as if he was trying to wring it dry. Twisting. Twisting.

Mammy put her arms around me. "Oh Rita, poor wee Daisy. Poor wee child."

I let myself be hugged and stroked, but I couldn't cry and I couldn't speak.

Mr Corrigan sat on the edge of the chair saying to himself, "Why Daisy? She was the loveliest wee girl ever was born. Why? Why? Can somebody tell me why?" he asked, still twisting his cap between his hands.

His face was the same grey colour as his hair. In his own house he shuffled about in slippers with trodden down backs. He used to get upset when he couldn't remember where he put his glasses, his sports page, or his cigarettes and matches and he often dropped food down his Fair Isle front. He could have heard wrong. Maybe Daisy wasn't dead. Maybe she was in hospital and would be better soon.

"No, Rita, Snow White didn't die. She didn't swallow the poisoned apple. She woke up when the prince kissed her. Honest Rita, she did. She did."

"I don't know why, Mr Corrigan. God must have thought it was for the best. Your Daisy's an angel in heaven."

Suddenly Daisy's quiet granddad, whose wife normally did the talking, stood up looking twice as big as he was.

"If your Rita was taken, would you say it was for the best? Would you?" he asked, his voice harsh with anger. "Just because Daisy was a bit slow, people thought she wasn't important, that she wasn't worth much, but no child was more loved than Daisy and no child gave so much back. Rita knows that, if you don't."

When he turned to leave, he was all hunched and small again.

Next day, Angela took me into a corner of the playground.

"You killed Daisy," she muttered, "You shouldn't have made her drink that poisoned water. You gave her cholera."

"No I didn't. And it was your idea. You made me."

84

"Me make you?" she snorted. *"I was only joking but nothing would stop you. All you wanted was my shilling and you didn't care what happened to Daisy."*

"I did care. I really cared. Anyhow, nobody gets cholera in England. Not any more."

"That's because nobody's forced to drink water full of cholera and malaria and other horrible diseases the way you forced Daisy."

Neither of us had an idea of the effects of cholera. We knew it was as fatal as smallpox and still existed in Africa.

After school, I slunk home through the park, even though I had been forbidden to go there by myself. I can see it clearly. One of those murky days we had so often, the park gloomy and dense with threat and shadows, fallen leaves in slushy piles, trees almost bare of foliage, stark against a leaden sky. I stopped at the pedestal. If I drank the filthy water, I would get ill and die too. I bent down over the water but a lump blocked my throat and my mouth wouldn't open.

I couldn't face Angela after that. Her accusing eyes. Her cruel tongue. The fear she would tell Mammy or Mrs Corrigan and I would be sent to a reformatory and then to prison to be hung. I wondered how long it would take for my neck to break. Our mammies thought we'd had another row and we would soon be inseparable again. But I missed Angela, missed being seen with her and looking forward to meeting her every day. She and I were the cleverest girls in the school, neck and neck, streets ahead of everyone else. The best singers, winners at every sport. One of us always first in tests, the other a close second. When Mammy learned that I had been top in every subject in the summer exams, she had danced round the kitchen with me singing, *"You beat Angela. You're a genius, Rita."* She bought me a tartan skirt and a red jumper in Robinson and Cleaver's and took me to The Picture House in Royal Avenue to see the Marx Brothers in *"A Night at the Opera."*

Mammy and I never danced or sang together after I killed Daisy.

She treated me like an invalid and made sure Daisy's name was never mentioned in my presence. Mr and Mrs Corrigan moved away shortly afterwards and Daisy was forgotten by everyone but me. I heard Mammy telling her friend I was in shock but I'd soon get over it.

But I couldn't get Daisy out of my head. Or her Granddad.

Coming first didn't matter any more. Nothing mattered. I didn't bother to finish any of the scholarship papers and was relieved when Angela got a place at the Dominican Convent on the Falls Road. My parents had to pay to send me as a boarder to a convent far away up in Portstewart.

I was fifteen when Mother de Lourdes wrote to my parents. She was worried about my health, because I was very pale and had no energy. The all-seeing eye of an x-ray machine saw through flesh and bones. It looked into my lungs and detected the stain of TB, or consumption as we called it. A shadow on my lung and a shadow on my life and on the lives of my parents. There was talk of iron lungs, of sending me to Lissue Hospital near Lisburn to lie outside in the fresh country air. Consumption was a shameful illness, a sign of poverty, of dirt and neglect and it could be caught by breathing the same air as the victim. If anyone found out, word would spread as fast as the disease and no one would dare drink in my parents' pub. As I was supposed to be at boarding school I would not be missed. So, I was imprisoned in my bedroom lest I contaminate innocent passers by. I had to lie in bed for about eighteen months and drink a bottle of porter every day from a crate that was hidden in the wardrobe. When the doctor came to see me, he shook his head and said poor child, I would have a better chance in a sanatorium on a mountain in Switzerland. I often heard Mammy sobbing beside my bed and begging God to spare me. But I was happy. Consumption was the big killer in those days and the answer to my prayers. It wiped out whole families. It had killed each of the seven girls in the McCarthy family from Magheragall. All I had to do was to wait till I was dead.

Dead like Daisy.

"A shadow on her lung!" Mrs Malloy sucked in her breath and said in a stage whisper, "A shadow, Jesus, Mary and Joseph! God spare the child. A shadow, that's awful. Mind, a spot's worse, if that's any comfort to you."

Mrs Malloy boasted that she knew more than any doctor. Ma often consulted her on medical problems and paid for her diagnosis and her discretion. She never came further than the bedroom door and spoke through a man's handkerchief which she had clamped over her mouth and nose. She reminded Mammy that TB was very catching. She'd seen it run like woodworm through families.

86

"That lovely looking O'Hara girl had a spot on the lung and she was in the ground within six months. God rest her."

Mrs Malloy, who had a rhyme to suit every occasion and believed everyone should be ready for the worst, went on to recite,

"From a Munster vale they brought, from the pure and balmy air
An Irish peasant's daughter with blue eyes and golden hair.
They brought her to the city and she faded slowly there.
Consumption has no pity for blue eyes and golden hair."
Spots! Shadows.

Spots came with measles and chickenpox. You could see them. Touch them. Scratch them. But shadows had no substance. If you put your hand through them, it was as if you were slicing through air. You could watch your own shadow growing longer, but you couldn't walk on it. Shadow puppets danced on walls and disappeared leaving no trace. They did no harm. But shadows could block out the sun and make a day feel cold. And an eclipse of the sun could turn day into night. I didn't understand that. Anyhow, the sun didn't shine inside us.

Before I had to leave school we had a retreat conducted by a very old priest with a smiling face and a confidential way of talking, even though he made slurping noises as if his phlegm was choking him. The junior girls were dismissed from chapel. This was to be my first sex talk. Into the circle the priest had made with the thumb and first finger of his left hand he kept plunging his right forefinger.

"This is what Daddy and Mammy did so that you could be made into a baby and grow inside Mammy."

Plunge, plunge, faster and deeper and him slurping as if he would drown in spit. Plunge, plunge as he bounced on the balls of his feet.

"Now, girls or young women, as I should say, do you all understand what Daddy did to Mammy to create you in God's image?"

I didn't believe one word of it and neither did my friends. Poor old fellow, he was ancient – and besides, how would a priest know what men and women did?

I still had a child's skinny body when I caught TB. While I was lying night and day in the steamy heat of my bed I developed breasts and a slender waist. When my parents were asleep I'd pull the light cord above my bed, take off my nightdress and caress my beautiful body. I thought of the priest and what he said. And all the while, my head was bursting with the immoral thoughts he had warned us against. Thoughts that were every bit as sinful as impure actions and had to be suppressed under pain of dying in a state of mortal sin and spending eternity in Hell. I was going to Hell in a handcart for killing Daisy, so I might as well enjoy my impure thoughts. And I did. I decided that young people with consumption were probably sent to the freezing cold of a Swiss mountain to keep their minds as well as their bodies from overheating.

I drag myself from my seat and shuffle to the kitchen. I fill the kettle, anchor it on its base and mop up the water I've spilled over the draining board and floor. My fingers fumble to press the switch. I can't cope with loose tea right now and I don't know where the teabags are. I look in all the cupboards before I find a packet that Rose must have hidden on a shelf above the sink. I drop a bag in a mug and add milk. A scum forms on the surface. Rose is always hiding things. She's got me all of a dither. Where did she put my pills? I had them a minute ago. I'll be fine after a wee rest.

I shouldn't have started thinking about Daisy. I wasn't ready. That's what made me act like a doddering old woman. No point in blaming Rose, though I always need somebody to blame. Angela went to Dublin, or was it London? She's not going to come back and have me sent to prison, not after all these years. I did see her again. Where was that? I'll remember later. She won't come back. Not now. She might have died for all I know. She was two days older than me after all. I'd better sit by the window for a while and read the death notices.

Chapter Nine

Grace and I rode with his father in Pat's car, heading for the hill town of Scerni, where Fred had been billeted before and after the battle of the Sangro. He said how pleased he and his comrades had been to leave Africa and arrive in the cooler climate of Italy; to give 'bully beef' a rest, eat fresh meat and vegetables from local farms and drink good Italian wine.

"General Montgomery came along one day as we were making our way up the Adriatic coast. He welcomed us and he said he was sure we would continue to be victorious in whatever battles we faced." Fred paused. With a half-smile he added, "Every time I stop to look at his statue at Whitehall, I see Monty standing on that small mound, somewhere near the Adriatic, making his address, praising and encouraging his troops. He was a great leader and it was a privilege to serve under him."

Their first mission was to capture the hilltop village of Scerni. Fortunately, the Germans had retreated several hours previously and the Allies had a great welcome.

"We stayed several weeks in the village and we got on very well with the local people. Their lives were very hard. The only light they had was from pieces of string dipped in saucers of olive oil that gave off a glow like candlelight."

"Did you get to know any of the Italians?" I asked.

"Yes," said Fred. "We were often invited to the villagers' houses for a meal and a sing-song and we made friends with several families. I remember watching them knock down the low walls at the side of their houses. They brought out bicycles, motorcycles, bottles of wine, salted pork, salami and furniture: anything the Germans would have commandeered."

Fred paused, reliving the memory. Then with a broad grin, he said, "We weren't allowed to talk to the girls of the village, but we enjoyed watching them fetching water from the well, going to the shop and to church. We hadn't seen girls for a long time and the Italian girls were lovely with their long black hair and their tanned skin. They used to stroll round the village in the evening, clacking past us on wooden sandals, laughing and giggling and pretending not to see us." He chuckled to himself when he added, "Our officer was amused when most of his soldiers suddenly became religious and needed to attend Mass on Sundays. It paid off. We saw a lot more of the girls and we had more invitations to eat with their families."

The twinkle in Fred's eye gave me a glimpse of the young lad who had volunteered as soon as he learned that England was at war with Germany.

Pat parked his car and led Grace and me down cobbled streets into a bustling square. I searched in vain for people of my age or younger, grandchildren of the girls Fred had admired in 1943. As in the towns I know on the Sussex coast, there were many pensioners. But in Sussex, lots of very young mothers can be seen pushing buggies. In the summer there are crowds of language students, tanned and smartly dressed, speaking noisily in languages other than English. I was wondering if emigration had robbed Scerni of its youth or if there hadn't been any births for fifty years, when I heard calls of "Fred!" and "Pat!"

A man and his wife kissed and hugged our English friends and greeted them in Italian. Soon others followed, kissing, chattering and hugging Fred. Pat introduced us.

"The first time we came to Scerni, Marilena was with us," he explained. "Dad showed the villagers photographs he had taken in 1943. Most of the people in the photos had died, some only recently, but we met their children and we are invited to their homes every summer. Always with Marilena."

Grace told the people who greeted Fred and Pat that her father had fought in the battle of the Sangro River. She watched their faces in hope as they repeated, "Antonio, Antonio O' Brai-an," as they scratched their heads and consulted among themselves. I saw her willing his name to trigger a memory of a soldier they might have met over sixty years previously, but, without a photograph, no one remembered Anthony O'Brien.

After a drink in a newly renovated bar and a promise to return, Pat took a road close to the route his father had climbed in 1943.

"It was a puff and a blow, as I remember," Fred said. "We left Scerni around two in the afternoon and climbed non-stop till around midnight. We were exhausted and hadn't the faintest idea of what tomorrow would bring." He pointed to Mount Calvo, a short distance

90

away. "The following morning we woke up and saw the Apennines covered in snow. You see that mountain to the east? It overlooks the Sangro Valley. It really was a lovely scene way back then." With a wry smile, Fred added, "Except that the enemy held the opposite bank."

He pointed at the sunlit slopes above the Sangro valley. Grass bent lightly in the breeze and the buzz of insects seemed to deepen the silence. Pat reminded his father that they had trudged through blinding rain and had been soaked before they reached the spot where they spent the night.

"After a couple of days here, our officer told us the battalion would establish a bridgehead over the Sangro. My section was the leading one in the patrol. We were to be the first over – a dubious honour," he said, wrinkling his brow.

"At midnight we moved to the actual position for the crossing – the bridge had been blown up by the enemy. We were to cross at 3 a.m. and our Italian guides had selected a safe, fordable place. We were to make for a clump of silver birches that shone in the moonlight."

His account of crossing the flooded river and reaching the silver birches was as vivid as a scene from many of the war films I had watched on the television. He spoke so fluently, it was clearly an incident he had often relived. They had crossed the river in almost total silence, developing a sort of rhythm by pushing their chests slowly forward in short bursts. When they were about halfway over, the silence was broken by a shout of, "Be Jazus!" from a very short Irishman, just before his head disappeared under the fast flowing river. Fred and another man had grabbed hold of the half-drowned soldier and everyone made a mad, noisy dash for the bank.

After a few hours' rest, Fred's platoon commander told him to select two men for a recce patrol. He pointed out a large house some hundreds of yards away. A solid looking structure, like a fortress. His brief was to see if it was occupied. Fred stopped speaking and said he didn't want to bore us with details, but Grace urged him to go on.

"I looked at the moon and lined it up with the fortress. I decided that, if I had to beat a hasty retreat, I should keep slightly left of the moon." With the grin of an eight-year-old, he turned at us and said, "It sounds daft, but it had worked in the desert. We went cautiously towards the building that was built of stone. Once inside, we crept down the passage till we came to the kitchen. It seemed empty, but there was so much food cooking. it wasn't hard to guess the strength of the enemy. We withdrew to the back door and lobbed two hand grenades down the passage. They exploded as we ran to take cover. We waited ten minutes. Nothing happened, so we returned and reported to our Company Commander."

They occupied the place, lit fires and made themselves at home. Fred said it was a relief to be surrounded by such thick walls. When the Germans began attacking the place, shells simply bounced off the walls.

"History books will give you a better account of the battle than I'm able to. My big regret is that many good comrades were killed when their vehicles were blown up by mines. The sad thing was their tactical role was finished and the Indian troops had already passed through our lines." Fred looked away, his mind apparently caught on the thread of a long-ago memory.

"After a week or so defending the area, my company was sent back to Scerni. Our friends in the village gave us a very warm welcome and a Christmas I'll never forget. They asked about the men who didn't return. When they were told, '*Morte,*' some were inconsolable. At Mass the following Sunday the congregation joined in prayers for the *Inglese.*"

In the car park at the Aragosta Grace thanked Fred for describing the battle so vividly. "My generation grew up without having to fight a world war. We can never repay the debt we owe to you and all the men you fought with."

"You're very kind, Grace. I was an ordinary soldier in war time, doing what I was told, only one of many."

Grace opened the shutters in our darkened room, letting in the noise of traffic passing along the road, the distant sound of the motorway and the scent of oleander.

"Pat told me his father was awarded the Military Medal for outstanding bravery in several campaigns. Fred's so self-effacing, nobody would have any idea." Still preoccupied, she kicked off her sandals and stretched out on her bed. A few moments later, she sat bolt upright and said, "I'm sure that Anthony O'Brien was one of the men killed when the fighting was over. It's something to work on."

92

Something to work on? We had visited Anthony O'Brien's grave. We had gone to Scerni, where he probably spent a few weeks. We had seen the site of the battle where he lost his life. What else could we possibly do?

When Liam and I visited cemeteries in France and Belgium, he often spoke to visiting groups who had come to see where their relatives were interred. Then they left with photographs and a mental picture of the gravestone and the cemetery.

I was standing on the balcony that overlooked the sea, restless, ready to move on to the excitement of Florence or Rome, to Pompeii and Naples. Now was the time for of the many questions I had not dared to ask Grace.

"How did you react when you saw your birth certificate?"

Grace thought for a few moments before replying. She got up and stood beside me. White knuckled, she clutched the metal rail of the balcony. "Mamma said nothing when it came in the post. In the column for my father's name, instead of 'Harold Sheridan' there was an empty space. I thought it was a mistake. I asked Papa if someone had forgotten to fill in his name. He had obviously been expecting the question and he answered quickly." Her voice was so low, I struggled to hear. "He said he had adopted my mother's baby, but I could not be more precious to him if he had been my natural father." Seconds, maybe a minute, passed before she continued, "I had been secure in my home life, the only child of adoring parents. That empty space took my breath away and it took away my certainty about who I was. Without wanting to sound too melodramatic, I'd say the bottom fell out of my world."

After a silence which I dared not break, she released her grip on the rail and said in a more matter-of-fact tone, "That was a lifetime ago. It wasn't a tragedy. Nothing changed in my day-to-day existence, so I'm not going to make a meal of it, except to say that as I grew older I became more aware of the missing person who was my birth father. I resembled my mother physically, but I was more like Papa in many ways. We had similar natures; liked the same books. I played tennis with him and chess. I loved going with him along the coast looking for fossils and studying rock formations. But," she hesitated, "another man was my real father."

"Did Aunt Kate not tell you anything about him? You must have asked her."

"Mamma was even more uptight even than your mum. Could you imagine Rita giving you any details about a man she knew when she was young?"

We both laughed. "Ma? God, no! Not in a million years. I wouldn't have had the nerve to ask her." The idea of Ma being able to have an affair was too ludicrous to think about. "But how was Uncle Harry after you learned that he wasn't your real dad?"

Grace chewed her bottom lip. "I think I told you he was worried at first, but he showed me a letter from the War Office with Anthony O'Brien's name, his regiment and where he was buried. He had got in touch with the War Graves Commission and we studied the papers they sent us." She smiled. "That's why I knew my way around the Sangro cemetery."

The ease with which Grace told me about what must have been a difficult time for her broke down the barrier I had been skirting since we left Stansted. I would have liked to ask why, since her parents obviously knew her birth father's name, it was not written on her birth certificate. Instead, I put my arm through hers and we watched two women settle down on the beach, undress their children and take them to paddle in the sea. Set beside a discovery which had shaken Grace to the core of her being, my grievances against Ma were insignificant and humbling. A luxury, as Liam had often told me.

She turned to face me. As if pleading, she said, "I hope you understand why I need to find out anything I can about Anthony O'Brien. Fred Cooper got in touch with the families of folk he knew in 1943 by showing them photographs. When we go home he's going to make enquiries among his friends at the British Legion. Anthony O'Brien will have had his photo taken when he joined the army. I'll find it, if it hasn't been destroyed, and I'll get in touch with other men from his regiment." She stretched her arms above her head and said, "It's been a long time since breakfast. Come on, Isabel, let's eat."

My dreams of visiting the Italy I knew only from book and films, of shining in glamorous company, of finding romance, however fleeting, vanished. For as long as she needed me, I would help Grace in her search for any shred of knowledge that might help her fill in a single piece of the life of Anthony O'Brien.

Chapter Ten

Though the dining room was only half full, it hummed with voices, of new arrivals rushing to greet those already at table, and with clatterings from the kitchen each time the door swung open. Franco placed on our table two cauldrons of soup in which open-eyed fish bubbled as if they were swimming in the steaming, tomato-coloured liquid and could leap out at any moment.

"*Zuppa di Pesce,*" he said. "A speciality of our hotel. *Buon appetito Signore*. Remember my wife Marilena comes soon with my son, Gianni."

"Marilena, Marilena," called a woman from a corner table.

Like a breath of summer, a young woman swept into the room. Clamped to her hip was a large, brown baby with the beaming smile of his mother. She could have been any age between eighteen and twenty-five. A short, white skirt showed off long, tanned legs and black hair fell in a ponytail down her red shirt.

"Here she is, Marilena, my wife, and my son," Franco said.

Gina appeared through the kitchen door, kissed her daughter-in-law and carried the baby into the kitchen. Like a whirlwind, Marilena kissed and shook hands with many of the guests before coming over to the table where Grace and I sat.

"Welcome, welcome to Abruzzo. It is Italy's best kept secret. I am very happy to meet you. Please, excuse me. I don't speak English for two years, except to Fred and Pat and they come too little. I talk baby-talk all the day. I have many plans for you," she said to Grace. "Firstly, enjoy your lunch. I go to see Zio Tiberio, Franco's uncle, maybe to wake him up. He knows I am coming. I telephoned him about you and why you are here. I come back when you finish." And off she dashed through a door at the far end of the restaurant.

"What a beautiful young woman," Grace said to me. "Just seeing her makes you feel good."

Marilena reappeared twenty minutes later, accompanied by a man who was probably in his seventies. Though shorter than his brother Claudio, he too had the features and profile of a Roman emperor. He had probably put on weight as he aged and had the solid build of many of the elderly men we had met in Scerni. He raised his right hand in an imperial gesture to friends seated at nearby tables, then cracked his fingers at a young waiter who returned almost immediately with cups of coffee and placed another chair at our table.

"This is Zio Tiberio," said Marilena.

Tiberio bowed to Grace and me. Then he and Marilena had a lively conversation, which I saw my cousin straining to follow.

"Zio Tiberio was at school with a man called Maurizio Rossi. This man spent many years in America and came back to live near a small town not too far away. Soon after the war's end, when he was about fourteen years old, his job was to find the bodies of soldiers who had been buried where they died," Marilena explained. A long and heated dialogue between her and Tiberio followed.

"After the bodies were found, they were buried in the British Military Cemetery. Zio Tiberio says Maurizio is the best person to help you. That is, if he wants to." Marilena's open hand made balancing gestures. "Instead of having his siesta, Zio will come with us to Maurizio's house to make him help. Zio telephoned this man just now and told him why we are coming." She gave Grace a pen and a sheet of paper. "Write your father's name, his regiment and the date of his death, please."

In Tiberio's car, Marilena explained that Maurizio Rossi had been given the location, the name and army number of each body which he dug up for reburial in the cemetery. Perhaps he knew something of Grace's father.

"Who knows? Maybe. We must be hopeful," Marilena said.

I think we all knew we were clutching at straws. I squeezed Grace's hand as we drove past gardens where pink and purple bougainvillea climbed against a blue sky, and white and pink oleander bloomed in dense clusters. The chances of Maurizio remembering the names of any of the corpses he had disinterred sixty years ago had to be negligible. I tried in vain to put myself in Grace's position. My father's background too was clouded in mystery. Sometimes he said he was from Innishmore, sometimes from Connemara, sometimes 'the west'. Ma called him the man from God knows where. But wherever he came from, he had been present throughout my life, except when he needed to escape from Ma.

We stopped at a neat bungalow where six-foot high sunflowers stood like sentries against the fences surrounding a paved area. Maurizio, a white-haired man with the same build as Tiberio, greeted us in American English which had not lost the lilt of Italian. Though they were the same age, the wrinkles that had carved deep furrows in Maurizio's forehead and cheeks and his pronounced stoop made him seem much older than Tiberio. With much ceremony, we were ushered into a room that was cluttered with heavy furniture, ornaments and photographs. In one corner was a bar stocked with an array of bottles of wine, spirits and liqueurs. A widescreen television was tuned to what looked like a quiz programme, hosted by a blonde woman wearing a seriously low-cut dress. A small, bent woman with jet-black hair shook hands and resumed watching the television.

"My wife, Anna. Thirty-six years in Florida and she don't speak English no more. Never did. Not really. You like English tea, coffee, wine, brandy, juice?" Maurizio asked. "Whatever you want, Anna gets it."

Marilena, Grace and I asked for tea, Tiberio for wine and water.

Maurizio indicated a large framed photograph. "My house in Taron Springson on the Florida coast. Beautiful, yes? Not bad for a guy who came to the U.S. in 1952 without a dime! See this: Casa Maurizio." Another photograph showed him talking to a group of customers at tables in front of a brightly-lit restaurant. "My daughter and her husband run my restaurant since I left. Clever girl, my Clara. I taught her everything. Twenty-four tables. You book weeks before to get a table on Friday and Saturday. Every week Clara phones, she says, 'Papa, how I do this? Papa, how I do that?' She misses her Papa."

"Why did you come back to Italy, Signor?" asked Grace.

"Why I come back?" Maurizio's shocked tone told us the question was superfluous. "Why I come back? All Italians are lonely for the place they were born in. They make big bucks and come home. Too much work. Too many Greeks. Too many hurricanes, every year more and more. Italy has the best weather in the world. Beautiful sunshine, no hurricanes."

Anna wheeled in a trolley, on which were a teapot under a chintz tea cosy, gold-rimmed china cups and saucers, bottles of wine and water, two glasses and a plate of biscuits. She smiled and resumed watching the television.

Tiberio erupted when he saw Maurizio produce an album of his time in the US. From the tone of their voices and their vigorous gestures, I thought the two men were about to come to blows. Anna giggled at a contestant on the television.

"Zio is telling him to get on with it, that you didn't come here to see his photographs. Men, they're all the same." Marilena shrugged and helped herself to another biscuit.

The competition on the television seemed to have reached a crucial stage. Marilena stood behind Anna and asked about one of the contestants. Tiberio jumped to his feet and shouted to Marilena. She pressed him into his seat and turned towards Maurizio.

"Grace's father is buried in the Military Cemetery. Maybe, maybe," she coaxed, "his name will come back to you. Grace will show you the details she has."

He glanced at the slip of paper and shrugged his shoulders. "What you want? One dead body looks like the next after a year in the ground. I don't look at faces. My job was to dig them up, match the information the English gave me with their identity discs and report to the officer. Nothing more." He refilled his glass and emptied it in one gulp.

Again, an argument sprang up between the two men. Marilena rolled her eyes and chewed another biscuit.

"He's asking Zio if he remembers what he was doing when he was fourteen and Zio says he does remember because he did the same thing every day. He worked and worked and worked to stop his parents starving. He tells him to forget about the money he made in Florida, to stop boasting and make an effort. Something like that. Not exactly." She spread her hands in a gesture of despair. Then she brightened up. "Grace, why don't you try again? Italian men like beautiful women. They like to be coaxed. To feel important. How you say it? Why don't you have a go?"

Grace moved closer to Maurizio and said, "Signor, please look at the name again, Anthony O'Brien. How many dead soldiers did you find whose names began with O'? Not many. Perhaps he was the only one. I know it was a long time ago and you have had a very successful and varied life since then, but please, please try to remember, for my sake."

"You know how to persuade, Signora, but I was not the only one…" he hesitated, "doing that job."

He picked up the sheet of paper, shook his head and thrust the paper down beside his glass. He raised a hand to quell an outburst from Tiberio, called to Anna to fetch his glasses and peered at the details Grace had given him. He turned and spoke for several minutes to Tiberio in a voice that held more doubt and anger than conviction. Tiberio answered with the passion of my male colleagues in Croydon when they talked football. Eventually, with a ring of triumph mixed with exasperation, Tiberio shouted and pointed at Grace, "*Racconta a la Signora.*" He filled his glass and that of his friend.

"Maurizio thinks he remembers the name, but he is not sure," Marilena said. "Some years after the war when he was working for the English, a woman came to see him. She gave him a name. It might have been like your father's, and she gave him what was a lot of money at that time." Maurizio nodded agreement. "He thinks she lived near Gorla. It is better he tells you."

With reluctance, Maurizio spoke, "I remember her, but not well. She was dressed like a local woman, but she was not a peasant. That was clear." His forehead knitted. He frowned at the floor, as though expecting the polished parquet to reveal the woman's face. "She spoke our dialect badly and I only knew a few words of Italian at that time. But I understood what she wanted. I was fourteen, maybe fifteen. My family was poor. The English paid me not much money and gave me cigarettes. I sold the cigarettes. I didn't smoke at that time and I sold the boots I took from the dead soldiers if they were still in a fit state. Well, they didn't need them and we had no money for bread." His shoulder rose to the level of his ears. He opened his arms wide. "I was glad of her money and I did look for the man she called Antonio. I wanted to find him before the others did." After more floor-searching, he lowered his voice, "I did find his body. What was I to do? What was a fourteen-year-old to do?"

He paused as if waiting for one of us to solve his dilemma. Slowly, he emptied his glass, spoke sharply to his wife who went to the kitchen and returned with a tumbler and another bottle of water. Grace, on the edge of her seat, twisted her hands. Twisted, twisted. She leaned forward. "Yes, yes, Signor, what did you do?"

"I asked my father what to do. He said any Italian woman who went with foreign soldiers, English or German, was a *putanna* and should be strung up like the Duce's whore. He told me to give him

99

the money, to tell nobody and forget about her." Maurizio's hand swatted away Tiberio's attempt to interrupt. "I gave him some of the money, more than he deserved, but I did not forget her. She came to find me one day. This time she had a kid with her. I said I had not found the body. What good would it have done? I ask you." He stared defiantly at Tiberio, Marilena and Grace as if he expected them to challenge his decision.

Grace swallowed hard and leaned forward. "The kid you mentioned, was it a boy or a girl?"

A bemused smile flicked over Maurizio's face. "Signora Grace, a fifteen-year-old boy remembers a beautiful woman and I could see she was beautiful. She had an… an air about her even in her rough clothes, but a small kid, bah!" With a backhand wave and a curl of his lip, Maurizio dismissed the idea.

Grace leaned back in her chair. Anna laughed out loud at the television. Tiberio and Maurizio engaged in a lengthy conversation, which Marilena translated.

"Zio will find out. He loves hunting and he loves gossip. He is the best hunter in the area and he knows everybody. He won't give up till he finds out all there is to know."

We thanked Maurizio and said goodbye to him and his wife. Tiberio talked non-stop for most of the way back to the Aragosta.

During a lull in his monologue, Grace said, "I was at school with a girl whose parents met while her father was fighting in France and another girl whose mother was German. I know that many children were born to soldiers who were away from home during the war."

Marilena laughed and said, "There does not need to be a war for men to meet foreign women."

She went on to tell us how her father went to Switzerland to earn money to support his wife and four children, because there was no work in Abruzzo. When he stopped sending money, her mother's family made enquiries and found out that he was living with a woman in Geneva by whom he had another child, a boy. Marilena's two grandfathers, old men who had never before left their village in the mountains, went by train to Geneva, dragged her papa from his Swiss lover's arms. They forced him to return to her mother, three brothers and sister.

100

"And if they had not made him come back," Marilena raised her shoulders and laughed, "I would not be here with you and Grace and you would not be going to meet my Gianni."

As Tiberio turned into the Aragosta car park Grace asked, "Did you never want to meet your half-brother?"

"Meet him?" Marilena spluttered, "I have three brothers already. Three too many."

Gianni leapt from his grandmother's to his mother's arms. We patted his cheek, asked his age and said what a fine boy he was. With promises to meet up the following day, we waved goodbye to Marilena and Gianni. Tears brimming her eyes, Grace embraced Tiberio and said, *"Grazie, Grazie, Signor"* at least twice. With wide gestures, Tiberio brushed aside her thanks, kissed her on both cheeks and said, *"Piacere, Signora, piacere."* He went towards his flat, having promised to find out all he could about the woman from Gorla.

Grace and I walked barefoot along the beach past families with young children and young men and girls with lithe, tanned bodies who were playing with a ball in the sea.

"I can't believe what Maurizio told us. It's like a miracle. Too amazing to be true, if it is true. I'm still punch drunk. Still haven't taken it in," Grace said.

The implications of an unknown woman and child chased round my head. I would have been beside myself with excitement, but Grace's nature was temperate and she belonged to a generation where feelings were not so openly expressed. I phrased and rephrased my question about the mysterious woman with the small child before blurting out, "And the woman who came looking for your father. How do you feel about her?"

"How do I feel, Isabel? I'm not sure. I know I shouldn't get too excited. Maurizio could have confused the soldier's name. He could have made her up to get rid of Tiberio and me, but deep down I believe she existed. There are many reasons for caution, but the truth is, I want to believe him."

Her right foot made coiling patterns in the sand. She studied the ever-widening shapes before answering my next unspoken query.

"My mother told me nothing about Anthony O'Brien and she side-stepped my questions. I could understand why. It must have been awful for her way back in the forties, but it's different for me. Every time I look in the mirror I see my mother's face, especially now that I'm older. But Anthony O'Brien was my father. I inherited his genes, his strengths, his weaknesses. Half of him is me and I seize on any crumb of information I might learn about him. You understand that?"

"Of course, and I am just as excited as you."

"I may be throwing caution to the wind but I can't wait to go to Gorla with Tiberio tomorrow."

"Why shouldn't you be excited? Throw caution to the wind, Grace. It's the best place for it. We're not following a will-o'-the-wisp. We have something to work on." I pointed towards the promontory at the end of the beach. "Race you to the top of that hill. Are you ready? Ready, steady, GO."

Our heels sank in soft sand as we ran along the shore to a spot where a stream flowed into the sea. After catching our breath, we paddled through shallow water and scrambled up a steep incline where bright blue flowers and foxgloves bloomed and low shrubs were heavy with purplish berries. The plateau we reached gave a wide view of the Adriatic and its blurred horizon. To the west, gently rolling countryside, dotted with houses and clumps of trees, stretched to the foothills of heat-hazed mountains. I watched Grace raise her arms to the sky and inhale gulps of cooler air. It could have been her dishevelled hair. It could have been the way she threw herself down and lay spread-eagled on the grass, but the age gap between us had narrowed.

102

Chapter Eleven

I had been aware, the following morning, of Grace's quiet movements around our room before I dozed off again. Half-asleep, I assumed she had gone to Gorla with Tiberio and was surprised to find her in the breakfast room. Tiberio had made many phone calls and had already left before she came down. Franco had said that village folk mistrusted strangers and a foreign woman asking questions would arouse suspicions. If they thought she was prying, word would spread like a forest fire and she would be greeted with silence and hostility.

"My uncle Tiberio is born here. He knows everybody in the area. He goes to shoot with men from Gorla. They hunt together since they are young. He likes to know about people. He has a very nice manner, when he wants," Franco pulled a face, "and he has his ways to find out. How you say? Round and about." Franco smiled as he drew wide circles in the air. "He will be happy to do this, Signora. It is good he has something to do. He is lazy, because his wife died before two years."

Grace was going to find an internet café and email her sons. She asked if I would like to go with her. Suspecting that she would be glad to spend a morning without me tagging along, I said I would read for a while and have a walk later.

I waved to her as she drove away and settled down in the shaded area in front of the hotel for another session with *Buongiorno Italiano* Lesson One. Words and pictures swam before my eyes. Grace's hopes were too high. The woman Tiberio sought could have emigrated to Australia or America as many Italians did after the war. She might never have returned to Italy. She could have died or moved back to wherever she had come from originally.

Gina came out of the hotel and sat beside me. With visions of men and women in jodhpurs and red jackets following a pack of hounds over fields and ditches, I asked her what animals did Tiberio and his friends hunt?

She laughed as she replied, "Italian men love carrying guns. They shoot any wild animal that moves."

She was going to see her parents in Casalbordino, a town about eight kilometers from the hotel. It was market day. Would I like to look around?

I was glad of a change of scenery in the company of Gina, who was lively and interesting. My spirits rose on the journey, part of which I recognised from our visit to Maurizio's yesterday. Besides, I enjoyed speaking French to Gina. Perhaps because of her Italian intonation and because she was used to speaking French to non-Italian guests, I found her much easier to understand than the French. And she made allowances for my lack of vocabulary. She told me that she and her husband's family all came from a village in the mountains which was almost de-populated now because there was no work for young people and the land was barren. They still had a house there which they like to visit whenever they had time.

Our progress through the market town was slow as Gina stopped every few yards and had an animated conversation with almost everyone we met. Watched by wary stallholders, women prodded melons, aubergines and peaches with the concentration of miners sifting for gold. They measured wraparound aprons, blouses and sleeveless dresses against themselves and bought warm bread, buns and meat. I stopped at a fishmonger's stall. At home I could recognise cod and haddock, salmon, herring, mackerel and jellied eels but I had never seen anything as vicious looking as swordfish armed to the teeth or slithery sea snakes. Lobsters and crabs stretched their pincers beside stingrays, flat as pancakes, and white fish that vaguely resembled sea bass. And I had no idea that the circles of fish in last night's fried platter were slices of the creature that Gina identified as calamari. She told me that the green creatures covered in spikes were not underwater flora, but sea urchins that could be eaten raw with lemon juice.

"You won't find them on the menu at the Aragosta." With a reassuring nod, she added, "We have a high reputation. We would never serve scavengers."

Men chatted in groups, smoking and eating rolls filled with slices of roast pork for which women and children queued at a steaming van. At a stall which sold ornaments, jewellery and toys, I bought two dancing puppets for Gianni. I tried to manipulate the puppets as the stallholder had, but they flopped over the pavement. Gina said Marilena would make them dance.

104

Her parents, who were small and dressed in black, reminded me of photos of Irish peasants in the nineteenth and early twentieth century. They spoke a local dialect to their daughter and Italian to me, which she translated. When she told them the reason for my visit to Abruzzo, her father showed me his left hand. He had lost two fingers from frostbite when he was a prisoner-of-war on the Russian front. Her mother, who had her daughter's liveliness, remembered stories which Gina translated. Before the German army withdrew from Casalbordino in the autumn of 1943, they slaughtered all the pigs they could commandeer and hung their carcasses to bleed from the trees surrounding the main square. They would be made into salami and sausage and joints would be cured to feed the soldiers when they dug in for the winter on the Gustav Line north of the Sangro. Having a pig confiscated meant hunger for families who had also counted on its meat to sustain them through the winter.

Grace was sitting on the veranda of the hotel, drinking coffee with Pat and Fred.

"I've had a great morning," she said. "I had a look around the town. It's a good size and I found an internet café. I looked up the war in Abruzzo, Fred, so I know a tiny bit more about the Italian campaign." She drained her coffee and turned to me. "I emailed Simon and David and I've just had a text from Simon. Guess what, Isabel? Rita has invited my two boys and their families to her birthday party." My mouth gaped open. "I thought you'd be surprised."

A shadow settled over me. What was Ma up to? Was she calling us to heel, manipulating us as the stallholder had manipulated his puppets? The woman I called my mother was a blurred shadow behind net curtains that I used to glimpse from the corner of my straight-ahead-looking eyes as I came home from school, hand in hand with Minnie or my father. She was the polished nails and the knuckles of two hands closing heavy curtains; closing out sunlight together with her daughter.

When Marie came to see me in Brockley last week, she'd said that nature equips us with a faculty for forgetting pain and remembering joy; so why were my surface memories of Ma so selective? The urgency and pleading in her voice on my answer machine returned to nag at me. Maybe she wanted to make her peace with me and with Rose and Linda. Maybe her doctor had told her she had a terminal illness. I could easily have phoned her again and spoken to her

From under a mound of buried memories came images of my mother applying poultices steeped in vinegar, before bandaging my sprained ankle; changing them every two hours. By my bed during the nights when I had bronchitis, wiping my face with a damp cloth, feeding me sips of lemon and honey drinks, putting brown paper on my chest after rubbing it with Vick. And the glimpse of a smile at the edges of her lips when she said the old remedies were sometimes best, though she didn't hold with rubbing a live snail over chickenpox spots and burying it under a cabbage plant.

Bronchitis, half sitting, half lying in bed, propped up on pillows because of a wracking cough and choking phlegm. Ma changing sweat-soaked sheets, her hand cool on my brow; whispering that I was sweating out the fever, and would soon be better. I remember the smell of her pink moisturiser and the slow rhythm of her hand on my skin. I remember sinking into her softness and her holding me in her arms as if I was the love of her life, more precious than gold, more precious than sunlight or star-shine. In the morning I reached out for her, but she had gone. Minnie, who was sitting in her chair, said I could get up for a wee while.

I was seven or eight when Ma disappeared to hospital for about two weeks. Women's trouble, Minnie said. Daddy said nothing, though he and Minnie visited her separately each day.

"Poor Mrs McGlade," I overheard Minnie tell a neighbour, "She's had everything taken away. Everything."

We did not discuss anything to do with reproduction or ailments in our house. When I told Minnie I was having my first period, she threw her arms round me. "Congratulations. You're a woman now. Fancy that, my wee Isabel's a woman."

Ma did not acknowledge the event, though a packet of sanitary towels in a brown paper bag was left on my bed each month.

She had to stay in bed after she came back from hospital. The district nurse said Ma must not pick up anything for at least six weeks. She was so hunched and haggard, I saw in her the ghost she would soon become and wondered how she could survive with an empty inside. One day I saw her through the open door lying so still,

I thought she was dead. Panic made me creep into that room I had been forbidden to enter.

"Don't die, Mamma, please don't die," I whispered and kissed her skin-and-bone-hands, her lank hair, the pale hollows of her cheeks.

The day of Liam's funeral. Grace's phone call. The happy family meal disintegrating into a brawl on hearing I was going to Italy. Me self-righteous and in a huff, itching to get away from Kenmara. I could easily have gone to the sitting room before I left. I could have said goodbye to her like a daughter, instead of sending a message through Una. So many occasions when I could have gone a little bit more than halfway. Since Liam's email I had begun to think of Kenmara as my home, the place where I grew up and where all my family had lived. The house in Brockley that I had shared with Liam was empty and hollow, a house of painful memories, a house whose beating heart had stopped. I could leave it without a backward glance.

The arrival of Tiberio's car and a call from Grace cut through my thoughts. My cotton dress was cool against bare skin and the shaded sun warm on my arms. I finished my drink of freshly-squeezed oranges, moved out of Ma's shadow and squinted up at the cloudless sky. It was good to be with Grace and our new friends on the Adriatic. I would make it up to Ma when I saw her on the ninth of July.

Smiling fit to burst, Tiberio rushed over to Grace, seized her hands and kissed her. His every gesture, every word told of success. When Grace asked him to speak slowly, he enunciated in loud, monotone bursts, which she struggled to translate.

"The woman Maurizio spoke of did live in Gorla. Her name was Elisa Fronelli. She was married to a local man and they had one child. She came from somewhere in the north."

Tiberio nodded in agreement and continued.

Grace covered her mouth with her hand. In a tone drained of expression, she said, "She died about ten years ago in Vasto, a town about fifteen kilometers down the coast."

Before we had time to absorb what Grace had said, Tiberio's wide, dismissive gesture and his benevolent air reassured us. Before us stood a general exhibiting the fruits of victory, not a defeated and empty-handed soldier. Resonant with pride, he resumed his account to which everybody listened, trying to guess at its meaning.

"I'm not a hundred percent sure. I think he says that Elisa's daughter and her husband emigrated to the States with the mother. They came back some years ago and now live in Vasto. The husband's name is Carlo Pace."

As Grace kissed Tiberio warmly and thanked him, Marilena's Fiat screeched to a halt. I hurried to the car, held out my arms to Gianni and carried him to the group on the veranda. I showed him the puppets, while Tiberio retold his news to Marilena.

"Elisa's daughter lives in Vasto with her husband. They have two sons. No problem, Grace. My parents live near Vasto and I have many, many friends there. I telephone. I find out everything."

Pat controlled the dancing puppets while Gianni, on all fours, was torn between grabbing at their strings and chasing the figures that Pat managed to keep from his reach.

Tiberio had made no mention of a Signor Fronelli, husband of Elisa.

While we waited in the restaurant for Marilena to return, Grace toyed with spaghetti carbonara, which she struggled to keep on her fork. She relaxed when Marilena burst into the dining room to greetings from friends and waiters.

"Good news. I make many phone calls." She drew up a chair and helped herself to fish and salad. "The father of one of my friends knows Carlo Pace. He works with him in the Post and Telegraph. We looked for him in the phone book." Like a victor bringing home a trophy, she gave the telephone number and address to Grace.

"Does Tiberio know what you found out?" I asked.

"Not yet. Zio always has a sleep in the afternoon. A very long siesta. You were honoured, Grace. Yesterday, he gave up his sleep for you. Today he gives up his siesta for nobody, not even if the Pope comes knocking at his door."

While Marilena consumed a bowl of chocolate and coffee ice-cream, we decided to phone from our bedroom.

In the space of two days, Grace had been buried under an avalanche of information, half told stories and expectations of a man about whom she'd known nothing except the place of his grave. I massaged her neck and tried to ease the knots of tension in her shoulders. "Take it easy. Let Marilena make the call. She has the know-how, and she does speak the language. Tell her what you want her to say."

Marilena was to say that a guest at the Aragosta from England would like to talk to Signora Pace. Her father, Anthony O'Brien, had fought at the Sangro in 1943.

I closed the shutters and closed out the thrum of the motorway and the noisy goodbyes of guests leaving the Aragosta. When Marilena said the name of Grace's father, a long silence ensued. Grace's knuckles whitened; every line of her face stiffened. Her eyes fixed on Marilena begged for an explanation as the young woman dictated the phone number of the Aragosta and the number of the bedroom. Then she said goodbye and hung up.

"*Tutto bene.*" She put her arms around Grace and sat beside her on her bed. "You are shaking. No problem. I think the Signora was more shocked than you are. She will talk to her husband. Soon she telephones."

Marilena's prattling and encouragement did not lighten the atmosphere in Room 107. Minutes dragged by. I opened the shutters enough to glimpse the road and the low hillside covered by olive trees, which Tiberio said were hundreds of years old. Would a new set of characters be introduced into the drama, or would it fizzle out with Signora Pace's refusal to see Grace and her denial of any connection to Anthony O'Brien?

One thing was certain. Grace would not give up. If it took weeks or months she would find out why Elisa Fronelli wanted to know if Antony O'Brien was alive. She would learn what had become of Elisa's child and I would do all I could to help her find out.

Grace jumped to her feet as the sound of the phone ripped through the bedroom. Marilena picked it up on the second ring. "The Signora wants to speak to you, Grace."

Grace sat down on the bed. Her voice quivered as she said, "*Buon Giorno Signora Pace. Mi chiamo Grace. Parla Inglese?*" and continued in English summing up her reason for coming to Italy and describing her visit to Maurizio. The voice at the end of the phone must have been reassuring. On a notepad she wrote, 'Antonella Pace, Via Pisino 42. Ground floor.' She thanked the caller and hung up.

"We are to go to this address today between four and five," Grace said. "It's all happening so quickly. I can't believe we could have found this woman so easily. On my own, I could have searched for weeks and gone home empty handed."

"It is normal," Marilena said. "This is a small community where nothing much happens. You bring excitement. You give us something to think about. Everybody in the area knows somebody, who knows somebody else. If they do not, they have ways to find out. It is an occupation, a hobby, and Zio Tiberio is an expert." She tapped the side of her nose. "He also has a very long nose. Very well trained."

"It is better you go together and I take Gianni to see my parents. By now, they will have learned the whole history of the Pace family. Come to reception when you are ready. I find a street map for you."

As I searched in the wardrobe for a jacket the back of my hand brushed against the dress Marie had chosen for me. My pulling dress. Ah well, I could wear it to Ma's party.

We arrived at a wide square in Vasto. With the help of Marilena's map, I directed Grace to Via Pisino. Number forty-two was in a block of flats. The building, one of four similar blocks, was a slab of green painted stucco. Each was surrounded by a garden, shaded by palm, pine and eucalyptus trees. Pink, white and red geraniums and hibiscus in window boxes softened the effect of decorative iron bars on the ground floor windows. Women, mainly middle-aged and wearing wraparound aprons, similar to those I had seen in Casalbordino, sat in groups under pine trees chatting and knitting and calling out to children who played around them

"Here goes." Grace scanned the names on a plaque beside a closed gate and pressed the name Pace. When a voice told us to come in, the gate swung open. The dark-haired woman who opened the door smiled and welcomed us. She was about Grace's age, more striking than pretty. Her deep-set eyes were almost black. She wore a blue, sleeveless dress which showed off her tanned skin and slim body. A middle-aged man, whose steel grey hair was cropped close to his scalp, shook hands with us.

110

"I am Antonella and this is my husband, Carlo." The woman spoke English with an Italian lilt in her American accent "You are welcome, Grace, and this is your daughter?"

"No, this is my cousin Isabel, my much younger cousin."

We entered a lobby and were shown into a room where shutters closed out the glare of the sun. Carlo invited us to sit in low armchairs and offered juice, wine and Amarretto biscuits before sitting on the green sofa beside his wife. Though Carlo could not have been more polite, I sensed a wariness in him, a need to hold back. To be presented with evidence.

A biscuit cracking against my teeth was the only sound to break the silence of the room until Antonella spoke. "I am very pleased you have come, but I'm curious to learn how you found out about us and where we live." On the edge of her seat, she clasped and unclasped her hands, fidgeted with a bracelet and pushed a lock of hair behind her ear.

Grace sat upright, as if in a dentist's chair, and related in a staccato tone the reason for her visit to Abruzzo. I glanced round the room. On an oval table under the window was a framed photograph of our hosts with a young man and a woman. The same couple appeared in a photograph on the wall beside a china cabinet.

Grace was relating the encounter with Maurizio Rossi, how he decided not to tell the woman from Gorla that he had found Anthony O'Brien's body, when Antonella uttered a cry and clapped both hands to her face. In obvious distress, she spoke to her husband in Italian. Carlo calmed his wife and seemed to urge her to explain.

"My wife was the child who accompanied her mother. She doesn't remember going but her mother told her about it."

"I hate that man. He was a thief and a liar." Each word rose in an angry crescendo. "My poor Mamma, she gave him all the money she had saved. He kept it all and he told her lies, lies, lies." With trembling hands Antonella picked up her glass of orange juice and drained it. She grimaced and shook her head as if she was casting off a bitter memory. "Please excuse me. Mamma had so little and she had to work very hard."

Then, as if a new truth had been revealed to her, Antonella clasped both hands over her head. Open mouthed, she stared at Grace. Again, she spoke to her husband. A rapid flow, punctuated by the raising of questioning hands.

"My wife thinks that you may both have..."

"I think you and I had the same father." Antonella jumped to her feet, held out her arms to Grace and burst into tears as the two women embraced. After much hugging and tearful laughter, she said, "It was my first thought, my first hope, when you phoned and told me the name of your father. Carlo said I must not make wild guesses and end up disappointed, but, the moment I looked at you, I knew it must be true. But why did you wait so many years to find me?"

While Carlo brought in fresh glasses and opened a bottle of sparkling wine, I hugged Antonella and Grace. In contrast to the warmth of Antonella's embrace, my cousin's body was stiff and unyielding. I willed her to relax, to let go, to show the lovely, warm person she was. Antonella and Carlo must not get the impression of a standoffish, stiff-upper-lip English woman, incapable of feeling or of expressing emotion. Grace didn't have the gift of the gab which my family had in spades. Ma said that my father didn't need to kiss the Blarney stone, he was born with a lump of it in his mouth. Grace's family was understated and reserved – the McGlades didn't know the meaning of the words. Her tranquil English household had not been disturbed by the ructions between my father and my brothers, or by my parents' frequent screaming matches. Her training as a librarian had instilled into her a need for order, for filing systems, nothing taken at face value. I wanted to tell Antonella and her husband that Grace's qualities were pure gold. She was reliable, generous and discreet, a loyal friend and a devoted mother. I wanted them to value her as I valued her, to appreciate that she had just emerged from the twilight life of a carer, her own needs stifled by the constant attention demanded by her parents.

Grace might disapprove, but I would make sure the Paces knew that my cousin was special, and they would love her, not just because she and Antonella had the same father, but because knowing her would enrich their lives as it had enriched mine.

"Why did I take so long before finding you?" Grace said. "Until yesterday I had no idea you existed. I only found out when I was sixteen that I was adopted and that my birth father was dead. And I didn't have the opportunity to come to Italy until now."

She gave a summary of her life – her job as librarian in Brighton and Hastings, marriage to a pharmacist who died of lung cancer when their sons were small, her father's death fifteen years later, her mother's frail health and terminal decline. Then she asked Antonella to tell her what she knew of her own mother's relationship with Anthony O'Brien.

Antonella went over to the window, rested her hands on the sill and gazed out through slats in the shutters before speaking. "I don't know where to begin. It was years ago since Mamma spoke about her life. I was about seventeen when she told me who my father was." Brows furrowed, she looked at her husband who nodded to her to continue. "Perhaps the best place would be the beginning. When Mamma was four and her sister Anna was six, their father died in an accident in Rome. The family had been living there. Their mother took her two daughters to stay with their grandmother in Venice. She then returned to Rome and disappeared from their lives."

Antonella sat down, took a deep breath, and continued, "Mamma kept a diary. It must have got lost. We moved house many times in the States before we came back to Italy. I'll do my best to remember, especially the part that concerns my father. She was keen to tell me as much as possible about him, though their time together was short. I haven't thought about it for a long time. Please make allowances for mistakes I make."

Her mother's time with Anthony O'Brien was very clear to Antonella, but the early part of her life before and in Venice was hazy. Antonella apologised. She had no idea of the sort of water transport that had been used there during the war, or what life was really like. Carlo assured her that didn't matter. His wife should start with the September day that changed the course of her mother's life.

Chapter Twelve

Elisa's Story

September 11th *1942.* The presence of armed troops oppressed the sweltering city. The grey-uniformed men who patrolled Venice were correct and disciplined, but an army of young men had to be fed and supplies of food available to the population of Venice were dwindling fast. On that day, it wasn't the soldiers that sent Elisa hurrying to the crowded landing stage at S. Marco. It was the sky, the colour of clotting blood. Some said maybe what they were seeing was no more than a spectacular sunset. No one remembered such a sun. They averted their eyes, only to find them drawn to the colour reflected by the sky on the Grand Canal.

Elisa's sister, Anna, had warned her against going into Venice. Anna was sensitive to barely perceptible variations in the atmosphere, to sudden changes of wind direction, to the slightest tremors that preceded an earthquake. But when had Elisa paid attention to her older sister? All the same, Anna's warning had come back to her as she waited at the jetty at S. Marco. She was out of breath from her futile attempt to catch the boat, which had just left the landing stage without her.

A stranger from another country watching her might have been struck by Elisa's beauty, though in a city of beautiful women she was not remarkable. She fingered the gold ring Nonna had given her last Sunday for her sixteenth birthday and wondered what her grandmother would find to add to the nightly pasta. Fresh tomatoes, tiny sardines, fat black olives? Poor Nonna, she knew that serving food on smaller plates did not disguise the meagre helpings on offer and that doubling the amount of garlic and herbs didn't really compensate for the absence of meat. The deeper waters of the Adriatic were now dangerous to shipping and the only fish not commandeered by the German army was whitebait, too insubstantial to satisfy a growing girl's hunger. Slogans on bill boards warned, "If you eat too much, you rob your country." Elisa thought about suppers her family had eaten before the war. Pasta coated with meat sauce, soup thick with fish and vegetables, steak, ice-cream, freshly picked apricots, cherries and peaches, but black market prices were beyond her Nonna's limited means. She wrinkled her nose. A young girl should have other matters on her mind than her next meal.

Elisa found a seat on the slower *vaporetto*. Passengers left the crammed boat at each stop, and were replaced by others. By the time it headed towards S. Elena, they numbered about twenty. Elisa slung her bag over her left shoulder, and clutched the satchel of books she had anchored between her feet. As she stood up and prepared to disembark, rain started to fall. Not the downpour of a summer storm but a stabbing torrent, dark as thunder. It lashed the boat. Elisa huddled with other passengers on the jetty, deafened by the noise of rain which pounded the roof with the thud of hail. None of those who had left the *vaporetto* with Elisa dared venture on to the quayside. Instead they sheltered under the roof of the jetty. She sat on the edge of a metal stool that was bolted to the floor and waited for the deluge to cease.

Up till then, her fellow passengers had been little more than shapes, changing figures on the stages of her journey. But she would remember for the rest of her life the brown baby who grabbed at her dress and clutched a bunch of cotton roses between his fists. She would see the apology on his young mother's face as she disengaged her son's dimpled hands. She would picture each one of a group of women, shawled in perpetual mourning. She would remember the smell of ripe cheese from their half-empty baskets, the panic in their voices now raised to screaming pitch.

The *vaporetto* had just sailed away from the jetty when the motorbus came into sight. At that moment the tornado struck, with a sound as ear splitting as it was sudden. It picked up the motorbus and the jetty and hurled them twenty feet into the air. As in a trance, Elisa, still seated on the stool, saw the boat at the same level as herself. She saw it poised, a giant bird or an airship at rest, before it turned upside down and the passengers who crowded the deck were tipped into the lagoon. Those entombed inside the cabin fell like flies from deck to ceiling. The vessel nose-dived and plummeted into the vortex of the tornado. How long did Elisa sit in mid-air, her eyes riveted to the stricken boat? One second? Two? Maybe three?

Only a handful of the passengers survived to recount the horror of the scene – to describe what was beyond description.

As the airborne jetty pitched into the Lagoon, the force of the tornado peeled her clothes and shoes from her body and tore her grandmother's ring from her finger. Elisa sank to the bottom, convinced this was the moment of her death. Though she had tried many times, she had never learned to swim. Then the same force hurled her up to the surface of the water. Struggling against an undertow that threatened to pull her under again, she grabbed a floating plank. Other swimmers fought to reach the quayside. They buffeted past her, men, women and children. Then they disappeared below the riotous waves. Bodies and parts of bodies floated past. A torso. Disembodied legs. A naked child. The sister of the brown baby? She reached out but as she touched the little girl's shoulder she knew that she too was dead. A head brushed against her as it bobbed past.

Time was suspended. Searchlights flooded the water. Sailors in dinghies paddled through the wreckage in search of survivors. Elisa heard their voices calling to each other. She heard them say they had found only corpses, there were no survivors. She opened her mouth to speak, to yell, "Help me. Help me." The words stuck in her throat. Still clinging to the plank, she moved three fingers of her left hand. The slightest movement, frantic in its slowness.

"There's one alive over here!" An urgent voice nearby. "Quick. She's still alive." Seconds later she was hauled, face down, into a dinghy. Her back was pummelled till she emptied her lungs of the filthy water of the lagoon. A sailor covered her with a blanket.

From that day on, Elisa, a survivor of the catastrophe, was regarded as a curiosity. Some said the hand of God had protected her. She was a holy person, saved for a life of sanctity. For greater things. Others muttered that witches could not drown. It was well known that the devil looked after his own. She heard, S*trega, strega* hissed, just within earshot in the near silence of her classroom. *Strega* streaked along streets leading to her home. *Strega* echoed over canals and pathways.

Impervious to accusations of witchcraft, Elisa herself believed she must have been spared for a purpose. That she was indeed destined for greatness.

116

For many months before King Victor Emmanuel signed the documents which placed Italy on the side of the Allies and before German troops garrisoned in Venice became an army of occupation, Nonna had feared for the health and safety of Elisa and her sister. Each morning they queued for hours for bread, for vegetables, fish and milk and very often returned empty handed. Nonna decided to go with her granddaughters to Abruzzo in the south of Italy where most of their mother's relatives lived. Anna flatly refused to leave and threatened to kill herself rather than be separated from Michele, the medical student she was to marry. Nonna could not abandon her elder granddaughter and decided that Elisa should travel alone. Elisa agreed. Whatever lay ahead was her destiny, the life for which she had been saved.

In April 1943 Nonna and Anna said goodbye to her at the railway station. Her suitcase, which was bursting at the seams, was intended only for the clothes and footwear that Nonna considered suitable for a rural life. However, Elisa had managed to stuff two floral dresses and a pair of high-heeled sandals into an empty corner. As presents for the family in Abruzzo, Nonna had sent most of her jewellery, silk scarves, handkerchiefs, scent and socks and caps she had knitted.

To Elisa the ten-hour journey, that mainly followed the Adriatic coast but occasionally wove inland past lush fields and large towns, was spellbinding. The rise and fall of the countryside, high mountains in the distance, miles of sandy beaches, springtime in newly leaved trees, the yellow, blue and pink of flowers and shrubs. She left the train at Vasto railway station where an old peasant woman met her with a donkey and cart. She jabbered in a language of which Elisa understood nothing and vented her fury on the skin and bone donkey that took them along potholed lanes to Gorla, the hamlet where she was destined to stay.

A woman, who introduced herself as Zia Nerina, welcomed her. She wore a black and white wraparound apron over a black dress. A black headscarf concealed her hair which she pushed back out of sight. She led Elisa into the kitchen of a small farmhouse where the ashes of a fire glowed in a circular fireplace. The only furniture was a table, six upright chairs and a wooden cupboard along the length of one wall. The plastered walls and ceiling were black with soot. The brick floor was cracked and uneven. At a shout from Zia Nerina, a crowd of children swarmed into the kitchen – two girls about the same age as Elisa and four little boys and girls, barefoot and wearing patched and patched again clothes. They hovered around her, chattering, touching her face, hair and clothes to giggles and whisperings. Their threadbare clothes made her realise how out of place were her heavy coat, best jumper and pleated skirt.

Elisa gave Nonna's presents to Nerina, who tried necklaces, bangles and brooches on all the children, dabbed scent on them all, even the little boys, and tied a purple silk scarf round her neck. When their mother's back was turned, the older girls poked through the suitcase, stroked Elisa's dresses and jackets and held up her knickers and night-dresses to hoots of laughter. Their eyes and hands asked permission to look at her diary. When photograph albums were passed from one child to the next, Elisa was close to tears lest they destroy her only memories of the person she had been in Venice. At a word from Nerina, all her belongings were put back into the case. Elisa smiled her thanks and gave a dress to each of the older girls. She would have no need for fine clothes in a dump like this.

A meal of minestrone, pasta and omelette filled her with a sense of well-being and sleep. Her cousins, Sylvia and Tina, aged about twelve or thirteen, escorted her by candlelight to a bedroom where they all slept in a large double bed. She woke, sandwiched between the girls, to the sound of Nerina calling and banging on the stairs.

Each day followed the same pattern as the last. Eating regular and plentiful food, working on the land, cooking, washing and cleaning. Most days she accompanied her cousins to the fields where she was given an implement, something like a hammer on the end of a pole, and instructed to break the baked crust of Nerina's land. After the first day, her hands were raw and blistered and the muscles in her back and arms screamed with pain.

Apart from Zia Nerina, who spoke some Italian, all the others knew only dialect. Dumb in a world of busy tongues and lips grown elastic through non-stop chatter, Elisa found herself an object of pointed fingers and barely suppressed laughter. Apart from small boys and old men smoking pipes in the shade of their doorways, the village appeared to be inhabited only by women and girls.

"Where are the men?" she asked Nerina.

"La Guerra," Zia Nerina replied with a bitter shrug and a wide, empty-handed gesture.

118

On Sunday mornings they trooped to Mass in a whitewashed chapel. Our Lady of Sorrows, after whom it was named, wore a black satin gown, a black, moth-eaten veil and an expression of grief to chill the blood of any sinner in the congregation. Nerina introduced Elisa to the parish priest, Padre Rocco, who spoke to her in Italian. He said how much safer Gorla was for a young girl than Venice, which he heard was rife with German soldiers.

Without newspapers or a radio, the only measurements of time were nightfall and daybreak and Sunday Mass was the only fixed point Elisa's week. Her next visit to Padre Rocco was several months later. Zia Nerina accompanied her to the priest's house.

"Signorina Elisa," he began, his expression solemn.

"It's Nonna, it's Anna. What's happened to them?"

"No, Signorina. This is not sad news. It is happy news." A smiling pause. "You are to be married the day after tomorrow." He beamed as if expecting a reward for his miracle of turning tragedy to joy.

Married! She hadn't met a man. She hadn't even seen one from a distance. She dreamed of falling in love with a handsome young man like Anna's fiancé, an educated Venetian who spoke Italian, who liked to read, to listen to music and to dance.

As though speaking to a backward child, the priest explained that the King and Field Marshall Badoglio had made an alliance with the British and the Americans. Italy was now at war with Germany.

"Now that the Germans are the enemy, any unmarried woman could be seized and sent to work as slave labour in Germany..." Father Rocco lowered his voice to a shocked whisper, "...or worse." The man your aunt has chosen is Renzo Fronelli. He lives with his invalid mother on a small farm about eight kilometres from here." With unexpected gentleness, he added, "He is not the person you would have chosen, Elisa, but he's a good man and you will be safe with him. I have written to your grandmother, explaining the situation. She replied saying we must do everything for your safety."

Stunned and disbelieving, Sylvia and Tina wept with her on hearing the news and Elisa sobbed through the next two nights in the arms of her weeping cousins. They were too young to be married, but were to be sent to stay with their father's relatives in Foggia.

Before she left for the church, Zia Nerina took her to one side. Grim-faced, she said, "You will share a bed with your husband,

Elisa. You must always submit to all his demands and bear his children. It is a wife's duty. In return you will have food and a roof over your head." She burst into tears and held Elisa to her, "And you will be safe, my little child."

For his marriage, Renzo Fronelli was dressed in a crumpled suit and shirt that looked as though they belonged to a bigger man. He was said to be thirty-two years old, but would have passed for fifty. His shock of dark, unkempt hair was shot with grey and he had the ruddy complexion and stocky build of a peasant. He made his vows in dialect in a low and faltering voice. When he put a ring on her finger, Elisa shuddered at the thought of his callused hands touching her naked body. She signed her name and Father Rocco indicated to Renzo Fronelli where he should make his mark. Not till she left the altar with him did she notice the limp, which twisted his body with each step.

He drove her down a rutted track to his home in a cart, drawn by a look-alike of the donkey that had conveyed her from Vasto to Gorla. Since the tornado Elisa had become fatalistic, believing that whatever happened to her had been decreed by God, though many times since leaving Venice she wished she had drowned in the depths of the lagoon. Never more so than on the day of her marriage.

At the end of the track Renzo stopped the donkey at a one storey hovel. A broken shutter hung over the only window. Numbly she entered the near darkness of a room with a dirt floor and blackened walls. She made out a gas ring and canister beside a scratched table that was covered with a few cracked plates and mugs, a food-encrusted saucepan, a hammer, nails and an oil lamp. Ashes spilled from a fireplace above which hung a crane for hanging cooking pots. The only seating was a bench against the wall. Elisa almost choked in the putrid atmosphere and was about to run outside to fill her lungs with clean air when she made out the source of the stench. Renzo's mother, a dishevelled old woman wearing a filthy shift. She lay in a bed at far the end of the room under a ragged blanket that looked as if it had never been changed since she became bedridden. She smiled at the woman who scowled and turned to face the wall.

Behind this room was another with a plank bed. Renzo indicated that this was where Elisa would sleep with him. Rooted to the spot, staring at a half-full chamber pot, she shook with panic. All day she had been numb, going mindlessly through motions. The brief ceremony at the church. Nerina and her cousins' tearful goodbyes. The journey in the donkey cart. Her disgust at the filthy hovel where she was to be trapped for the rest of her life. She had to escape. To run away. To run. Run till she dropped. But there was no escape. Nowhere to run. No one to run to.

She had grown up with a romantic notion of love and had no idea what to expect on her first night with the stranger she had married. And she had no idea what a naked man looked like. She sat on the bed weeping, hugging her knees and rocking to and fro till darkness fell and Renzo came in. She heard, rather than saw, him strip off all his clothes and climb into the bed. He pulled her in beside him. She screamed when he penetrated her, but he stroked her gently afterwards, wiped away her tears and the words he spoke sounded kindly. Almost loving. She lay awake all night while Renzo snored and snorted in his sleep. After what had just happened she was bound to her husband by a bond that could never be sundered. Since this was her destiny she had no choice but to accept it. Her own mother had abandoned herself and her sister Anna in Venice and their Nonna had been obliged to bring up her two small grandchildren. And Renzo's mother, what choices had she had, or the women in Gorla who worked like drudges in the fields and in their homes, often with babies tied on their backs and five or six other children to care for?

Since Elisa was doomed to live in the home Renzo shared with his mother, she might as well make it as habitable as possible. Not wanting to be faced with the old woman each time she entered her new home, she remade the bed she had shared with her husband. On it she put sheets and pillowcases given to her by Nerina. Then she indicated to Renzo that she needed water to wash his mother. He went outside and returned with a bucket filled almost to the brim. From her luggage she took a large towel and one of her new nightdresses.

"My name is Elisa, Signora, Elisa," she said, pointing to herself, "Elisa."

Holding the frail old woman, she was overwhelmed with pity. Pity for the terror in the poor creature's eyes, pity for her trembling body and for the dread she must feel of this stranger who peeled off her filthy rags and wrapped her in a towel. Elisa spoke in a gentle, low voice while she washed the old woman's skin-and-bone body and drew the new nightdress over her shoulders. She called her

husband and indicated to him that he was to carry his loudly
complaining mother into the bed in her new surroundings. Under his
wife's instructions, he lit a fire outside the house and burned the
stinking bedding, together with the mattress which had already shed
most of its dried grass filling.

She opened the door and window in both rooms. On the crammed
table, Elisa made a space for the food Nerina had given her. She
poured some milk on bread and found a spoon which she used for
feeding Renzo's mother. With a broom she swept years of debris
from the floors of the dwelling. She washed dust and dirt from all
surfaces and made up the bed. In the brief time she spent with Renzo
Frenelli, she realised that the priest was right. He was a good man,
and not the brute she had feared. He treated her like an exotic
helpmate, specially chosen for him by Father Rocco.

He took her to an outhouse where he brushed straw away from
part of the mud floor. He pulled back rusted bits of an ancient plough
and several boards to reveal a hollowed space underneath. He
indicated that this was where she was to hide if the Germans showed
up. With much difficulty and coaxing, he taught her to milk the cow
he kept tethered in a hollow close to the house, well out of sight of
the enemy or of poachers.

There was no warning the day six soldiers emerged from the truck
that Renzo and Elisa heard rattling to a halt outside their home.
Renzo shoved his wife into the window side of his mother's bed and
piled blankets over her. His mother's yells rent the room when she
found Elisa tight up against her. Though almost deafened by the
woman's fury, she heard the soldiers shouting and banging, opening
cupboards and drawers. One of the Germans must have asked Renzo
what was wrong with his mother.

He replied with one word, *"Tifo."*

She heard voices ask, *"Tifo?"* and fear in the reply, "Typhus."

The dull thud of boots kicking her husband out of the house fell
muffled on her ears.

Whether the rumour of typhoid at Renzo's home had spread
through the neighbourhood, whether the constant rain of the past
weeks had made the track to the farm impassable, whether Sylvia
and Tina had been sent off to a safer part of the country, they no
longer came to see Elisa. She missed their company and the bread,
salami, sausage and pasta Nerina used to send with them. She feared

her husband had been murdered and his body dumped, as it was unlikely the Germans would have taken a suspected typhoid carrier with them. She searched the fields and the track to the farm for trace of him, but without success. Life in the sole company of a demented old woman was lonely and frightening. She looked after her as best she could and waited for her husband to return. She chopped wood, cooked and made bread the way Nerina had taught her. Each evening she wrote her thoughts in her diary and dreamed of returning to her family in Venice.

One morning on her way back from milking the cow, she decided to go further than usual into the wood to search for a plant Nerina used in salads. As she picked her way through rain-soaked grass, she almost stumbled over a young man curled up against the trunk of a tree. He woke with a start. Terror glazed his eyes.

"No *Tedesco, Inglese*," he stuttered and sat up. "*Inglese, no Tedesco.*"

He tried to stand but his face twisted and his left ankle gave way.

Elisa motioned him to sit. She tried to speak the few words of English she had learned, but fear locked her throat. Fear for the skinny young man, shivering in threadbare shirt and trousers. Fear for herself, if she was discovered with an enemy soldier. Fear lest the men who had carried off Renzo might steal on silent, muddy feet through the wood. Fear of Fascist spies whose reputation for brutality dared only be whispered.

She held the rim of the bucket of milk to the man's lips. He drank greedily and said, "*Grazie, Signora.*"

Though she eased the boot off his left foot with care, he made a sound between a yelp and a squeal and blood drained from his face. "Shush, shush," Elisa whispered and gasped when she saw his blackened and badly swollen ankle. She ripped a wide strip from her overall, dipped it in milk and bound it round the ankle.

"I come back," she said in Italian, raising the bucket once more to his lips.

At her house, she filled a bottle with milk and put salami and bread in a bag. Then she heated milk on the embers of the fire and made a herb poultice, which she wrapped in a pillowcase before setting off with one of Renzo's shirts round her shoulders.

She placed the still warm poultice on the man's ankle and bound it as she remembered her Nonna doing when she was little. He ate the bread and salami and he talked in a language of which she understood nothing. He must have escaped from a prisoner of war camp. She had heard of such places. She laughed and nodded at his swimming gestures and guessed that he had swum across the river to the north of Gorla. Before changing his tattered shirt he took a cellophane wallet from the pocket and put it in Renzo's shirt, which was too big for him, but at least it might help him to pass for an Italian farm worker.

"I come at night," she mimed, pointing towards the sky and indicated that he must not move.

"Yes, yes. Thank you," he said as she left.

Elisa drew back the heavy bits of plough that covered the hiding place Renzo had shown her. It was too small for a tall man, however thin. Fortunately rain had dampened the soil that she scooped out with a trowel. After digging for an hour, she lined the space with oilcloth from the kitchen table, and a blanket. At twilight she crept to the wood, armed with a heavy stick for the man to lean on or to fend off attackers. But would he still be where she had left him? Nights spent in almost total darkness had accustomed her to the gloom of the wood but what if she wandered into local Fascists, or a patrol of Germans?. She retraced the path she had memorised earlier that day. With relief, she almost stumbled over piles of sticks she had left as markers. He was still where she had left him. She helped him to his feet, placed the stick in his right hand and put his left arm round her shoulder.

"*Grazie, Signora,*" he whispered.

Scarcely daring to breathe and with many stops, they hobbled to the house where she rekindled the ashes to warm the shivering stranger. Alert for any sound outside, she led him to his hiding place in the outhouse.

"Thank you, Signora." He pointed to his chest and said, "Tony, Tony."

"*Elisa. Elisa. Buona notte, Toni.*"

At daybreak, she released him, stiff and chilled. She helped him to the kitchen area and gave him a bowl of coffee made from acorns and hot milk. From his gestures, she understood that he had been released, or escaped, from a camp north of the river and was heading south to join the British army. She put a fresh poultice on his foot and tied a piece of flat wood to his leg to act as a splint. If they heard

124

anyone coming, Toni was to climb through the window in the old woman's room and hide in the woods.

The days he spent with her were the happiest of her life. She taught him the words for hens and for the cow, for food and household objects. As his ankle healed, he chopped wood, mended the broken crane over the fire and milked the cow with expert hands. They were often forced to cover their mouths to muffle the sound of their laughter when they misunderstood what each other said, or when Toni tried to do a hobbling dance round the kitchen with a broom for a partner. Rain, which continued to lash the countryside, seeped into his hiding place and turned it into a sodden mess. Elisa decided that Toni should sleep on the floor in the house. A short step from there to sharing her bed. A tender and passionate sharing.

Having no common language, she had submitted in silence to Renzo's clumsy fumblings and his urgent demands for sex. Toni and she had no need for words. Their hands and mouths spoke the same tongue and she understood the gentle names he called her. "O love, o love," she repeated, and smiled to hear him murmur something like, "*Amore mio. Amore mio.*"

This was how she had dreamed love would be, dissolving into each other, in harmony, as if they were one and the same person. Lying beside Toni silenced her fears of the ink-black darkness surrounding them. It blotted out cries from Renzo's mother as it blotted out the creaks and groans of the crumbling house and the sound of rain hammering against the window and drumming on the roof. As each day passed and Toni no longer needed a stick to help him walk, their loving grew sweeter and wilder in the unspoken knowledge of his inevitable departure. She willed time to slow down, to stand still, but hour followed hour and a new day followed hard on the heels of yesterday.

Not knowing who to trust, Elisa mimed going to Padre Rocco, who might be able to advise her. Toni helped her hitch the donkey to the cart and watched her set off along the muddy path in driving rain.

"How long has this man been in your outhouse?" the priest asked.

"Since this morning."

"You must not allow him into your home. It is not right for a married woman to be alone with a stranger, you understand."

He said the British army had forced the Germans to retreat from Scerni, a small town not far from Gorla, but German soldiers were still around. He would talk to local partisans who would take the Englishman back to his people. They would come at nightfall as Elisa must not spend a night alone with this man. Besides, there was a large bounty for each prisoner captured and the Fascists were ruthless bloodhounds.

"I will give my rosary to the men I send as proof they come from me." He showed her an amber coloured rosary.

Zia Nerina welcomed Elisa with joy and tears. She had sent Tina and Sylvia to stay with relatives in Foggia, which was in British hands. Her heart was broken without them and without Elisa. She would arrange for her to come back with Renzo's mother and stay till her husband returned.

Elisa and Toni made love one last, tearstained time. Her finger tips and lips memorised the thin line of his mouth, his straight English nose, freckles on cheeks and reddened arms, a hint of auburn in sun-bleached hair. His body lean and strong. The slats of his rib cage, the arch of his instep. They spoke no words of farewell, for they were not lovers parting in the hope of another meeting. They knew they would never meet again.

Two men came in darkness. They showed Father Rocco's rosary to Elisa and Toni, wearing Renzo's oilskins, left with them.

Elisa and Renzo's mother and their belongings were brought by cart to Zia Nerina's home. The following year Elisa gave birth to a daughter. Several months later a letter arrived from her sister Anna, which she read with horror. Anna's fiancé, Simone, had been arrested and shot by soldiers who were rounding up all the Jews in the city. Some time afterwards, a hundred men were hanged in Saint Mark's Square in retribution for the death of a drunken soldier who had been discovered floating in one of the canals. The citizens of Venice had been compelled to watch the hangings. Nonna died shortly afterwards. Her death certificate stated that she had died of influenza.

Like many men from the area, Renzo never returned home.

126

Chapter Thirteen

I shivered in the silence which followed Antonella's telling of her mother's story. Elisa had followed the road where she believed destiny had led her. It was well she never knew where other roads might have led.

"Poor Elisa, your poor mother," Grace choked back her tears.

"It was war time, Grace, and many suffered much more than Mamma. She loved Anthony O'Brien. She told me that the days she spent with him were the happiest of her life, even though they both knew their time together was limited." She gave her husband a rueful glance. "They didn't know each other long enough to have rows like most married couples and she was happy that I was his child and not her husband's."

Grace took Antonella's hand

"It is true, it is true," she repeated, "You are my sister. All these years we have lived not knowing of each other's existence. My mother said she was lucky to have me. She said I was a miracle, but I always wished I had a brother or a sister."

The two women laughed and cried. They marvelled at each other's faces. The shape of their eyes was the same, though Grace's were the piercing blue of her mother's. They remarked on their similar straight noses and even teeth. I smiled to myself. Carlo smiled too. Many sixty-year-old women look like each other. But today was for searching for similarities, not for saying how Antonella's exuberance contrasted with Grace's restraint, or how Grace's skin seemed even paler compared with Antonella's olive complexion, or for comparing Grace's slim figure with Antonella's more rounded shape. Both women revelled in each discovery. Like Grace, her half-sister had two sons. Antonella's dress was almost the same shade as Grace's shirt. Blue was their favourite colour. Again I smiled with the indulgence of a loving parent. Blue must be the most popular colour in the spectrum. They both enjoyed cooking, reading and swimming. Grace said she would have loved to travel as the Pace family had, but there had always been demands on her time.

"Now's the time," said Antonella, gabbling her words with the enthusiasm of a child who can't wait to tear the wrapping paper off a present. "Carlo, we'll take Grace around Italy. We'll see Toni in Rome first and then we'll go to Umbria and Tuscany and the Amalfi Coast. And we'll visit the family in the Alps and we'll go to parts of Italy we don't know. Then we'll take you to the States and stay with Marco and his family."

"I can't believe it. Here I am making plans to travel the world with my new sister and brother-in-law." Grace shook her head in amazement. As Antonella prepared to speak, she said, "England's a lovely country. We have wonderful castles and mountains and London's a great city. You must meet my family too, and we'll go to Ireland where Isabel's family lives and where my mother was born."

"We'd love to go England and Ireland," Carlo said. "We met lots of Irish in the States. Half the population of New York seemed to be Irish."

Grace and Antonella talked non-stop, interrupting each other, making plans, fixing dates. I listened to Grace's voice as she described her sons and her granddaughter. She would not need any reference from me.

Photos of Antonella's sons were produced. The elder, Marco, a taller replica of his father, was an architect who had studied in the States. He lived on the coast of Maine in a small town north of Boston. He was married to a girl from an Italian family and had two daughters and a son. We saw page after page of smiling children from infancy through to nursery school, their affluent home, holidays on beaches in Maine and in Vasto.

Antonella's younger son, Antonio, was an engineer who worked in Rome for the Electricity Board. He had his mother's cheekbones and deep-set eyes and he was absolutely gorgeous. He had been engaged to a local girl, whom he had known since their schooldays. She had been unwilling to leave her large family and wanted to stay in Vasto, where there were fewer job prospects for Toni. I perked up on hearing that his childhood sweetheart had married a local man. And he was still single.

Grace continued to gaze in rapt attention at snaps of her new family, while Antonella telephoned her younger son. A film formed over my eyes as other albums showed the boys' childhood in New England, in Vasto and in the Julian Alps. I felt a stab of envy at the

128

obvious affection and ease between the two sons and their parents. Arms round each other's shoulders, happy faces. I'd seen similar, if more restrained, photographs of my brothers with my mother and father; never any of me with both my parents.

Black and white snaps of Elisa woke me to wide-awake consciousness. Elisa, the girl who had sheltered and loved Grace's father. A handsome woman, dressed in peasant clothes, holding her daughter's hand outside her school, mother and daughter in Sunday best in front of a church, a matronly figure at Carlo and Antonella's wedding. A woman grown plump with time, whose unlined face gave no indication of the hardships she had endured.

"This is Antonella's mother before she left Venice." Carlo took a silver-framed photograph from the china cabinet.

A young girl who had the dark colouring, classical features and the intelligent, eyes of a Renaissance painting. I looked closely. She could have been the model for *La Bella,* by Titian, which I had first seen at an art history class that Marie and I had attended last autumn. Grace and I studied the likeness of the girl who had been married off to Renzo Fronelli. There was a hint of mystery in her half smile. To my sentimental mind, it hinted at the dreams of the Venetian girl who had left her native city, brimful of hope for a bright future.

Antonella's voice broke into my thoughts. "Toni's coming tomorrow. He is very excited about meeting you. You will come? We will have a special meal to celebrate finding each other."

"Of course we will and, on Sunday, Isabel and I invite you and all your family to the Aragosta." Grace said. "I want you to meet the Celucci family, especially Signor Tiberio and Marilena, who helped me find you."

"We would be happy to meet your friends and to thank Signor Cellucci for the wonderful job he did." Antonella swayed as if she was about to glide round the room. "Carlo and I planned to spend a lazy afternoon. Instead, my new sister and my cousin are sitting here with us in our home and it's a miracle. But there is one other snap you must see." She took a small wooden box from the bottom of a chest of drawers. It contained a rough edged black and white snap of a young man who could have been a farm labourer.

"Antonio O'Brien," she said. "Mamma took it with a box camera she brought from Venice. She had it developed years later."

I heard Grace's sharp intake of breath. A lean man, whose hair was fair or light brown, stood, feet apart, in front of a ramshackle country dwelling. He could not have been much older than twenty. The rolled-up sleeves of a checked shirt revealed arms that were strong and sinewy. They were outstretched as if to fold in an embrace the person holding the camera. His lips were parted in a wide smile that lit up his face.

After his escape from the prison camp, he had probably swum across the Sangro before weeks of rain had turned it into the torrent the allied forces had been forced to cross. I saw Anthony swimming in rhythmic silence in the hope of rejoining his unit. Swimming into German occupied territory on the opposite bank; swimming towards his death.

Grace studied the blurred image as though she was committing each feature to memory, as though she was searching for distinguishing marks or some feature she shared with the nondescript man she believed to be her father.

Was she glad he had known happiness with Antonella's mother, or was she disappointed that he had not remained true to her mother? She must have been relieved that Kate had never known about Elisa, that she had held on to the memory of her young lover as he was when they last parted. She returned the snap to Antonella, who closed the box and put it back in the bottom of the chest of drawers, a sacred relic to be produced only on rare and special occasions, like the Shroud of Turin or one of the many nails said to have pierced Christ's hands and feet.

"Mamma told me he carried a photograph of a young girl, in a cellophane wallet," she said, as if aware that Elisa's story must have seemed to Grace like a betrayal of her mother. "It was very important to him. On the back she had written a message. Mamma said she was somebody he loved and hoped to marry." She sighed. "Things happen in war, Grace."

"I know. Thank you for telling me that and for showing me his photo. I would like to copy it, if I may."

"I'll do that for you tomorrow, Grace." Carlo promised and asked if we would stay and have supper with them.

To my relief, Grace did not accept the invitation, saying she needed time to absorb all she had learned that afternoon. She said we looked forward to seeing Antonella and Carlo the following day and to meeting their son.

I drove back to the Aragosta. "You must be totally exhausted. I know I am and I haven't met my new sister, or found out about my father, or seen his photo."

But Grace didn't want to lie back and close her eyes. She and I went over the afternoon from the moment we met Carlo and Antonella, reliving every minute, 'do-you-remembering' like children still high after a ride on a Ferris wheel.

"I think I knew Antonella was my sister from the moment I saw her, but I was my usual cautious self, afraid of being too hopeful. Needing proof. Afraid of being let down." Grace burst out laughing. "What a pain they must have thought I was."

After a moment's silence she said, "Antonella is lovely. She's so warm, so relaxed, so trusting and great to be with. I want to spend time with her and meet her family even if I find out it was all a mistake."

"It's not a mistake. No way. I was there too, remember."

As we drove slowly along the road to the hotel, we talked about the coincidences that had brought us to this point. Had we arrived at the British Military Cemetery a day earlier, even an hour earlier or later, we would not have met Fred and Pat and we might have gone to another hotel. It was unlikely that we would have met anyone who spoke English as fluently as Marilena, or anyone with her charm, energy and willingness to help. We recalled how she introduced us to Tiberio. Was it coincidence that Grace should meet Maurizio, recently returned after many years in Florida, whose revelations led Tiberio to find out about the woman from Gorla?

"I like to think it was destiny or fate, whatever you want to call it, that led you to Antonella," I said. "That it was meant go happen."

"Do you know, Isabel, I used to think I had to be in charge, organising, directing events, leaving nothing to chance. Since being with you I've begun to think that there's a lot of truth in that saying about a Divinity who shapes our ends, rough-hew them how we will."

"Elisa thought so as well. You remember Antonella telling us her mother believed she had been saved from the hurricane for a purpose."

We talked of the long chain of events, and her belief in her destiny, that had brought Elisa from Rome, via Venice to her mother's relatives in Abruzzo. And Anthony O'Brien? Was it merely the fortunes of war that led him, an escaped prisoner of war from a camp near the Adriatic, to hide in a place in the woods previously unknown to Elisa, and from there to her bed? A man and a woman, from different countries with different cultures and without a shared language, colliding like stars in space.

I told Grace that my father was teased, often maliciously, about my birth. I was referred to as a mistake, an accident, Barney's blunder. Such remarks infuriated him. "Don't you ever dare call my daughter a mistake. Isabel is a gift from God. She was meant to be born. And she has her special place in the eyes of God as much as any of you," he would say and threatened to beat up anyone who disagreed with him.

As I parked at the Aragosta, Grace stretched her neck and arms and sank back in the seat. "I can hardly take in what we learned today. It all happened so quickly. It seems totally unreal. Like a dream."

"Well, I was in the same dream and I'm wide awake. Would you like me to drop you off at the beach to recover from the emotion of finding a new family? If I can get hold of Franco, I'll let everybody know what happened and when you come back we will all drink a toast to your new family."

"No, no, please come with me, Isabel. You're my hold on reality. Besides, you and I can be quiet together, but you're quite right. I do need time to let everything sink in."

A wind ruffled the sea where white-edged waves broke on the shore and billowed around rocks and submerged breakwaters. We kicked off our sandals and walked over sand that was cool to the skin.

I told Grace the story Daddy used to tell me, where I was the youngest of King Lir's children and I described my recurring dream of finding my older sister.

"I was very lonely in Kenmara. When I was very small I lived with the hope of finding Lir's other daughter, the sister I was parted from when I was a few days old. I already had the brothers. I usually have the dream at a time of high emotions, like when I came back to London after offending most of the family. The trouble is that I always wake up just when I am within a wing's tip of touching her."

Grace held me to her and stroked my hair. "Isabel, little Isabel. Life has been hard on you. All that is going to change. Don't ask me how I know, but I know it. Believe me."

Grace didn't pluck such statements out of the air. She didn't make wild forecasts, nor did she conjecture without evidence. We sat on the sand, letting its grains flow through our fingers. The breeze was warm with the subdued heat of the early evening sun. I was listening to the lapping sea and enjoying our companionable silence, when Grace spoke.

"Fionnuala! That's the name of Lir's eldest daughter," she exclaimed. "I've been racking my brains and suddenly the words of a song Mamma used to sing have come back to me." In a low, sweet voice she sang:

Silent, O Moyle, be the roar of thy water
Break not, ye breezes, your chain of repose
While murmuring mournfully, Lir's lonely daughter
Tells to the night star her tale of woe.

" – I'll spare you the other verses." She took my hands in hers. "Believe in your dream, Isabel. It will come true, just as mine did. The best has yet to come."

Our steps were light as we took the longer road back to the Aragosta. When we were within sight of the hotel, Grace stopped and said, "I love Jack's version of the children of Lir. It certainly adds another dimension to the story I learned. when I was small."

As we entered the foyer of the Aragosta, a thought struck me with the force of a wind straight off the Atlantic. On one of the most momentous days in Grace's life I had managed to shift the centre of focus from her to me. And hard on its heels came another equally selfish thought. Now that Grace had found a new family, who could tell what Destiny had in store for me.

"You make your own luck," Marie often said

I would seize the day – and Antonella's younger son *was* drop-dead handsome.

Chapter Fourteen

Kenmara

I've invited John and his wife to dinner. It's a one-off occasion. John is usually too busy with his extra-curricular activities to spend time with his mother and he seems to enjoy any company other than his wife's. Not for one minute do I believe any of the rumours that even my closest friends hint at. Success breeds jealousy among small-minded nobodies. Many of them are beside themselves with envy of my clever son and his expanding practice. I soon scotched the rumours Mary Farrell was circulating by asking her, point blank, if her Seamus was still a drunk. She looked daggers at me, but she got the message. I can read John like a book and I'll soon spot any lies he thinks he can get away with. My other reason for asking John and his wife is to hold out an olive branch to Rose. To tell the truth, I miss her doing the shopping, reading out the bits of the newspaper that I can't see, and keeping me posted on the ins and outs of my family. And I'm ashamed of the way I treated her.

I check the dining-room table. Three places are laid with silver cutlery, the best Waterford glasses and the dinner service that Rose gave me and Jack for our fortieth wedding anniversary. It's plain white with a gold rim. Jack said a medal for hard labour would have been more appropriate.

I've searched everywhere but I can't find my own willow pattern plates that I wanted to use. Minnie Burns must have hidden them in that bag she carries and taken them away one at a time. Or it could have been the woman who came to cut my nails. She was so busy admiring my ornaments and furniture, I had to tell her she should keep her eyes on my feet because, if she didn't mind, I wanted to hold on to all ten of my toes. Maybe Linda thought I wouldn't notice a half dozen missing plates. Her family smashes everything they lay their hands on. When she comes, I'll ask Rose if she's seen my plates. I'm not exactly living off the clippings of tin, but I can't stand the thought of somebody stealing my belongings under my very nose.

The menu I've chosen for the meal is foolproof, even for a lousy cook like me. I sloshed half a bottle of wine into my stewed beef casserole and christened it *Boeuf Bourguignon*. It needs another hour in the oven. I scattered a handful of flaked almonds over the trifle I made yesterday and decorated it with a glacé cherry. Oh, I forgot to mention the starter – salmon paté from the supermarket with slices of tomato, avocado and cucumber. I am very pleased with my efforts.

I steamrollered over all the excuses John gave for not being able to come this evening and insisted that he and his wife arrive together. There are matters I have to discuss with the pair of them and it will do John good to spend time with Rose, whether he wants to or not. He was keen enough to marry her shortly after he qualified. Jack and I talked ourselves blue in the face. He refused to wait till he was in a position to look after a wife and family.

John's wedding. A showy affair, three bridesmaids in pink taffeta and Isabel, in a white frock, clutching a horseshoe. I haven't time to think about something that happened years ago. I have to change, do my face and look my best for what may well prove a tricky evening. But no matter how much I try to think about my missing plates, I can't shake the day of their wedding out of my head. Every detail of that sunny August day in 1978 is as clear as if it happened yesterday. Not John, beaming and handsome in morning suit and top hat or Rose, a slim bride in full white regalia. Of course they were there. They had to be, but they are only shadowy figures in the background of my memory. Centre stage is Angela. Angela after forty-odd years. Come back to rake over the past; to taunt me with Daisy's death.

Like a lizard on a hot stone wall, the photographer darts up to re-position Rose's train, to adjust the angle of her bouquet, to prod my son an inch closer to his bride. We're in the grounds of the Deerpark Hotel, posing for the group photograph. Angela is suddenly right beside me in full wedding attire, and a forty-one-year-old chasm is widening between us. How do I break the silence? Should I ask who invited her to my son's wedding? Shall I ask her how she's keeping, or tell her she looks like a bunch of daffodils in her yellow dress? I'm hunting for the right words when she turns to me.

"Rita, do you ever think about Daisy?"

Just like that. No small talk. No lead up after all that time.

Typical. She could always read my mind, so she knows her arrow has hit home.

"Rita, did you hear what I said? Do you ever think about Daisy?"

There's a roaring in my ears. My brain, that had been empty of everything except the hope that Rose will be kind to my son, is a cauldron of scalding memories. I'm thinking of making a run for the car when John stops gazing at his new wife and redirects his smile towards me. And despite Angela's question, my heart turns over as it did each time I saw him waiting for me at the school gates. Jack often said I loved John too much and accused me of mollycoddling him. How could I tell him, how could I tell anyone, why nobody but me could be trusted to look after my son? How could I explain why I had to protect him constantly after what I did to Daisy?

"Next, the happy couple and their parents. Over here, please. That's right, bride's mother and father beside their daughter. Mother and father of the groom on his right." I move close to John. "Very nice. Big smiles everyone." The photographer demonstrates, baring a row of sharp teeth crowned by a thin moustache.

Do I ever think about Daisy? Her memory will haunt me till the end of my life. Not a day passes without me seeing her – her knitted pixie, muck from the bird bath stuck in her eyebrows and round her mouth, the skin under her nose raw and weeping.

"Now then, groom's mother, this won't do. You're at a wedding, not a funeral. Think of it this way. You haven't lost a son. You've gained a daughter-in-law. Somebody to look after him, to cook for him, do his laundry." He titters as if he's said something funny. "So, give us a big smile. That's better."

John squeezes my arm. "All right, Ma?"

At least, while I'm here, Angela can't get to me. A multi-coloured wall of guests stands between us, but once the photograph of the immediate family is taken, she'll be back and she won't give up till she's raked over every last detail of that day in October 1937.

After much shuffling and re-arranging, the group photographs are taken. John and Rose are shepherded off to pose beside a fountain and against various flowering shrubs. I chat to members of Rose's family and smile at polite comments from John's friends. But all the while Angela's yellow shape hovers in the corner of my eye. How am I to avoid her? My mother must have invited her. At times she can't remember her own name, or much else, but she hasn't forgotten how to cause trouble.

"Rita, I need to talk to you. Please."

I look around. No escape. Angela's arm guides me down a quiet path out of sight of the chattering crowd. My heart is beating so loud I'm sure she can hear it.

"It's about Daisy." She stops under an arch of pink roses and faces me. "We didn't kill Daisy. We had nothing to do with her death. She was run over by a car."

I stand open-mouthed, unable to grasp the meaning of her words. All I hear is 'we' not 'you.' 'We,' after forty years.

She looks into my eyes and repeats, "We didn't kill Daisy."

A voice I don't recognise as mine, whispers, "How do you know? You can't know for certain."

"When the invitation to John's wedding arrived, I was happy. I hoped maybe you'd forgiven me." She pauses, and goes on, speaking deliberately as though she's reciting a speech she knows by heart. "I couldn't get Daisy out of my head. Or what her death had done to us. So I did what I'd been scared to do all along. I found out where I could see her death certificate." She puts her hands on my shoulders. "Rita, she died from injuries when a car knocked her off her trike."

My head is filled with cotton wool, so thick I hear only an echo of Angela's words. She tells me Daisy was knocked down outside her home in Dundrum. She lay in a coma for three days and died on the ninth of November.

"Her death had nothing to do with us. We were wicked and cruel and I was a spiteful brat. Can you forgive me, Rita? I was more to blame than you."

My eyes widen in amazement. The ghost of a smile plays on her lips as she adds, "After all, I'm three days older than you."

I want to speak, but the same silence as when I first heard about Daisy's death, freezes my throat. How can Angela be so certain? What if she made up the story about an accident? For forty years, the certainty I had killed Daisy has been a weight pressing me into the ground. It has grown with me. It has made me the person I am and I don't know if I can survive without it.

I walk away from Angela and back towards the hotel, towards the sound of chatter peppered with laughter. I need time on my own to think; to grasp what she has just told me, but there is no time. Today is about John and his bride, not a day for raking over a quarrel between two wilful children. I look back. Angela stands motionless on the gravel path, twisting her hat in her hands. Her hair is dishevelled. Her face is bleak as winter.

"Rita, where have you been?" Mammy bustles towards me, scolding. "We're going in for the meal any minute. And where's Angela?"

"She's coming. We were ... we were having a talk."

"Were you? That's good. I'm really pleased to hear that. And about time too." She nods her head, beaming. Then she propels me into the hotel. "You have to hurry. Your place is beside John and Rose. You and Angela will have plenty of time to talk afterward."

Maybe. I'm not sure. I'm not ready to face her. Maybe some other time. Jack's growling at me to get a move on and Rose's mother is heaving sighs you could hear in Dublin.

I'll talk to Angela later. Maybe. Maybe not. I don't know.

"Mammy, look at me. Please Mammy, What's wrong? I'll call the doctor." John's on one knee by my chair, worried, pleading. "Look at me. That's better. My wee Mammy, you were so far away, I was afraid something had … Are you able to stand up? Give me your hand. You still look a bit dazed."

"I must have dozed off. Stop fussing, John. You're not rid of me yet." I rise to my feet, brushing away my son's helping hand. I smile at him. He stopped calling me Mammy when he started going to school. He's such a handsome man, my son, though his belly is expanding as fast as his bank balance and it sticks out when he's off guard. Rose hovers behind him, shifting from one foot to the other. How can she have changed so much in such a short time or is it because I've never taken time to look at her? Flesh has fallen off her face and the bags under her eyes are the colour of stewed tea. It can't be because I ordered her out of Kenmara. Can it? I hope not. She could do with a facial and a good moisturiser. I stroke my own well-nourished complexion. Well-nourished it may be, it's still as wrinkled as a crepe bandage.

"We were very worried, Rita, when we saw you. Were you just having a wee doze?" She hangs back, subdued, no longer the brisk know-all. Obviously, she's learned her lesson. "I hope you weren't over-doing things."

138

"Not at all. Just day-dreaming," I swallow the acid comment that's souring my tongue and kiss the air near my daughter-in-law's cheeks. "Oh my goodness, I forgot to put on the vegetables."

"Would you like me to switch them on, Rita? Is there anything else you'd like me to do?"

I'm concerned about Rose. I think I prefer the old, spirited Rose with the voice of a fire alarm to this mouse scuttling to the kitchen.

John pours sherry for me and a gin and tonic for himself. "So, Ma, everything's fine with you now. You're sure? Good, good, good. So that's grand now."

"I'm not ready for the knacker's yard for a while. At least, I hope not. How about yourself and Rose? I hope you are both well." Ignoring the cloud of annoyance darkening my son's face, I continue, "She's a good woman. She's lonely now that the children have left. You need to spend more time with her and less on your own activities." My raised hand quells his next outburst. "I know I'm a fine one to talk, considering the way I treated your father, but it's not too late for you." I fix him with a gimlet eye. "That is, if you value your marriage and if you want it to last."

"And just what's that remark supposed to mean?"

"You can interpret it any way you like. I may be an old woman but I'm neither blind nor deaf. Call Rose in from the kitchen. I've something to tell you both."

"Why can't you tell me now?"

He waits for me to inform him. John is not used to being kept waiting. I insist that he fetch Rose. I'm really enjoying myself, enjoying the feeling of power, especially over my clever son. Just like the old days.

Followed by his wife, he returns to glower at the window. "What's so important, mother? I had to cancel two appointments to come here. And there's no need to sneer."

"And I am suitably grateful." I motion Rose to the armchair beside me. "I'm having a party on the eleventh of July for the whole family and I'd like you to come and your children, if they are able to. Hugh, Linda and their children will all be here."

"The eleventh of July. That's your birthday, Rita. What a great idea. Of course our children will come. That is... if they're in the country. Would you like me to do the catering I could... "

"Why this year, Ma? It's not a special birthday?" John moves quickly to lean over me. Furrows crease his forehead. "Has something happened? Are you ill?"

"I'm getting on and there are a few things I need to settle with my family before I die. You will come? It's not an order, Johnny. It's an invitation. "

"Try keeping us away," John strokes the brown spots on my hands that frequent coatings of peroxide and concealer don't hide any more. "Rose will organise the catering as soon as you know the numbers. Is my sister coming?"

"Of course she is and Grace too. I've asked her sons as well."

"Her sons! What made you ask them? We hardly know them."

"Well now's the time to get to know them. They are family, you know." What's the matter with John and how dare he question who I'll ask to my own house? "I want a big family gathering. I've already organised the catering. Rose, I think the vegetables will be ready and, John, you can deal with the wine."

After his first drink John stops pushing back his white cuff and glancing at his watch. Rose limits the scope of her conversation to buttering me up.

"Rita, this meat is so tender it just melts in the mouth. And the sauce has such a delicate flavour." She goes on to gush over the trifle, which she says is so heavenly and luscious that words fail her. My own mother would turn a few times in her coffin if she knew I had bought ready-made custard in a carton.

"If you can read a recipe, you can cook." I clamp my lips tight before the words squeeze through. It's very hard to undo the habits of a lifetime. "It's really kind of you to offer to do the catering, Rose, but I've been in touch with a firm that Norah Larkin recommended and I've asked them to make the cake."

"Well, that's grand, Ma. I was a bit worried when we received the summons to come today. I thought we were due for a dressing down. You know, I'm a grown man but you can still put the fear of God into me. Here's to many more years." John and his wife raise their glasses. "Anything you need, Ma, say the word and Rose will see to it. I married a very capable woman."

"And a long-suffering one. See you don't take her for granted or you'll have me to reckon with. Actually, Rose, on second thoughts,

140

I'd really prefer it if you'd make the cake. Nobody makes a better fruit cake than you."

It was a good evening. The ice has been broken and diplomatic relations established between me and Rose once more and not a mention of Bridget or that stuff she brought up last time she was here. I stretch my arms and set out for my nightly tour of the shrubs and flower-beds. I have to hand it to Jack. He had a gift for making a blaze of colour out of a barren patch of ground. There's colour not only in annuals and perennials but also in the pink, white and dark blue clematis, in honeysuckle that climbs over the summer house, in the different greens of shrubs and trees and in rambling roses running wild through the shrubbery. I always seem to think of him whenever I come into the garden. Jack, the man from God knows where. There were worse husbands, God knows. Much worse. I never really gave him a chance. I resented him for being my father's choice. For being fourteen years older than me. For not being Jemmy.

Jemmy! I trip. Grab at a bush. Almost fall. That name. Where did it spring from? Oh God! Heartache. Heartbreak. Jemmy! Where did he come from? I shouldn't have started thinking about Daisy. I wasn't ready. There's too much that's best forgotten.

Jemmy? The name of the yard boy, who came to work for Pa the first summer that I was well enough to go out after all those months in bed with TB. Pa called all the cellar men Jemmy. It was simpler, he said. The real Jemmy, a red-faced man who could carry a barrel of beer on his belly, had been laid up for weeks.

No. I'm not going there. Not going to think about that. I've spent enough time in the past for one day. But why is my early life as clear as yesterday, when sometimes I hardly remember what I did last week? I've heard it said that when a man is drowning, the closeness to death makes him see his life pass before him in flashes. Resurfacing buried memories has the same effect as drowning on me. I've been told that the pains in my chest are in my mind. In my mind they may be. They hurt, just the same.

A picture of young Jemmy's face swims before my eyes, clear, focused. Then it fades. An image disintegrating on water.

"Rita, don't you know us? It's Jemmy. I work for yer da." A grin from ear to ear.

Too thin for carrying crates from the delivery lorry to the cellar. Too slight for the heavy loads of bottles he lugged down the concrete steps from the bar. A joking lad, cycling with me along the coast towards Carrickfergus, hair blowing over his face. Bikes thrown on the grass. Arms round waists, leaning into each other on the path along the shore to Whitehead. Waves foaming over rocks, over our feet, backs pressed against a wall of rock. Miles away from Ma's beady eyes. Miles from the clack-clacking of neighbours' tongues. A long, warm summer and Jemmy free on Wednesday afternoons – Ma and her sister look at pubs for sale in more select parts of the city every Wednesday. Free as the wind to ride beside me. Puffing uphill. Freewheeling downhill, his feet on the handlebars. White-bellied gulls swirling above us.

"You're beautiful. I think about you first thing in the morning and last thing at night and I dream you're lying in my arms."

Me saying nothing. Drinking in every word.

The day he said, "Yer da had a word with us yesterday. Jemmy's coming back to work on Monday. I'm out of a job."

Tears in the voice that told me there was no work in Ireland. He couldn't expect his mother to keep him. She had a crowd of children to rear and her with no man any more. Three of his brothers had gone to England where there were plenty of jobs in factories and on farms. Money to send home.

"I'll be back for you, Rita. Wait for me. I promise I'll be back no matter what. You can count on that."

That was the last I saw of him.

Calf love. Foolish. Impossible. The sad thing is that those brief summer weeks were the only time in my life when I thought I was in love. The only time I felt my heart leap each time I caught sight of someone. The only time when desire for a man raced through my veins. Maybe that's why I turned into such a discontented old woman, angry because I missed out on life.

If my father had found out that I was seeing his cellar man, too menial to be given a name of his own, he would have locked me up or stuck me into a convent till I came to my senses. I well remember my own anger when Hugh said he was going to marry a girl from Ballymurphy.

Hugh was a grown man. He married Linda across my teeth.

My sister Kate had managed to produce only one single daughter and my father needed grandsons to take over the business. He said it was time I had a strong man to sort me out, to make me see sense. He produced Jack McGlade, a big, *sauncey* fellow who drank in his bar. He was said to be well-heeled, a man of stature. And he was looking for a wife. Pa said it was best to make no mention of TB. A man like Jack, could have his pick of the basket when it came to women. He would want a healthy wife and he'd be off like the clappers if he heard there was consumption in the family. Jack was a reluctant suitor. He said he'd be proud to have such a fine-looking wife, but my coldness could freeze whiskey. So, to increase his daughter's market value, my father bought Lake View. Jack, believing he would be joint owner, fell in love with the house and agreed to accept me and a dowry of a thousand pounds.

Before we were married, he announced that he was going to call his future home *Hy-Brasil*. Since I was to be sold like a piece of furniture to a stranger, who was years older than me, the name of the house was the least of my concerns. Jack said that *Hy-Brasil* was a hallowed island out in the Atlantic that rose to the surface as a haven for anyone who was shipwrecked. The Irish name meant Isle of the Blest. I never admitted to him that the name pleased me. It was unusual, had a touch of class. My father would have none of it. He didn't believe in houses with foreign names.

Jack was full of such stories. Full of shit, his sons said. They lost interest in the yarns from his past and in the legends and tales that he loved to tell them. In Isabel he found an avid and an attentive listener.

"Will you take me to Clare and to Innishmore to see my aunts and uncles and cousins and can we climb to the top of the cliffs and you'll show me where to look for Hy-Brasil, Daddy?"

"I'll do that. To be sure, I will. You and me, we'll take the boat from Galway and we'll climb up to the Dun Aengus and I'll show you where to look. You'll see it, to be sure you will. You're my daughter. We'll go, just the two of us. One of these days. That's a promise."

143

I go back indoors. Typical of Jack. An old cod, full of fine words and empty promises. Isabel never stopped believing in him. My poor daughter, she didn't have much luck with her parents. A liar and a big mouth for a father. A sour, old woman for a mother. And that monkey-faced fellow from the back streets of the Ardoyne for a husband.

Pain again. I must stop raking over the past, resenting what I've lost, what I can't change. That's what's causing it. It's how old people fill their lives. Digging into the past, because they're scared there may be no future. Opening doors that are better unopened, for fear of what they'll let loose. Please God, let me last another few weeks. That is all I need, though I want a lot more. Years more.

Chapter Fifteen

As soon as Franco heard about our visit to the Pace family he telephoned Marilena. She wanted all the details from Grace, who heard her relay them with shrieks of delight to her parents and to Gianni. Pat and Fred had gone upstairs for an early night.

They joined us for breakfast on the patio behind the dining room. They had already heard a summary of our visit from Gina, but were hungry for information about Antonella and her mother, especially her time with Anthony O'Brien.

"What a story, Grace. Dad and I said that meeting you really made our holiday," Pat looked at his father who nodded his agreement. "We haven't had so much excitement since the year we met the families of Mauro and Francesca from Scerni. You remember we told you about them? Dad knew their parents in 1943."

"Pat's right, Grace, it's like something out of a book, and learning so much about Anthony O'Brien." Fred paused, his eyes fixed on a spot somewhere beyond the gardens of the hotel. "I could well have met him in Scerni. I remember escaped prisoners joining us there. They were in a terrible state – in rags, filthy hair and beards, covered in muck. Two lads, dressed like peasants, turned up one morning." He paused again as if he was trying to separate the memory from others buried in forgotten crannies of his mind. "It was before the Sangro crossing and they were soaked through. One was leading a donkey on a string. The other had a dog. They told us after it was to make them look like Italian peasants. They gave their names to the officer and collapsed. It was their boots that made him think they might be British soldiers. What was left of them." Fred remained deep in thought before turning towards Grace. "Your father would have been very proud to have a daughter like you. It's a shame your mother didn't live to make the journey with you."

Grace and I exchanged glances. Had she come with Aunt Kate, she would have made sure her mother learned nothing about the young Italian woman who had sheltered Anthony O'Brien and given birth to his daughter.

"Isabel told me about your wife and your other children, Fred. You're a lucky man." Then Grace questioned Fred about his family. He told her about his marriage to Sophie and the birth of Pat, their first child, in 1948, followed by two more sons and a daughter, Joan. A contented life clouded by Sophie's death.

"She would have loved coming to Italy on holiday with me and she would have been proud to know that our children have been so good to me."

He looked at his watch, stood up and said they would leave Grace to prepare for meeting her new family. Pat was taking him to the hillside town of Atessa, which he liked to visit each year. While he had been waiting for the order to cross the Sangro, he remembered hearing Allied bombardments of the town which the German army had already occupied.

Grace said she was going to spend the rest of the morning at the rooftop pool, swimming, lazing about and thinking about how lucky she was.

I turned left out of the hotel and walked till I came to a narrow road and a path which led up a gentle slope to a tree-lined horizon. Not the long established oaks, pine and beech that isolated Kenmara from the outside world, but slender trunks of saplings and young, not yet thickened, hedges. Seeing a For Sale notice, I stopped at an abandoned house which had been built half-way up an olive grove, close to a narrow strip of vines. Masses of red and pink roses and white oleander flowered in a long, neglected garden. I navigated my way over missing floorboards, cracked concrete, broken tiles and glass till I came to a balcony with a sweeping view of the sea from the promontory in the south to the escarpment in the north. As I looked over the surrounding countryside, my head emptied of the headlong events and revelations of the past weeks. They had hurtled so quickly past; although I raced after them, I might as well have been trying to catch hold of my shadow. I was aware, as from a great distance, of the occasional car on the narrow road below, the buzz of insects and the whisper of leaves, but inside my head was nothing. Only the silence of no noise. Hardly daring to move, I let my gaze wander over the sheer blue of the bay, over the foothills of the Apennines and I felt behind me the reassurance of an olive and vine-covered slope. I could be contented here at the centre of this panorama. It would be like floating on a millpond under a clear sky. I would restore the garden, turn the uneven ground into a lawn, cultivate the nameless, overgrown plants and rebuild the house to its original design. I would come here with Grace and her family each summer and at Christmas my friends would fill it with the vitality of Hugh and Linda's busy home.

Liam had disliked the privileged situation of Kenmara with almost the same intensity as he loathed my mother. His childhood and youth had been spent in the troubled streets of the Ardoyne, where areas were separated by what became known as the Peace Wall, built to stop warring factions tearing each other apart; where flags and images painted on the gable walls of both communities left strangers in no doubt of whose territory they had entered. Liam loved the noise and the tensions of the city and mistrusted a lifestyle that might take him too far from his roots. He would not have lasted two days in an olive grove, or a vineyard.

I could sell my house, rent a flat and buy this place in Abruzzo. It would have its ghosts, but not the ghosts that haunted me in London. I left the balcony and walked round the house viewing it from all angles, my mind busy with plans and dreams. A lawn in an olive grove? Maybe. Maybe not. I'd have to talk it over with Grace.

Grace threw open the doors of the wardrobe and we stared in. What to wear to Vasto? She rejected a navy trouser suit. Too dark, too librarianish. A print, silk dress with layered skirt? Too showy. A cotton blouse and matching skirt? Not chic enough for Italy.

A cream linen suit was stretched on the bed, a black camisole inserted under neat reveres. No. Black wouldn't do for a family celebration. Brown, dark green?

"The trouble is, I'm used to blending into the background. If I were a book I'd be filed under 'Historical' with 'Smart, but colourless,' written on the flyleaf."

"Not any more you wouldn't. You're a new woman on the brink of a new life. What would go with the suit?" I plucked a crimson silk camisole from my drawer. "There you go. Perfect. Keep the silk frock for tomorrow night's do. Remember, you want to arrive cool and calm today, so I'm driving."

"Isabel, you're an angel. I wish I had a daughter like you to advise me."

"Steady on. You've acquired a sister, a brother-in-law and two nephews. All I'm looking for is a boyfriend."

"Not a husband?"

"No, a handsome boyfriend, who adores me, will be just fine," I said as I slipped on a short denim skirt and a bright green top. Marie said I looked fit in that outfit. I studied myself from all angles and decided it would do.

At Via Pisino, the scene was similar to yesterday. Groups of women sitting under the shade of pines nodded and smiled at us. As soon as we got out of the car, children ran to knock on the door of the Pace flat to announce our arrival. Antonella, in a sleeveless yellow frock, and Carlo hurried out to embrace us, to hold us at arm's length and say how smart we looked. For the first time, I really did see a family likeness between the two women: the same straight nose and crinkly smile. And something of Antonella's liveliness had rubbed off on Grace.

A black sports car stopped outside the gate.

"Toni arriva!"

"Ecco Toni!"

"Eccolo!"

A group of boys, aged about nine or ten rushed through the open gate as a tall young man emerged from the car, called to his parents and attempted to take a bag from the back seat. He ruffled the hair of the small boy who was carrying it. He moved through the children, answering their torrent of questions. *"Ciao Toni, ciao Toni,"* called the women. *"Ciao Dina. Ciao Gianna. Ciao Marisa. "* He waved to them and approached his parents, arms wide open.

Toni's arrival reminded me of the first time I saw Liam burst into the East Slope Bar on the campus in Brighton. My first thought was. "He loves himself." My second was, "Why wouldn't he?" His photos had shown nothing of his energy, his vitality or the delight with which he embraced his parents.

He was about two inches taller than his father, whose aquiline features he had inherited. His hair, which was short and black, grew into a peak in the centre of his forehead. He gazed at Grace before putting his arms around her.

148

"My new aunt and every bit as beautiful as my mother. I can't take it in, even now when I see you side by side and I have only to look at you to know that you haven't made up the whole story." He hugged Grace again.

Carlo introduced me as Grace's cousin.

"I'm not your uncle, am I? Or some other close relation?"

"No, you're not, I'm sorry to say. I'm Grace's cousin. Our mothers were sisters, but you and I are not related."

"Don't be sorry. I'm very pleased." Toni said and kissed my cheeks.

As we drank iced tea, the story of Grace's visit to the British Military Cemetery, the encounter with Fred and Pat, Maurizio's revelations and the meeting of Anthony O'Brien's two daughters whizzed around the sitting room, Antonella and Grace interrupted, one continuing the narrative, the other filling in forgotten details.

"He must have been quite a guy, this father of yours. Nonna often spoke about him. All I got from him is his name," Toni said.

"We called our first boy Marco after my father. It's the custom," Carlo explained, "Italian parents expect to be obeyed and my generation did what we were told. More or less. When Toni was born, it was right that he be called after his other grandfather."

Toni chatted to his parents about his job, his flat, holiday plans, sometimes lapsing into Italian. Then he said, "I think Isabel needs a break from all this family talk." He turned to me, "Would you like me to show you around Vasto and leave the older generation to talk among themselves?"

"I'd love to see around Vasto with you." I jumped to my feet, pleased to escape from hours of family chat and photographs and to be alone with him.

"When do you want us to come back, Mamma?" he asked.

Whatever reply his mother gave, she hugged her son and laughed.

Once outside and through the gauntlet of Toni's admirers, I said, "Thank you for asking me to come out with you. I am delighted that Grace and Antonella have found each other, but I am glad to..."

"Get away from it all? I can believe that. Don't thank me. When Mamma said that Grace's cousin was with her, I expected a much older person. A very different person." Toni laughed and held the car door open. "I am pleased that you are you, and not a much older or a different person, Isabel."

I smiled to myself. When you meet someone for the first time, depending on the impression you want to make, you decide which of your many faces to show. Which aspects of your character you will highlight. Which you will keep under wraps. I hoped Toni would like what he saw.

"It's not far to the town, is it?" I asked.

"No, but Italians aren't like the English. We don't walk. We like to be seen in our cars, getting into them and climbing out of them. It's called *bella figura*. Looking good." He grinned. "All very shallow."

"First of all, Toni, I'm not English. I'm Irish, from Ireland."

"I am sorry. That is a big mistake, I know. Half the kids at my school in Brooklyn were Italian, the other half Irish. We were in gangs and we used to beat each other up a couple of times a week, but we were good friends." He laughed and said, "My first girlfriend was called Kathleen O'Shea. We were both ten. She was lovely. You're Irish, like Anthony O'Brien?"

"He had an Irish name but his family may have emigrated to England. A lot of Irish did."

"Well, Isabel, let's have a look at Vasto. There's a big church in the square and a famous medieval castle though I can't remember what it's famous for. It's one of the smartest towns in Abruzzo. Every evening, young girls from the town like to walk up and down showing off their new clothes. This happens all over Italy. It's known as the *passegiata*."

He parked the car in a square dominated by a fifteenth century castle which was closed. Toni translated its history from a plaque on the wall. After visiting the cathedral we strolled around the town to the Piazza Rossetti, where a statue had been erected to Gabriele Rossetti, father of Dante Gabriel and Christina. Toni told me he had been a revolutionary, forced, under threat of death, to leave Italy. We strolled high above the Adriatic, passing the house where Rossetti had lived before fleeing to England. Toni said the town had been built on a hill about a thousand years before the Roman invasion. A landslide in the 1950s had left part of it sloping to the sea.

We sat outside a bar framed by yellow and purple bourgainveillea, and with a panoramic view over the bay at Vasto.

While Toni ordered drinks I remembered my first meeting with Liam. Within seconds, we had sussed out each other's religion, class and education and we had pinpointed the districts in Belfast in which we had grown up. By contrast, apart from a few items of background, Toni and I faced each other fresh as blank sheets of paper.

"My mother only spoke about Grace when she phoned yesterday. Understandably, I suppose. I know they're the same age and I think you are much younger than me."

"Where did you learn not to ask a woman how old she is?"

"In England. Where else?"

"Of course," I smiled at him. "I'm twenty-seven, going on twenty-eight. Only a couple of years younger than you. Your parents told Grace and me about you and your brother."

He shook his head. "I'm quite sure they did. Italians are very wrapped up in their families and expect everybody else to be interested. It can be very boring. You're not married?"

An Englishman would have phrased the question less directly. "I got married when I was nineteen, in my second year at university. It didn't work out. We separated years ago." I hesitated, unwilling to cast a shadow over the afternoon. "He died recently in a car crash."

"Oh Isabel, I'm sorry."

His hand rested briefly on mine. Dappled shade, the scent of bougainvillea and the kindness of this stranger who was Grace's nephew, had lowered my guard. I'd met men with as much personality as a lump of lard, whose idea of courtship was a swift drink in a pub and bed. I'd learnt to spot them a mile off. Toni's liveliness was infectious. I wanted him to know a happy me, interesting and interested, someone he would wish to spend time with, to be seen with, not a widow, wallowing in sorrow.

My smile of reassurance said to him, please like me, Toni, not because your mother asked you to look after me. Not because I've a pretty face. Not because I'm your new aunt's cousin. Please like me because I'm me, because I long to be the happy girl I used to be and to feel that I'm worth loving. It need only be for today and maybe tomorrow, until you return to your life in Rome. You're the first man who has attracted me since I emerged from my self-imposed shadows. Please like me, Toni.

I reminded myself that I wasn't a star-struck teenager on holiday in Italy, falling for the first good-looking man who showed an interest in her. But my blood was rushing to every nerve ending and I

151

was aware, as I had been on arriving at Pescara, of the luminous quality of the light, how it radiated from objects and was not merely painted on the surface. How vibrant were the yellows, reds and purples of the bougainvillea. How intense the blues of the sea and sky compared to the rain-damp colours of Ireland.

"Thank you, Toni, thank you for... for taking me to this lovely place. Now, tell me about yourself?"

He hadn't wanted to leave Brooklyn, especially when his brother decided to stay in the States, but his grandmother pestered his parents to return. He had studied electrical engineering in Rome, where he lived in a flat which his parents owned. He had been engaged to a local girl who had married someone else.

We stood at a railing overlooking the blue-green sweep of the bay which curved around Vasto. His arm rested lightly over my shoulder as he pointed out the grey slab of the Maiella and sandy beaches along the coast, which he said were visited mainly by Italian families

I told him I'd grown up in a house that overlooks Belfast Lough – "I love the sea, even in winter. Just as well, since we don't have Italian sunshine all year round."

He had been to Blackpool, Manchester and Brighton and he wanted to hear about my home overlooking the sea. His job took him to England several times a year to conferences, to buy plant for power stations, to visit engineering companies and on health and safety courses.

"Next time I visit," he said, "we should meet up."

"That would be great," I said. "After all, we're almost related."

He paused, pursed his lips, as if working out where we should go next. "My parents want to introduce Grace to Papa's family tomorrow and they're talking about going to the Sangro Cemetery. I'd like to take you to the Gargano, to one the best beaches in Italy." Before waiting for me to reply, he added with a half smile, "The truth is I'd like to spend a whole day with you, Isabel, to get to know you, that is, unless you would prefer to meet Papa's family?"

He had Grace's habit of raising his left eyebrow. A question? A request? I was about to shout yes, yes, when an image of my headlong falling in love with Liam stopped me. "There's nothing I'd like better than to go to the Gargano with you. I could meet your father's family another day. It doesn't have to be tomorrow."

152

"Good. We'll swim at Vieste and we'll eat in the old town and I'll show you around the area. What time will I come to your hotel? Eight o'clock, nine o'clock?"

"Nine, I think." I'd have to wash my hair and decide what I'd need for a day out with Toni.

"Nine o'clock it is. And now, we must go back and taste my mother's cooking."

At Via Pisino the table was covered with a white embroidered cloth and already set for five. While his parents busied themselves in their narrow kitchen, Toni chatted to Grace, asking her about her family, her job and her life in England, as much at ease with his new aunt as he had been with me. Not remotely like the stereotype Latin lover of the come-to-bed eyes and oily tongue I would have avoided like chickenpox. Were all Italian men born with the knack of making the person they were with feel really important, or was it a skill they acquired? There was something of Liam in him, the same lightness, same quirky sense of humour and zest for living. Women make the same mistakes over and over again and I was no exception. It was no big deal. Toni had invited me to spend a day on the beach with him. He hadn't suggested setting me up in a flat in Rome.

We ate lasagna, followed by veal cutlets and salad. In the pause before having the cake to welcome Grace into the family, she told Toni about her sons and invited him to accompany his parents to her home in Hastings.

"Of course, I'll come. I love England. I love fish and chips and ploughman's lunch. You live in Hastings. The Battle of Hastings is the only date I know in English history." With a half smile he asked, "Shall I see you too, Isabel?"

"You most certainly will. I look forward to meeting you all. I'll show you around London if you like."

"Antonella and Carlo are coming to England at the beginning of August after we've been at your mum's party. I have to be home before the end of next week, Toni, to see my family and get ready for Ireland," Grace said. "I promised Isabel we would spend a few days in Rome before we leave Italy. We'll probably go to Pescara Airport on Monday morning and say goodbye to our friends, Fred and Pat Cooper. Then we'll drive across to Rome."

153

If the pitch of the discussion between Toni and his parents had been any indication of the subject under discussion, they might have been preparing an assault on the residents of their block of flats, with each of them fighting to lead the attack. Grace and I should stay with the parents in their apartment in Vasto and we would all go to Rome in the middle of next week. Toni said the best solution was for Grace to hand the car over at the airport on Monday, say goodbye to our friends and drive to Rome with him.

Thoughts exploded inside me like fireworks. My mind rushed ahead, weaving plans, hoping hopes. Nobody was waiting for me in London. Nobody looked forward to my return. My neighbours would notice my absence and get on with their lives. I dreaded returning to my empty house, to the noise and loneliness of the city, to dog-fouled pavements, to pubs belching out drunks and knife-happy gangs, to being groped on crowded and late-running trains. To the implied threat in that anonymous letter. After Grace returned to England I would stay in Rome until it was time to return to Kenmara. When Liam left me, I became a forty-year-old. One afternoon with Toni and I was a sixteen-year-old looking forward to her first date, counting the hours till tomorrow and the Gargano.

Chapter Sixteen

Being dumped by Liam, with a final confirmation from the grave, had battered my self-confidence. Suppose Toni didn't turn up. Suppose he had telephoned some excuse to release him from a promise made on the spur of the moment! I hovered at the top of the stairs, unclenched my fists and took deep breaths. The outing to the Gargano was no big deal. Something between a blind date and a set-up engineered by his parents.

The moment I caught sight of him in the foyer chatting to Gina and Claudio, all my fears vanished.

"Isabella," he said, taking my hands and kissing my cheeks.

Gina and Claudio wished us a good day and waved us off.

"The Gargano peninsula used to be an island." I read from my guide book. Reading was easier than making small talk with a man I had known only for a few hours. "It's a very mountainous promontory quite separate from the Apennines. Think of it as the spur of the Italian boot."

"The spur of Italy? OK I suppose it is. You probably know more about it than I do." Toni pointed to the hazy sea. "The Tremiti Islands are over there, somewhere. You can see them from here in winter when the Tramontana blows from the north. I wish we had time to go there, but that's for another day."

Another day! Sea and sun-baked countryside flying past, black hairs on Toni's arms, long, confident hands on the steering wheel, eyes dark-shadowed behind sunglasses, his smile as he turned to speak at me. A coastline of coves, grottoes and cliffs, sandy beaches and a sea the blue-green colour of postcards; the shade of beech and oak in the Foresta Umbra.

Liam and I had only rarely explored the Sussex coast or walked on the Downs. We'd spent most of our time in bed, time snatched between his lectures, time when I should have been attending lectures, but lacked the will to tear myself from sheets still warm from him. Two almost-strangers, who had seen only the in-love sides of each other, thrust into a marriage neither of us needed or wanted.

Toni stopped the car and pointed. "That's Vieste. We'll have a swim, relax for a while and find somewhere to eat in the old town. There's a castle in the town," he laughed, "so famous I know nothing about it, but I expect you do."

"I read something about it but I've forgotten what it was." Trying to avoid launching into full gushing mode, I said, "Toni, thank you for bringing me to this beautiful place."

"You don't need to thank me. I'm selfish. I only do what I like doing and I do like to be with you. Very much."

He chose a spot on the beach, gave me a striped beach towel and slipped off his white T-shirt and navy shorts. God, but he's handsome, I thought again as I watched the muscles on his arms and shoulders flex with the effort of righting the umbrella he had brought with him; as I wondered about the scar along the lower part of his backbone, a thin white line against the deep tan of his skin.

Though I enjoyed swimming, windy Irish beaches or the shingle at Brighton and my pale Irish skin do not encourage sunbathing. On school trips to Newcastle or Bangor we used to rush into the sea, huddle in towels while we ate our tomato and ham sandwiches out of plastic lunch-boxes and play rounders wearing shorts or track-suits.

My green bikini showed off my shape, but I would never have the confidence to promenade along a beach like the beautiful Italian women and girls in tiny bikinis that enhanced their tanned and voluptuous bodies. Next time I was near a shop I would buy a smaller and brighter bikini and a bottle of instant bronzer.

Toni and I swam parallel with the shore. As I floated on the warm sea I raised my eyes and gazed into the fathomless ocean of clear blue sky before following him towards the rocks which separated the two beaches at Vieste. He waited, treading water, and stretched out his arms when I reached him. He climbed on a flat rock and pulled me up to lie beside him. Brown thigh beside white thigh, brown shoulder close to pink, twin rivulets flowing back into the waves which foamed below us. He reached into a rock pool and gave me a cockleshell so delicately coloured an artist might have painted the stripes, ranging from dark brown to lightest fawn, and the base edged with fluted cream.

He told me he was often sent to collect *telline,* small clam-like creatures that could be found under the sand or as you walked in the sea. All you had to do was dig your toes into the water and you discovered lots of them. His mother added them to pasta with parsley, garlic and Parmesan. They were much harder to find nowadays.

He stopped speaking, leaned on his elbow, looked at me and said, "Isabella. *La bella.* You are well named. You must have been told many times that you're beautiful."

I shielded my eyes from the sun, squinted at him and laughed. "Once or twice, I believe."

I had only to move a fraction closer till we touched. I had only to raise my head till my lips met his. I had only to cast off my doubts as I had cast off the clothes I'd left in a pile on the shore. Instead, I sat up and slipped back into the cold and weightless freedom of water, where he joined me. Wet skin brushing against wet skin, invisible limbs touching, floating apart. Shoals of tiny fishes. Lengthened arms slicing through water. Drifting to the push and pull of white-edged waves. Floating under a sapphire sky, where birds soared and hung on the air, still as pictures. Our companionable swim to the shore.

"If I sit in the sun, I change into a lobster. Maybe I should have one of the suits those little boys are wearing." I pointed towards a mother playing with two small fair-haired children who wore suits that covered them from neck to ankle. Any visible skin was plastered with cream.

"No, don't do that. I watched you stepping from the sea just now and thought how beautiful you looked, like a goddess coming out of the waves."

"You have a way with words, Toni. You know how to flatter, though I've never seen a goddess with wet hair dripping over her face."

"It's not flattery. When I first saw you yesterday, you reminded me of one of the figures in a painting by Botticelli that my brother has in his house in Maine. A copy, that is. My sister-in-law told me she's called Flora. She's my idea of a perfect woman."

Liam had made the same comparison, the first time we were naked together. How many women have been told they looked like Flora?

We showered under a basic shower at the entrance to the beach and settled under the shade of our umbrella.

"Let me put some cream on your shoulders. My mother will be annoyed with me if I allow you to burn. Lie down and I'll do your back."

His hands moved slowly over my skin. "You have the most beautiful scarlet back and shoulders I've ever seen."

"The scarlet woman, a little known painting by Botticelli, damaged by over-exposure to sun and sea."

I told myself to lie still, to content myself with the rhythm and the pressure of his hands on my skin; to imagine the feel of his cropped hair and the roughness of his chin. I closed my mind to harping voices telling me that in two weeks or so, I would be in London and Vieste would be nothing more than a memory to be filed away with the Breton coast, the beach at Arromanche, the dunes and the golden stretch of Camber Sands. And happiness, light and bubbly as champagne surged through me. Happiness in the shushing waves, in the tuneless cries of seabirds, in shaded sunshine, in Toni's account of his life in Rome and his need to escape from the sweltering summer to the lakes and hills close to the city or to the beach at the mouth of the Tiber. And happiness in the joyful outcome of Grace's visit to her father's grave

After about an hour, Toni said, "I could lie here all day with you but we had better go, Isabel. You must be hungry. I am, and we've have lots to do before the day's over."

I shook out the beach towel and Toni brushed sand from my shoulders before he dismantled the umbrella. He took my hand to help me up and held it as we climbed through a maze of narrow streets that were dim and shaded from the glare of early afternoon sun, past courtyards where cats lay stretched in shady corners, where vivid red, white and yellow flowers bloomed against the brightness of white-washed walls. We wove through alleys full of bars and tiny shops, whose roofs almost formed an arch above us, the bright blue of the sea at the end of each street. We went into a bar in an alley overlooking the promontory. Toni ordered mixed antipasti, pasta and fish, wine and salad. I gasped as one dish after another arrived. I had roasted peppers, courgettes and onions and giant prawns but gave the squid a miss. I told him the octopus tentacles tasted like salted elastic stuffed with screws. I skipped the spaghetti course and had a melt-in-the-mouth fish called *dorata*. A passer-by might have looked fondly

158

at us, sitting close together drinking white wine, and seen a couple blessed by nature, in love and untouched by pain or loss.

"There's a magic in this country," I said. "I can't explain it. Maybe it's the slow pace of life, the vivid colours, the feeling of weightlessness, like when we were floating in the sea. I feel as if I've been asleep for years, as if I've been pressed down under a heavy stone. Suddenly it has dropped from me and I'm awake and more alive than I've ever been."

"In the story, the beautiful princess pricks her finger and sleeps for a hundred years until she is wakened by a kiss. Like this." Toni kissed my lips. "I'm not the handsome prince of the story but I'll do my best to stop you falling asleep."

Spoken in an American-Italian accent, his words were enough to make my heart turn upside down. Liam, in love, had talked like a poet. In our early months in Sussex words and images flowed from him in a glittering stream. He didn't quote fairy stories for children. He sang the passionate love songs of Diarmuid to Grania; he compared his love for me to Abelard's longing for Eloise and said my image stole between his God and him.

When Toni and I had lain on the rocks, I needed to remind myself that I was no longer a nineteen-year-old student, head over heels in love for the first time and that I had lived too long with the reverse side of passion. Not any more. Careless of the couple at the next table or the owner lazily wiping wine glasses, I put my arms around his neck and kissed him lightly, holding in check the desire racing through me. The kiss was for reminding me of the Sleeping Beauty, the story my father used to tell me if he looked into my room before going to bed and found that I was still awake. It was for being uncomplicated and for making me feel like the lively, out-going girl I used to be.

We walked to the end of the alley, below which waves crashed on shining rocks and sea birds swooped and dived to the sea. "This is how I imagine an Arab town, blinding whiteness and labyrinths of mysterious streets where strangers would struggle to find their way." I was leaning against a rail above the rocks while Toni took photographs of me. "I'm printing a picture of Vieste, the town, the twin bays and the open sea, into my mind to take out on grey November days in London when it seems as if the sun won't ever shine again."

159

"We have grey November days too in Italy. Vieste wasn't always as beautiful as it is today. The Gargano was a very poor area and folk like my parents emigrated in their thousands. That was long before the EU poured loads of money into the tourist trade and gave Vieste a facelift. It's still one of Italy's best kept secrets." Toni drew me towards him, kissed my forehead. "Do you know what I like about you, Isabel, apart from you being the loveliest girl I've ever met? It's your enthusiasm, your excitement. The way you enjoy everything you do."

It wasn't hard to be excited with him. Toni hadn't seen me on a wet day waiting at the station for a train that came ten minutes late or didn't arrive at all, or elbowing my way into a carriage already full to bursting. It wasn't hard to be lively and enthusiastic in a country where I carried no baggage and could reinvent myself, where I didn't need to keep looking over my shoulder and avoiding cracks on the pavement. And a place where the sun shone every day was my idea of Paradise.

Gina had told Grace and me that the tourist season was short and the winter months brought little income. Tiberio, Claudio, herself and many of her relatives had been forced to leave their families and spend years working in Switzerland. So did lots of young men and women from Abruzzo in order to send money to their families. They had worked long hours and were often employed in jobs too menial for the Swiss.

Before leaving the old town we paused to look through a window at a display of jewellery and bric-a-brac. Tempted, we passed through a bead curtain into an Aladdin's cave which smelled of spices and the same incense that used to drift from the high altar of our church on Sunday evenings. When my eyes adjusted from the glare outside to the dimmer light, I saw that the interior was crammed with Oriental wall-hangings, glazed jugs, vases and painted plates, carved boxes, wooden bowls and figurines, long strings of beads and pearls, black cats and polished dogs, all covered with a film of dust. Toni picked up a box containing a pendant on a gold chain. A golden sun was painted on china, its gilded rays on brighter gold; a filigree pattern wove round the shining blue of the base. As he slipped it round my neck, the owner of the bazaar came up to us and spoke at great length. With each gesture of admiration the

160

buttons of his shirt strained over his belly exposing hairy snatches of dark brown skin.

"What's he saying, Toni?"

"He says the bright gold is the colour of your hair, the darker gold is the glow of your skin and the sky is the deep blue of the Signorina's eyes."

My sky-blue eyes widened into saucers and I returned the grin pinned on the man's face

"You're making that up. I said you have a way with words."

"No, I'm not. That's exactly what he said and I agree with him. He also said that the craftsman who made it had you in mind." He smiled as I managed not to laugh out loud. "I hope it will remind you of our time in Vieste, but don't wait for a grey November day to wear it."

While Toni followed the shop owner to the till, I admired the pendant in the dim light of a mirror and ran my fingers over the smooth gold of the sun and sky, over the raised surfaces of sunbeams and filigree. In the subdued light I really did look beautiful.

On the way back to the Aragosta Toni said, "We have so many great buildings in Italy, we take them for granted. I'm going to have to do a lot of homework before you and Grace come to Rome." With a grin he added, "I've got a better idea, you can see churches and monuments during the day while I'm at work and we'll all go out on the town in the evening."

Grace, wearing a coral-coloured frock with short sleeves and a scooped neckline, was rehearsing the speech she would make later on. After admiring my pendant, she told me she had spent a wonderful, but exhausting, day with Carlo's parents, met lots of his relatives whose names she had instantly forgotten and she had eaten far too much. She had gone with Carlo and Antonella to visit Antonio O'Brien's grave. The two women clung to each other and wept for the father neither of them had known and for the men who were interred beside him.

"Antonella's son, Marco, phoned from the States and I had a chat with him and his wife. They're full of plans for meeting up, maybe later in the summer." She paused, bit her lip and said, "I've decided not to tell Simon or David my news till I'm back in Hastings. They might think I've gone mad and decide to come out here and drag me back to England."

I put Toni's shell on the dressing table, went to the balcony and peered down at the veranda where two waiters were arranging tables under Claudio's instructions. There was no sign of Toni.

"Is that really me, Isabel?" Grace asked as she studied her reflection in the full-length mirror on the wall.

"It's you all right and you look wonderful. As they say·back home, our wee holiday is doing us both a power of good."

She came to the balcony and stood beside me. "You know, if Mamma had come with me, none of this could have happened. And if you hadn't phoned to tell me about Liam's death, I would have come here on my own. You gave me the brass neck to keep going."

"Things don't happen by chance. My friend Marie says we can shape our lives, but we must seize the moment with both hands. I'm having the time of my life and I don't want to go home."

"Talking about going home, can I ask you a favour?"

"Of course."

"If you see Rita before I do, would you mind not mentioning anything about Anthony O'Brien? She's a bit touchy at the moment. I think she wanted me to ask her to come here instead of you." I was about to say I would do as she asked, when she continued, speaking as if she was plucking words out of the air. "I'd like to tell her myself when the time's right. And I'll have to decide how much she needs to know."

At that moment my mother could have been on another planet. "Ma and I are barely on speaking terms, so that won't be a problem. Now, if you don't mind, I have to beautify myself too."

My London dress slid over my shoulders and fell in shivery folds against my thighs. There are clothes which, by their cut and texture or some other intangible quality, transfer their beauty to the wearer. Such was the blue chiffon dress I saw in the mirror. I twirled, and admired the cinched waist and the deep V at the back and at my neck where Toni's pendant lay on my breasts. And however pallid I had felt compared to the hour-glass Italian women on the beach at Vieste, every bit of me reflected the glow that made my heart beat faster and fixed a vacant smile over my face.

Grace raised her arms in a mini version of the bazaar owner's gestures.

162

"You look radiant, Isabel. What a transformation from the careworn girl I picked up in the early hours of Tuesday. I take it you had a good outing?"

"I loved the Gargano and Vieste. We had a swim and lunch and a stroll around the lovely old town."

"And Toni? He's quite nice too?"

"Yes, as you say, he's quite nice." A blush flooded my neck and face. I grasped her hands. "Grace, your nephew is utterly, totally gorgeous and I'm fighting to stop myself falling in love with him."

"Don't fight too hard, love. You deserve to be happy. Do as your friend said. Seize the moment with both hands."

Chapter Seventeen

Like the dowdy offspring of swans, the daughters of beautiful women live in their mothers' shadows. My mother did not actually disown me, though for most of my life she ignored my existence. She had been an outstanding beauty. Everyone, herself included, said so. Daddy told me that her beauty had bewitched him and he had counted himself fortunate to have a wife who turned the head of any man who saw her. As I grew older, she stopped referring to me as her ball and chain and confined her comments on my appearance to pointing out my untidy hair or telling me my skirt was too short.

I didn't lack love or admiration. Daddy and Minnie adored me, said I was the prettiest child on earth. After Liam left I had lovers who overwhelmed me with compliments, but Ma had imprinted on my mind's eye the image of a plain and shapeless girl, unfit to be seen in her presence. During the early months with Liam I used to look in the mirror and thrill to see the girl of his love poems, the girl his fluent tongue described, the girl he introduced with pride to friends and colleagues. After Grania's death, Liam's loss of interest and his final rejection, my head separated from the rest of my body and my rare glance in a mirror revealed the haggard face of a woman for whom life held little hope or prospect of happiness.

This morning I had crept down the broad stairs of the Aragosta, heart pounding, hands shaking. Ten hours later, I made my way confidently to where Toni waited with his parents. I admired Antonella's black frock and said how smart Carlo looked in his pale linen suit. I didn't notice what Toni was wearing, but I remember thinking he was the handsomest man I had ever met. Having grown up in a culture where children were praised and admired, not kept in their place in case they grew too big for their boots, I suspected he already knew that.

Marilena, wearing a slim-fitting red dress, introduced her parents who had come to take Gianni back to Vasto. Her mother was a big-busted woman in shining black, whose lined face had retained the delicate features of her daughter. Her father, a wiry little sixty-year-old, with a few strands of brown hair combed over his bronzed pate, held me at arm's length, said I was *bellissima,* and butterfly-kissed my hands and wrists. Meanwhile, Marilena, in a torrent of breathless English, reminded me that her father was the chap who had to be dragged from his Swiss lover's arms by her two grandfathers and returned to his wife and children. Then she introduced him to Carlo and the two men talked about all the folk they both knew in and around Vasto. Her mother, who was probably a few years younger than Antonella, told her she remembered her as a young girl, always accompanied by her mother, a handsome, but proud, woman who kept strictly to herself.

Toni took me aside and pointed out the Maiella silhouetted against a salmon sky and, in the far distance, the Gran Sasso's jagged outline on the red-gold of the sunset. Corks popped. *Spumante* bubbled and sparkled in glasses. Names repeated and names forgotten floated around me. More handshakes, introductions and kisses. I smiled, repeated each name, said, *"Piacere"* and tried to look as if I understood every word. Summer warmth on bare skin. The pale sliver of the new moon tilting to the right. The subdued blacks and greys of older guests, the intense colours and the chic black of younger women of the Cellucci family, who stopped to greet us on their way into the restaurant. Fred, immaculate in a pale grey suit, white shirt and regimental tie. Pat by his side, a cotton jacket slung over his arm. Both men surprised and delighted to welcome Mauro and Francesca, their friends from Scerni, whom Grace had asked Marilena to invite, unbeknownst to either man.

Toni translating, his hand on my elbow. Tiberio in his element, explaining to Antonella how he, single-handed, had solved the riddle of her mother. Grace introducing Carlo and Antonella to Pat and Fred and to the Cellucci family, moving from group to group welcoming, consulting with Claudio. At ease with her Italian guests and with Carlo's parents, whom she had invited during her visit to their home. The music of Italian, the lightness and excitement of female voices, the darker and noisier booming of the men. And though Grace, Fred, Pat and I spoke in a lower register, our voices too had acquired a new excitement. A new intensity.

I looked at each person seated at the large circular table, and at Claudio in a pale suit and embroidered waistcoat, as he supervised the arrival of each course and chatted to guests at other tables.

Tiberio was holding forth to Carlo, his conversation sprinkled with "Maurizio" and "Gorla." Antonella was asking Fred about his family and his other war experiences. Before meeting Grace, she too must have wondered about the young soldier in the black and white snap – her father. Had he survived the war? Had he married the girl whose photo he carried in a cellophane wallet? Like Grace, Antonella had not learned of her birthfather's existence until she was sixteen or seventeen. This same symmetry had been reflected in Aunt Kate's and Elisa's lives. They had both kept safe the secret of their relationship with Anthony O'Brien and died without revealing his name to anyone except their daughters and their families. Apart from my immediate family, Grace was my closest relative. On meeting us, strangers could tell that we were closely related, yet she shared more DNA with Antonella than with me.

A war in Europe, which had ended sixty years ago, linked most of the guests Grace had invited to celebrate her meeting with Anthony O'Brien's other daughter. Toni and I, like Marilena, were part of another generation. I squeezed his hand and thanked whatever destiny had taken me from Kenmara, to London, to Italy and him from New York via Rome, to Abruzzo to share the company of his parents, his grandparents and all those we had met, thanks to Fred and Pat Cooper.

After a selection of antipasti, Grace stood up. Speaking in English, which Carlo translated, she thanked Fred and Pat for taking us to the Aragosta and introducing us to the Cellucci family. She also thanked me for my company and for putting up with her single-mindedness.

With the confidence of someone who had rehearsed her speech and was able to laugh at her own mistakes she switched to Italian, thanked Gina, who had been summoned from the kitchen, for letting her practise her limited command of the language and for calling in Marilena, our lively guide and interpreter, who had introduced us to Tiberio. Everybody laughed to hear how he had sacrificed his daily siesta to enable us to meet Maurizio and how, on the following morning, he went off shortly after daybreak on a fact-finding mission to Gorla.

We had a choice of mixed fish, steak, salads, courgettes and aubergines. In the pause before choosing fruit, creamy desserts or home-made ice creams, Grace rose again promising this was the last

166

time she would interrupt the meal. For as long as I had known her, Grace had shunned the limelight. She was always in the back row in family photographs, in the kitchen making sure everyone was fed and looked after, attending her parents, mopping my tears.

"I'd like to tell you about a document from the Ministry of Defence. It is the citation my dear friend Fred Cooper received when he was awarded the Military Medal for outstanding courage and initiative. Carlo, my brother-in-law, has agreed to translate it into Italian.

This NCO has consistently shown the highest qualities of daring, devotion to duty and initiative from the Battle of El Alamein to the crossing of the River Sangro in Italy and especially in the period from 26 Feb to 23 April '45. No situation seems to daunt him and no enemy fire to diminish his valour.

After applause from everyone at the table and from guests who crowded around to hear Carlo's translation, Grace said, "Before coming to Italy, I had done research on the battle in which my father died, but meeting Fred brought to life what had only been historical fact. I should like to now call on Fred Cooper to speak."

Fred stood with the bearing of a soldier. Pausing occasionally to glance at his notes, he said, "*Signore* and *Signori,* ladies and gentlemen, I would like to thank the Cellucci family for receiving me and my family every year. I think of the Aragosta as my second home. All year I dream about coming back to this hotel to meet my dear friends, and going to Scerni, where we were so well looked after before and after the battle in November 1943." He wiped his eyes and waited for Toni to translate. "I know, without any doubt, that the Allies could not have won the campaign in Italy without the help of the Italian people. Many Italians, who had hardly enough to feed themselves, risked their lives sheltering escaped prisoners such as Grace and Antonella's father, Anthony O'Brien. These brave people helped them to avoid re-capture and enabled many to return to their regiments. On their behalf, and on behalf of the men who fought in the Italian campaign, I thank you and propose a toast to the Italian people."

After a mumbling pause while Fred's words were translated, everyone clapped. Tiberio rose from his seat. "Fred, you must not thank us. We Italians are proud to thank you and all the Allied soldiers for what you did to save our country. I have not the words to

167

thank you all." His eyes bright with tears, he hugged and kissed Fred and Pat and ordered Marilena to tell everyone what he had said.

Guests seated at neighbouring tables came to congratulate Grace and Antonella, to shake hands with Fred and Pat. Toni translated the words of an old man who, with a friend, had escaped from the Germans dressed in women's clothes. Carlo's mother remembered her parents feeding two British soldiers, bandaging their feet and hiding them under straw in the stable till they were fit enough to leave. They were lovely young men, she said, who played cards with them in the evening and taught them *It's a long way to Tipperary*. She hoped they had long and happy lives. An elderly man embraced Fred. He was from Scerni and had been ten years old in 1943. He remembered his fear on seeing German troops parading in the streets and the excitement when the British army arrived. His older brothers had known many of the soldiers who liberated the town. The dining room echoed to the sound of talk and laughter. Stories of the liberation in 1945, digging up wine hidden during the Occupation, singing and dancing in the streets, sharing cured meat that had been hidden from the Germans. Some talked of the poverty after the war that caused many families from Abruzzo to emigrate to America and Australia. No one mentioned tomorrow.

"I need to be alone with you, Isabel." Toni said, as guests prepared to leave. "Why don't you show me the beach at Casalbordino Lido?"

Night silence wrapped itself round us, broken only by the pulsing murmur of the sea and by sounds from further along the beach, where the reflections of lights from bars danced on the water. A night I didn't want to lighten into a new dawn. His arm around my shoulder, Toni pointed out constellations in the endless vault of the sky over the Adriatic. He told me about winter holidays in the Julian Alps at the farm owned by his Nonna Elisa's father's family, a place where the heavens are boundless and the air so pure that the night sky is filled with stars such as he had never seen, even in the empty spaces of the Appalachians.

"We sometimes spent Christmas with my cousins. We skied every day at a resort not far from the Dolomites. I'd love to take you there, Isabel." He said the mountains turned pink at sunset and the slopes sparkled as if they were covered in diamonds. "So many places I'd like to show you." He stroked my face, kissed me lightly

168

and asked, "Do you have to hurry back to England with Grace? Is someone waiting for you?"

"No, no one at all."

"There's something I ought to tell you." Though he didn't move from where we stood at the water's edge, his silence hovered like a question mark between us and I felt him distance himself from me. "It's about Liliana, the girl I was going to marry. My parents said they talked to you and Grace about her. I didn't think I needed to say any more."

I waited for him to continue, to lighten the weight of silence.

"Liliana was the first girl I got to know when we moved back from the States. She was thirteen, a year younger than me. A lovely girl, quiet and shy. I missed my brother and I missed Brooklyn. I hated living in a small flat with my parents and Nonna, who was a cross old woman and jealous of my father." Again he paused before continuing, as if he was considering how much to tell, "Liliana didn't make fun of the way I spoke Italian or call me names. Because of her, I was accepted into the gang of kids who hung out together in cafés and played on the beach in the summer. I don't remember falling in love. It just happened. We were *fidanzati in casa* as they say in Italy. My parents thought I'd forget Liliana when I went to university in Rome. I didn't. I missed her very much. We were to get married as soon as I finished my degree."

He explained that Liliana had never left Vasto and didn't want to live in Rome. Her visits were a disaster. His flat on the eighth floor gave her vertigo and the Roman traffic terrified her. Her family was busily preparing for their wedding and accused him of not fixing a date and not trying to find some sort of work locally.

With a shrug he continued, "I would not have found an engineering job with the prospects of the one I had in Rome. I liked living in the capital. Compared to Rome, Vasto's a backwater. I accepted the blame her family piled on me." After a silence when even the waves made no noise, Toni turned to look at me. "Her sadness and her fears got on my nerves. I wanted to break our engagement and escape to the States, but that would have brought shame on her family and on mine. In the end I stopped coming to Vasto and she met someone else." Holding me at arm's length, he looked into my eyes. "I needed to tell you that I behaved badly towards Liliana, and I haven't told you the whole story." After a pause, he said, "I've fallen in love with you, Isabella."

He kissed me. I clung to him, unsure of what to say.

"We don't own each other's pasts. You say you haven't told the whole story. Toni, we never tell the whole story, not even to ourselves."

We had talked too much. Far too much. I opened the top buttons of his shirt and kissed the sea taste of the hollows of his neck.

"Isabella, Isabella." He buried his face in my hair, while I undid each button and kissed his chest, his waist. He held out his hands and drew me towards the shelter of the promenade wall where he spread his shirt over sand which was still warm from the heat of the day. My dress slid from my shoulders and we made love under a star-drenched sky to the rhythm of the waves. Our hands and mouths explored and marvelled at each other's bodies and we made love again slowly, with passion and with tenderness, as I had known we would when we lay side by side on the wet rocks at Vieste.

I hadn't led a nun's life after Liam and I parted. My affairs, if they could be called that, had fizzled out because Liam's restless presence always slid between me and the man I was with. I needed time, I said. I still loved my husband, I said.

Grace was asleep when I crept into our room. Still dizzy from the aftershock of love, I stood by the balcony listening to the shushing of the waves, looking for one last time at the narrow beach now silvered by moonlight, and searching along the dark horizon for the elusive hills of Croatia. I hadn't thought I was capable of falling in love again. I'd forgotten the yearning. How it rises from the pit of the stomach. I'd forgotten how the spine melts. I'd forgotten the weightlessness, like floating on clouds. The fun of it. The aching joy of it.

170

Chapter Eighteen

Kenmara

I am about to go alone, as always, for my daily constitutional up the gentler path towards the Castle. As usual, I dress with my customary care and attention to detail. It's the same principle as wearing clean underwear in case of an accident. On these walks I often meet women of my age and others considerably younger. I don't want to appear catty but some of them I can only describe as scarecrows in anoraks, wearing woolly hats pulled down over their ears, or headscarves. The Queen wears headscarves too, and somebody should have a word with her. Don't get me wrong, I have the greatest respect for Her Majesty. Given the chance, I could transform her fashion-wise.

I've always taken a pride in my appearance and check the back view as well as the front. I wouldn't be seen dead with a hem trailing below my outer garment or wearing colours that fight with each other, like the pink fleece and mustard trousers Kathleen Beirne was sporting the other day when I met her at the shops. She turned quite nasty with me, said she was only getting chops and broccoli for her Frank's dinner and not taking part in a fashion parade. Then she boasted about having a full head of hair, as if I cared. Some folk don't want to be helped.

I reposition the freestanding mirror. No twisted belt, no label sticking out at the collar. My legs were restored to their former shapeliness when I had those unsightly varicose veins removed, the ones brought on by Isabel's birth. A final check

Oh my God! I don't believe it. I cover my eyes, look again. It's still there. Disaster! It can't have happened overnight, so why have I never noticed the bald patch on my crown? Everybody must have been laughing behind my back. I know a lot of old women have pink and half-bald skulls, but my hair has always been my pride and glory. I have it washed and set once a week by Marilyn. Going to Marilyn's gives a purpose to my day, the way yoga or bingo does for some folk. Maybe her name should have put me off. When Marilyn has finished blow-drying, she waves a mirror over the back of my head. I say "very nice" and give her a pound tip, two if I have had a cut. I can't have gone bald since last Wednesday. I always have my hair blow-dried on Wednesdays when pensioners have reduced rates. There's no question of showing myself in public now. My heart's going hammer and tongs. I swallow two pills with a glass of water, remove my coat, sit at the dressing table and study the stricken area. It has not altered. I cover it with wisps from the right side and then from the left. I could weep. All I'm doing is opening up another bald patch. I'm stuck. I'm expert at putting on makeup. I know how to emphasise the bright blue of my eyes, the perfect lines of my cheeks and nose, hide the ravages of age, or at least try to. And I cannot think of any solution except a wig that everyone will spot a mile off. I'll be a laughing stock. I'd need months to choose the thing, have it fitted and practise wearing it behind locked doors. In less than two weeks I will be the centre of attention at my party. I've planned a trip into town with Mary Walsh to look for a suitable outfit, not that she will be any help in advising me, but she'll be company and she never says no to a free lunch. If only I had a daughter, I hear myself thinking. It's not fair. I have been so excited about this party and now I feel like calling it off. Worry has affected my whole appearance. My back has slumped into a dowager's hump and my skin has that uncooked pastry look that makes old women's faces look like masks.

Linda! Like a message from heaven I remember that Hugh's wife was a hairdresser. Poor Linda, I'm ashamed to think of how unfavourably I compared her to my solicitor daughter-in-law. Personally, I would never have forgiven anyone who had treated me with the scorn I heaped on her. Thank God, everyone doesn't have my nasty nature. I pick up the phone and dial the number for Hugh's garage. Linda takes my call.

"Mrs McGlade, what's wrong? Have you had a fall? Have you taken your tablets? I'll call Hugh and we'll be with you in no time."

Despite all the questions, Linda sounds calm. I've seen her with her own children when they have been in fights, burned themselves or fallen out of trees and opened up old scars. I tell her my predicament and wait. She doesn't make light of my anxiety and will leave the garage at once. If I can wait till this evening she will see if her elder daughter, Aisling, is free to come with her. She explains that not only is Aisling a beautician, she is a qualified hairdresser. I remember how I sneered when I heard she had to spend three years at college before being considered fit to practise her art. I had high hopes that my first granddaughter would go to university like her cousins and I was sorry to see a pretty child change into a sulky teenager whose only ambition was to go clubbing and to spend holidays in Majorca with friends of her own ilk. I had a row with her parents when Aisling appeared, aged ten or thereabouts, earrings dangling from pierced ears. Then, some years later, I caught sight of a shiny object on the side of my granddaughter's nose and a ring in her navel. I tell you that shocked me into silence. Hugh laughed when I found my voice. He said times had changed since I was young.

The phone rings. Linda has explained the gravity of the situation to Aisling who will come to Kenmara straight from work. I watch the minutes tick slowly by. This is what waiting for the results of a biopsy must be like, I think, as I make futile attempts to backcomb strands of hair over the frightful spot, but I'm only robbing Peter to pay Paul. At least, I don't have to worry about preparing food. Linda said she will come complete with scissors, mousse, spray and a takeaway. My daughter-in-law Rose would sooner starve than eat pre-cooked rubbish. As for me, I won't be able to look at food until my predicament is sorted, if it ever can be.

I hear Linda's car bumping down the drive long before it comes into sight. Una jumps out shouting, "Granny, Granny," puts her arms round me and kisses me. I am blessed to have such a sweet, unspoiled granddaughter and my delight in listening to her chatter puts the horror of this afternoon's revelation to the side of my mind for a moment. But only a moment. No sooner have we gone inside than Aisling arrives in a taxi. I'm so pleased to see her that I don't comment on her extravagance. I've noticed that the younger generation doesn't give a thought for tomorrow. Though Aisling is always hungry and grazes from morning till night, she says that Granny's wee bit of bother must be dealt with at once. We troop up to my bedroom where I can view proceedings in my strategically-placed mirrors.

The two girls are amazed by my furniture, my drapes, ornaments and the array of potions on the dressing table. They want to know about all the framed photographs and pictures.

"God Granny, it's like something from one of those black and white films," says Aisling

Her mother reminds her of the urgency of this gathering. She and Aisling pick up my sparse locks and survey the offending area.

"Your hair is quite thin, Mrs McGlade. A good cut will help. Maybe lowlights. What do you think, Aisling?"

Like a patient who has suffered under the hands of an incompetent quack and has been transferred to the care of two highly qualified consultants, I listen to the verdict and the recommendations of my daughter-in-law and my grandchildren. All three wear jeans and their short-sleeved tops look good on their slight figures. Linda is a natural blonde, I think, though these days you can't be sure. I am pleased to see that her hair is short and thick, good for going under cars as she puts it. Una, whose shoulder-length fair hair is tied in a ponytail, is as yet untouched by the horrors of teenage years. She says I look posh, like the Queen, and lowlights might be common.

Aisling greets her sister's remarks with scorn. "Don't talk daft, Una. Granny's got a great figure. The Queen's a dumpy wee woman and she's years older than Granny."

Aisling's dark, tightly curled hair has gone through many transformations and colours, none of which improved on what nature gave her. Her shoulder-length locks have been straightened and streaked. She assures me it's the fashion and adds, with a rather vulgar laugh, that you might as well be dead as out of fashion. She has consulted with the owner of her salon who has sent me books featuring coiffures for more mature ladies. Aisling may not be the granddaughter I would have wished for, but I can't help admiring her professional approach and her exuberant personality that has brought life to this mausoleum of mine.

Find a style that suits you and stick with it, Jackie Kennedy said. I am nearly seventy-eight, and I have followed her advice all my life. Jackie and I were contemporaries, give or take a few years depending on what age I own up to. I'm wondering if Jackie would have gone grey and abandoned her bouffant look, when Aisling presents me with pictures of women sporting short styles that give them a youthful, though not a mutton-pretending-to-be-lamb appearance.

174

A cut is decided on. It will be performed by Linda under her daughter's supervision after my hair has been washed. If I agree to lowlights, I will be taken to Aisling's salon for discussion with the senior stylist who will oversee the operation.

We have an Indian meal sitting at the kitchen table, very mild chicken korma with fried rice and vegetables. Aisling opens a bottle of wine for her mother and me. She finds several cans of beer in the drinks cabinet, which Linda insists must be drunk from a glass. My gloom has lifted and Aisling is confident of success.

"Sure if it doesn't work we'll get you a wee hairpiece and weave it through. Ach, sure it'll be alright. God, you should see some of the cases that come in. Yours is wee buns, so it is."

At the mention of buns, I am about to rise and produce some cake from a tin in the larder when Una presses me back into my chair. "Don't move, Granny. You've had a hard day and we're here to look after you."

Aisling's confidence is contagious. I submit to having my hair washed, cut and styled with lavish quantities of mousse and spray. Una, who has been holding my hand during the various processes, cries out, "God, Granny, you're lovely. Dead modern."

I stare into the mirror which Linda holds behind my head. They have worked a miracle. Tears of gratitude fill my eyes. My granddaughters and their mother hug me as if I've emerged from a coma after some hideous illness and I relax into their arms.

"I'll make an appointment for you in the salon with Tracey. She'll advise you about lowlights and check the cut. Then we'll enter you for the Glamorous Granny competition."

"What are you going to wear to your birthday party, Granny? Have you bought your dress yet? Mammy's got hers and it's lovely. Aisling and me went into town with her and picked it."

I tell them about my planned shopping trip with Mary Walsh. Aisling asks if Mrs Walsh is an expert on fashion.

"I know what we'll do," she says, "I have a day off on Thursday. Mammy, you tell Daddy you're going out for the day with us. We'll get Granny kitted out and have something to eat. I'm really, really excited. Granny, you take your mate out for a meal another day."

"Is Isabel coming to the party, Granny?" Una asks.

"Of course she is. She's coming a bit early to help me get ready."

"That's great," says Una. "Isabel's lovely and she's got gorgeous clothes."

"She'll see a quare difference in you, Granny," Aisling says. With a raucous laugh she adds, "That's if she recognises you."

With a mixture of envy and pleasure I observe the ease between Linda and her daughters, how they laugh together, how they touch and tease each other. On my rare visits to their cramped home, they have been on their best behaviour and probably scared of my nasty tongue. Because of my idiotic snobbery, I have shunned Hugh's wife and children, measured them against John's academic sons and found them wanting. As Linda drives off, Aisling and Una wave out of the windows, calling "Cheerio, Granny, see you on Thursday. You look gorgeous, Granny."

The scent of curried lamb and chicken lingers in my home, which seems to have retained the lightness and the laughter that swept in with the arrival of my granddaughters and their mother. Later on, the memory of them close together admiring their handiwork burns through me. Isabel would never have dared touch me or joke in the way that came naturally to Hugh's girls. I hope it's not too late to make up to her, to apologise and try to explain my behaviour. I hope she comes on Friday as she promised. I wish she'd sent another card at least. I pat the back-combed top of my head. It's lucky I discovered the bald patch. Lucky in more ways than I could have imagined.

I'm really looking forward to Thursday. Maybe somebody will explain lowlights to me.

Linda arrives by car and immediately phones for a taxi. I admire her grey trouser suit and crisp blouse and tell Una that she looks a picture in her peach, tulip-skirted dress. We are to meet Aisling in Royal Avenue. Like all my contemporaries, I use my bus pass for my occasional forays into the city. Today I enjoy the luxury of sitting beside Una and showing her Limestone Road where I was brought up and where I used to play with my cousin Angela. Aisling has made an effort. She wears a green printed dress and a short-sleeved cardigan. I refrain from saying that all those shades of eyeliner and eye shadow make her look like a panda and thank her for giving up her free day for an old woman.

176

"Where's the old woman? I don't see no old woman." She scans the street behind me, takes my arm and explains her plan of action. We won't trail around too many shops because Linda and Una might get tired. Instead, we'll go to Castle Court, have a coffee and visit a store that has loads of posh concessions for women with pots of money.

Over coffee, we discuss colours. I say I will probably go for a pastel shade, pale blue, lavender, grey or perhaps some shade of pink. Aisling frowns and assures me that pastels are totally last century, unless I want to look like the Queen Mother who's been dead for ages, or that aul' doll who wrote about ten romances a week and only wore pink. Linda says her daughters must not bully me, that I know what suits me and am always very smart. The search begins. The names of the various concessions are familiar. Safe and unspectacular. Aisling requests a chair for her grandmother. It is brought by an assistant, who looks like an advert for the cosmetics department. Aisling presents outfits for my inspection. Linda consults with me. Like her daughters, she has good fashion sense and dismisses them as too dowdy, a bit flashy, the wrong shape, a bad cut. Mindful of my age and conservative way of dressing, she keeps the girls' enthusiasm in check.

"Granny, this is so you. It's really class," says Aisling. "Keep an open mind. The style's right, the colour suits your complexion and it will go with your new hair style. You'll knock them dead in this."

I think the cherry shade is rather bright for a woman of my age. The assistant, with a lip-glossed smile, tells me the colour is known as cerise. Because I'm cornered, I try it on and the result amazes me. Linda and her daughters assure me that the classic cut of the dress and its optional jacket take ten years off me. They say it goes with my trendy hair cut. Pleased with my reflection, I twirl before my family. They agree with the assistant that I am a singularly handsome woman and I see no reason to contradict them.

Linda has booked lunch in a cool and, as yet uncrowded restaurant in a street that runs down from Great Victoria Street to the back of the City Hall. We all have excellent fish and salad followed by sticky puddings for my granddaughters and fruit salad for Linda and me. I tell them about the Carlton Restaurant that used to be close by, in Wellington Place. My mother and my Aunt Eileen used to take me and my cousin Angela for afternoon tea as a treat for our combined birthdays in July and for Christmas. Even as I speak, I'm not sure if the Carlton was in Wellington Place or Donegal Avenue.

"What's afternoon tea, Granny?" Una asks.

I explain that afternoon tea at the Carlton consisted of lemon pancakes that were kept warm in a covered dish, sandwiches and hot buttered scones, a three tiered cake stand for sliced coffee cake, fancy biscuits and cream sponge.

"While Angela and I ate our way through every item on offer, three musicians played in the corner, classical and Irish music. Each year they played 'Happy Birthday' to me and Angela. Do you know, girls, my idea of heaven was afternoon tea at the Carlton."

"God, Granny, it sounds like something out of a film," Una says, "Did you go to the Carlton too, Mammy, when you were a wee girl?"

"No love, my family weren't the sort to have afternoon tea at the Carlton or anywhere else. Besides, there were eight of us."

"It was probably closed down before you were born, Linda."

"Daddy took us all to Belfast Castle for our dinner for my eighteenth," Aisling says. "It was brilliant."

She goes on to describe the view over the city and the Lough from the dining room, what each one ate and what they wore. The girls tell me they wanted their mother to book a table at the Castle today. Linda explains that the main dining room with its wide views is only open at weekends. I ease the collar of my blouse from my neck and try to cover my face. I haven't blushed since I was a young girl and I don't expect my eyes to fill with tears in public. The memory of Angela and the Carlton Restaurant has unsettled me. Angela and me, inseparable before everything fell apart after Daisy!

Without warning, I'm grieving not only for Daisy, but for an eleven-year-old child stuffing herself with pancakes, sandwiches and cake, for Angela and the years we should have spent together, for the misery I caused Jack and Isabel. There was always someone else to blame. Angela for refusing to share the responsibility for Daisy's death. My mother for forcing me to make a life-shattering decision when I was too young to know what I was doing. My father for insisting I marry Jack. And Jack for being Jack and for making me pregnant at forty-nine. Now they have all gone, my parents, Daisy and Jack and there's no one left to shoulder the blame.

No-one but me.

178

While Aisling sends a text and Linda settles the bill, it's as if I have moved out of my body and am observing from a height a woman in a cerise outfit preening before her family and a shop assistant, soaking up their admiration. Posing, asking for more. A closer look shows that she's a mannequin, like the tailor's dummies you see in shop windows. Plaster eye sockets in a plaster face, forever frozen in the pose of a model. A shell of a woman, whose life was wasted in selfishness, who ignored her own daughter's existence and didn't even send a message of sympathy when her baby died. I watch that sham of a woman, sharp-edged and hard as steel and I ask myself what became of the girl I once was, of the woman I could have been.

I never bothered to learn the dates of my granddaughters' birthdays and I didn't even acknowledge Aisling's coming of age. I remember Hugh inviting me and Jack to their son Fergus' birthday party – a gang of rowdy five-year-olds careering like wild animals through the cluttered mess of Linda's house and hordes of loud-mouthed women with babies hanging from hips and breasts. I told Hugh it was a sinful waste for somebody in his circumstances to squander money on rubbishy food and take-home-bags for spoiled brats. Hugh and Linda may have had other parties. I was not invited. There was no fear of forgetting my other grandsons' birthdays. For weeks, Rose reminded me of the coming events. These parties were less rowdy than the one at Hugh's. There was room for me to escape in John and Rose's large home, and the visiting mothers were professional women who spoke with Malone Road accents. And they had fewer babies.

Belfast Castle overlooks my home. Jack liked to take the family to lunch for our boys' birthdays. He enjoyed showing us off to the headwaiter, who reserved a table by the window for him. I remember how I dressed up for the occasions, how I loved the views over the Lough and Cave Hill, how our sons put up with the ordeal to please their father. Every year on Isabel's birthday, Minnie produced a cake with icing and candles. Jack gave her a cheque to celebrate her eighteenth with friends at some club in the city. I don't forget that date. How could I, after all I went through to give birth to her?

I study my granddaughters' eager faces and say, "Linda, I have really enjoyed shopping with you and the girls and coming to this lovely restaurant. You've made me feel years younger. Thank you for everything. Thank..." Suddenly I'm tongue-tied, searching for words that have fallen into an empty pit at the back of my throat. Nobody, not even Rose, can hold a candle to me in arguments and I always manage to have the last word – as if that's anything to boast about – but I have never learned to say what I really feel. "Would you... could you... that is, I'd like take you all, young Jack and Fergus and your daddy, to lunch at the Castle on Sunday, if you're free. Please say you can come."

"We're free, Granny."

"Will Hugh come too, Linda?"

"Daddy will do what he's told," says Aisling and phones for a taxi to take us to Kenmara.

Chapter Nineteen

While Grace settled the bill with Gina, I went into the dining room to say goodbye to Franco and found a room transformed for a banquet to be attended by two hundred and fifty wedding guests. Diagonals of white lace spread over green damask. Sprays of fuchsia-like flowers in silver vases and chairs white-robed for a banquet. On each side plate was a packet of white-coated almonds in a silver box, presents for each female guest, Franco said. A coach drew up in the car park and a party of twenty-eight visitors from Switzerland poured into the foyer for the start of their annual holiday. Franco told me they had another wedding party on Wednesday and five First Communion celebrations the following Sunday. He said goodbye and hurried to help his mother behind the desk at Reception. Grace and I would quickly be forgotten by the staff, who had seen only a narrow aspect of our lives and who were now involved with guests they had known for years. Fred and Pat would always be remembered at the Aragosta, as we would remember our meeting with them at the Sangro Cemetery, which had set in motion such a momentous series of events. Destiny or coincidence? We look for patterns in life and ascribe meaning to what may only be chance.

Antonella and Carlo, who were already waiting at Pescara Airport, said Toni had left at dawn for an eight o'clock start in his office in Rome. Grace and I said a tearful goodbye to Fred and Pat and thanked them for helping Grace to meet Antonella and her family. We watched and waved as Pat, one hand carrying two bags, the other on his father's elbow, helped the old man across the concrete to their plane. We had only seen a slice of Fred's life. For us he existed in Italy. Through his account of events in the winter of 1943 we had forged a connection between him and this place. Pat had told us how proud his father was to be a member and subsequently chairman of the local branch of the British Legion, how he enjoyed the company of men who had shared his experiences.

The Troubles which began in 1969 had already been causing death and destruction in Northern Ireland for seven years when I was born. Though they continued to wage through most of my life, I had been insulated from the bombings and murders that tore families and communities apart. I could not begin to imagine the horror of fighting on the front line throughout the Second World War. Meeting Fred made me understand why those years had been the most defining and the most memorable he had lived. I had grown up sufficiently on this trip to realise that no one goes through life unscathed. We all suffer, either by the deaths of those we love, by illness, deprivation, the trials of old age, or the sorrow we inflict on one another. Pat had told me of the grief which consumed his father at the untimely death of his wife, how his family worried for his survival and Pat had to give up his own home to live with Fred.

When the motorway stretched over wide, cultivated valleys, tires thudded with the slow-train sound I remembered from our first drive in Italy. Towns climbed up mountain sides, the spires of their churches etched against the sky. Ridge upon ridge of the Apennines and walls of sheer rock directly before us. Carlo said that the tunnel we were entering was almost four kilometres in length, the longest of the Apennines. Signposts pointed to places with names that had the rhythms of poetry – Sulmona, Aquila, Castel Madama. And always mountains, folding, rising before and above us. Lengthy queues at toll booths, cars jockeying, veering from lane to lane to gain a toe-hold. The final stretch to Rome.

Rome: a place of high pines, city walls, aqueducts and ruins whose names I forgot the moment I caught my first glimpse of the enormous shell of the Colosseum. Through narrow streets and cars parked a hair's breadth from Carlo's Lancia to the quiet of the hotel, where Grace and I would stay during our time in the city. Toni's parents saw us installed, plied us with maps, guide book and suggestions about what we might see before they arrived to take us to dinner. After they had set off for Toni's flat, Grace studied the maps and unpacked. I kicked off my shoes, stretched out on my bed and fell asleep.

The noisy restaurant we went to with Carlo and Antonella had a vaulted ceiling and upper walls displaying pennants and flags of various Italian states. I sat beside Toni, listening to his parents singing the praises of the pasta, which they said was a speciality of Rome. I didn't admit that all pasta tasted the same to me, regardless of its shape or the sauce that accompanied it and I was pleased to leave with Toni for a tour of Rome by night. From his car we saw the floodlit Colosseum, more city walls, more ruins. Toni parked on one of the city's hills and we looked over tiled rooftops to where domes and towers of ancient Rome stood out against the night sky. I turned my back on scenes I vaguely remembered from A level Latin to face Toni, to feel his arms around me and to fold my body into his.

"I wish I could take you back to my flat, Isabel," he said, caressing my face as an archaeologist might a newly unearthed golden statue, "but my parents are sleeping in my bed. You will stay with me after Grace leaves on Friday?"

I could have told him I wanted nothing more than to be with him in this city where the wonders of the past existed side by side with nose-to-tail streams of shining cars.

"I'll stay until I have to go to Ireland," I said.

We lay together in Toni's car in the empty car park. Above us towered a statue of a horseman. Toni said he was Garibaldi. Then we drove down sleeping hills, through the ancient centre and past the main train station to my hotel.

For the next two days while Toni's parents shopped, did repairs to the flat and visited friends, I followed where Grace led in the blistering heat and dust of summer. We congratulated ourselves on neither coveting nor even liking anything in any of the exclusive shops in the Via Condotti. We drank coffee in the oldest and possibly the thinnest café in Rome and we had lunch in a restaurant crammed with larger than life plaster casts of emperors, popes, gods and goddesses.

Toni was reading a newspaper in the foyer of the hotel when we emerged from the lift wearing outfits we had bought in a shop in one of the less expensive streets of the city. He stood up and exclaimed, "Isabel, *tu sei bella, bellissima.*" He apologised to Grace and said how stylish and lovely she looked.

"Don't worry, Toni, I am not Isabel. I am your elderly aunt." Grace embraced him and thanked him for collecting us.

"Before we go to the restaurant I have been told I must show you the view from the Aventine Hill. Mamma wants you to see everything before you leave, Grace."

From the hill, Toni pointed out the dome of Saint Peter's, a white monument and many spires and towers of famous buildings whose names slid into that place in my memory where other basilicas, temples and ancient columns slept undisturbed.

"Now I'll show you something my brother and I liked when we were kids."

Through a keyhole in the thick door of a nearby building, Saint Peter's appeared close up as in a photograph, framed by an arch of greenery.

"Marco and I used to run from here to the far-away view from the Aventine and back. We never worked out how Saint Peter's could move so quickly. I still can't," he added.

The remaining days of Grace's stay in Rome were spent looking at churches and ancient sites. I remembered Saint Peter's, while the rest merged into one religious blur. On the morning of Grace's departure we decided to visit the white pyramid which Toni had pointed out to us the previous evening. Disappointed to find that it was not open to visitors, we turned to walk away.

Grace grabbed my arm. Gasping with excitement, she cried, "Isabel, look! The Non-Catholic Cemetery where Keats and Shelly are buried. I've read so much about it and here it is next door to the pyramid. I can't believe it."

I hesitated. I had been to more graves in the past couple of weeks than most folk see in a lifetime.

"And we've come on it by chance." Like a child wearing down a parent's resistance, she coaxed, "You believe in Fate. You say we should go where it takes us, isn't that so?"

Well, it was our last day together. We went into the cypress shade of the walled cemetery, into an oasis of stillness, where the fragrance of flowers and flowering shrubs hung in the air, where the silence was broken only by bird-song and the occasional meowing of cats from one of Rome's many cat colonies. We had read about them on a notice at the entrance to the cemetery. In a corner, close to the pyramid, we found Keats' grave. He had been eight years younger than Liam was when he died.

We made our way up overgrown pathways in the more crowded part of the cemetery. I side-stepped mounds of food left for cats that rubbed against our legs, or slept in the shade of tombstones which had been erected to men and women who had lived in this city and chosen to be buried among their fellow exiles.

I thought about Liam lying in the devouring wilderness of Milltown. I thought about Liam, but I couldn't quite piece together the face I had woken up to each morning and used to picture on his pillow long after he left. Am I a shallow person, or is this dimming of the memory Nature's way of helping those who are left behind to let go? I know that in many Mediterranean countries photographs of the dead are incorporated in tombstones. Maybe it's to make sure that they are not forgotten, or to remind the bereaved and passing visitors of the flesh and blood human beings they once were. In the non-Catholic cemetery, children of all ages were buried with parents. For the first time I wished that Grania had not been cremated. If she had been buried, I would have a place to remember her, where I would plant yellow crocuses and snowdrops to bloom in spring and yellow and white roses to scent the air in summer.

Grace and I wandered together, stopping to look at inscriptions in unknown scripts on Jewish and other non-Christian graves, and on some where wild flowers half-hid the names of those who shared their resting place. I was reading in the guidebook about the history of the graveyard for non-Catholics, when another entry caught my eye.

Letting Fate direct us once more, I took Grace's arm and led her across the road to a British Military Cemetery in which four hundred and twenty-nine men were interred in the shelter of the city wall. A tranquil spot in a bustling city to complete our pilgrimage. Lines of headstones marked the graves of men from Britain and the Commonwealth who had died in the battle for Rome in the Second World War. Geraniums, roses and daisies flowered on graves and a cover of pine sheltered us from the scorching sun. We saw in the atrium where the people of Carlisle had inserted a piece of Hadrian's Wall as a tribute to the servicemen buried in this spot.

Hadrian's Wall, built to keep out the Scots and other invaders from the North, had been part of my A level Classical Civilisation course. In my last year at school, our Latin teacher had organised a visit to the forts along the Roman Wall in Northumberland. Shivering in a biting wind, I felt sorry for myself and for Hadrian's soldiers whose lives had ended in the freezing cold of the bleakest outpost of the Roman Empire.

The neat rows of graves were of young men, whom the violence of war had robbed of a future. Men like Anthony O'Brien and Fred's comrades for whom he bought poppies each Armistice Day. My eyes blurred as they ranged over the white crosses erected to their memory. Here, death was the great leveller. Though the setting was magnificent and the cemetery was beautifully kept, each grave told of a life cut short. Each headstone, in spite of the personal message engraved on it, was identical in form. War had taken these soldiers far from their families and their homeland. It had killed them all in a matter of weeks and, in death, it had taken away their individuality. I stood, unable to move, overwhelmed by the sadness of it, by the wrongness of it.

In the Non-Catholic Cemetery death had been a part of life – childbirth, sickness, accident, old age. I had been struck by the peace of the place and that was how I thought it should be.

That was reality.

Swans with the power of human speech, a mystic island rising out of the Atlantic, a perfect father, a gifted and loving husband.

That was fantasy.

I prepared to explore Rome on my own, to study the maps and guide book Grace had left and decide how to spend my time. Toni phoned to say I should leave my suitcase at the hotel. We arranged to meet at the Piazza Navona at six.

I had learned to find my way around London on foot instead of popping up from the tube like a mole, my only connection between Angel, Paddington and Bounds Green being stations on a map of the Underground. London is a city of crowded streets and a population on the move. When you cross the Thames you are struck by the cranes and skyscrapers on London's ever-changing skyline – not so in Rome, where you walk on thousands of years of history. Grace and I had visited churches built on the foundations of pagan temples and on buildings from subsequent eras and religions. Toni had told us that the proposed Metro extension to the area where he lived had been shelved because of the discovery of pre-Imperial remains. I remembered a scene from Fellini's *Roma* where workmen are digging a tunnel for the underground and find themselves in a perfectly preserved Roman villa but, as they look, the colours of the frescoes start to fade when exposed to the atmosphere. And I wondered how many capital cities would cancel or divert developments to preserve their past.

Though Grace was an undemanding presence, it was good to sit alone in a shaded café on the Piazza Navona with a long orange juice. Not thumbing through guidebooks, identifying figures in fountains, not overloading my head with information before moving on to the next famous church, another beautiful fountain. Instead of appreciating the Piazza Navona, my heart was lurching in a mixture of anticipation and dread. Making love on the beach and in Toni's car had the teenage excitement of stolen love. Would we survive seven days and nights solely in each other's company, apart from the time Toni spent at work? Marie, who is an authority on such matters, reckons that any man and woman who are physically attracted to each other can have a happy and sexually fulfilling relationship for a fortnight, maximum. According to her, the essential component of a romance in a foreign country is the escape road to the airport. Once you're in the departure lounge you will either feel broken-hearted or relieved to be returning home from make-believe to reality. I didn't need an escape road. I had only to pretend that my mother was ill and I had booked an earlier flight. I've always felt obliged to create complicated scenarios that convince me, if nobody else.

"Isabel, Isabel." Toni weaving through crowds and my doubts melting faster than the ice in my glass.

He ordered drinks. We held hands. The smiles of children who have escaped their parents' all-seeing eyes wreathed our faces. He told me the piazza was built over an ancient stadium and he pointed out a church dedicated to Saint Agnes.

"I forget most things," he says, "but I remember Saint Agnes."

When she was twelve years old, Agnes refused to marry the elderly pagan who had been chosen for her. As a punishment for her disobedience, she was to be exposed naked in the square, but her modesty was preserved by a sudden, miraculous growth of thick hair over her whole body. I said I'd rather have married the pagan and we raised our glasses to the hairy Saint Agnes.

After an early supper in a narrow street close to the Tiber, we collected my suitcase from the hotel and drove past the main railway station through a built-up area with a flyover. We passed a park where children played, supervised by their mothers, where families and old men sat on benches and drank coffee at an outdoor café among pillars and remains of buildings built two thousand years previously.

Though his flat on the eighth floor had only one bedroom, it was spacious and uncluttered. A man's home, functional and impersonal. A place of transit for someone waiting for his next move. Someone unburdened by possessions. A few posters, a map of New England, a computer on a desk piled with papers and books, and a large-screen television. Toni said his mother had tidied everything and smiled as he added, 'in case he had company'. Sliding doors opened to let air into the stifling flat. There were awnings and deck chairs on the balconies of the street opposite us and roof gardens, where masses of red, yellow and purple plants climbed and trailed in a blaze of colour. Toni pointed out Saint Peter's, floodlit on the eastern horizon, a fraction of the close-up he had shown Grace and me on the Aventine. He said the lights along the hills to the right were of the *castelli Romani* on the Alban Hills and the Pope's summer residence where we would go tomorrow. I marvelled at the place names – Tivoli, Frascati, Castel Gandolfo – which sounded familiar, but which I found hard to identify with Toni's mouth on my neck, with his hands sliding over my breasts. I turned to face him.

I feel as if I have been drinking champagne. The frothy wooziness that comes somewhere between the second and third glass when I haven't quite lost control and don't care if I do. Toni places my hands on his chest over the thin layer of cotton between him and the heat of his skin. I splay them over his damp skin, over the pulse of a vein that throbs through my palms. His hands are gentle against my cheeks. He moves them slowly over my mouth, over my neck; he traces the crevices of my ears, my eyebrows and the lids of my closed eyes. And my hands touch the roughness of his chin and upper lip, his smooth brow. I open my lips and we kiss. Light, all-the-time-in-the-world kisses; hot, exploring kisses till we're gasping for breath. His body is pressed tight against me. If I were not wedged between him, the metal railings and the lights of Saint Peter's, I would slide to the floor.

188

A whole night to lie with him, to learn the lines and features of his body, to trace the scar on his back, the result of falling out of a tree when he was twelve; to watch, as he sleeps, the pulse in his throat, the rise and fall of his chest, the shadows on his face, and to know I have arrived at a place I had hardly dared hope to reach.

When he goes out to buy bread and milk, I put my arms round the space he has left and memorise the shape of him, the feel of him. For a moment I wonder how many women have slept in this bed. But only for a moment.

Two days alone with him in the cooler heat of the Alban hills. Roast pork and artichoke salad at a lakeside restaurant, a walk through the shade of spruce and pine, through thin, brown tree trunks and a memory of autumn in rustling leaves. A flock of green parrots on the Appian Way, blue-tipped wings soaring to freedom. Going up in a balloon anchored on a hill in the Borghese Gardens, Rome stretched out below, the Tiber a silver ribbon meandering through the city.

As the week passes we speak as if we have a future together. Toni says we will do part of the Appalachian Trail, stay in huts or sleep in a tent on summer nights. We will start with a walk in the White Mountains of New Hampshire.

He tells me how he had found Vasto claustrophobic, how life in his extended family is lived under a microscope and he intends to return to the anonymous freedom of the States. He says he will go to Abruzzo to see the ruined house I would like to buy. A place of our own, near his parents, but not too near.

When I ask about his grandmother Elisa, he paints a picture of a manipulative and domineering old woman who was possessive of his mother and jealous of his father and lived in the hope of being buried in Gorla.

"Though she came from an educated family, when she was older Nonna behaved like a peasant from Abruzzo, or one of the Italian grannies in Brooklyn."

He must have been about five when she first showed him and Marcus the clothes she had brought from Vasto to wear in her coffin. A black dress, shoes and stockings and her rosary all carefully packed in a big suitcase. And a crucifix on a silver chain. He remembered the shiny, unmarked soles of the shoes and told her she should get some wear out of them before she died.

189

"Our parents were furious with my brother and me when they heard us making fun of Nonna. Papa ordered us to show respect for her. She'd been taken from her own country to a place where she never learned the language and she was stuck in a flat all day looking after two badly behaved boys."

He says his Nonna had her way in the end. The family returned to Italy, leaving Marcus with his dad's sister, Zia Laura. Elisa died seven years after leaving the States. All the inhabitants of Gorla, mostly old people wearing black, navy or brown, followed the coffin on foot from the church to where she was buried beside her aunt Nerina. Not a lot happened in Gorla. It was a big occasion. They were investing in their own funerals and Elisa was one of their own.

He explains that old people in rural areas of Abruzzo still make sure their funeral clothes are ready and goes on to say, "When my great-grandfather died, Marcus and Papa's family came from New York. My father and his sisters got him ready for the journey into the afterlife. He was buried in Guilmi, the village in the mountains where he came from, with soap and a towel, a piece of bread, his reading glasses and some coins." By way of explanation he added, "Guilmi is the last village on the road. Nobody passes through, so traditions don't change."

He asks if I find this all a bit primitive.

"No, I don't. In Ireland we have many funeral rituals. I think it's because, like Italy, we were a rural society until recently. At my husband's wake, crowds waited outside his home to pay their respects and the huge church was packed for the funeral Mass. It's not morbid. Where I come from, death is a part of life."

When my next-door neighbour's husband died, only Glynnis, one of her daughters – the other hadn't spoken to her father for years – two neighbours and I attended his cremation. Was this city living or modern society in Britain?

Toni says we must look to our future and not to the past. I agree with him and say I've had a bellyful of cemeteries and death. But I can't get Elisa out of my thoughts. Though I had seen photographs of her as a middle-aged woman, I carry in my head a picture of a beautiful young Venetian girl. She would have been about the same age as my mother. How different their lives had been! Ma grew up in a country virtually untouched by a war that had made her father rich. She had led a secure life and, apart from her time at boarding school, had moved only a few miles to Kenmara from the home where she was born. Whereas Elisa had been taken from Rome, abandoned by her mother in Venice and sent to Gorla to escape starvation. She had lived under German occupation and been married off to an illiterate stranger. Then, in her middle age, she was transported across the Atlantic to a country where she was as isolated by her lack of language as she had been when she first went to Gorla. Grace used to visit Kenmara every summer with her parents to visit her grandparents whom Ma looked after for years. Minnie remembers a united and happy family. That was long before Ma was landed with me. As for secrets in her past, it would have been almost impossible for her to have kept anything hidden from the long-fingered probing of the society in which she grew up.

Friday morning at five o'clock, Toni drives me to the airport with a promise to come to England as soon as he can. In the departure hall the joy of the past week seeps from me. Am I half asleep or merely dreading my time alone with Ma and the problems between Rose and John in which I will be expected to take sides? Is my heart broken? I don't know. I have yet to spend two consecutive weeks with Toni. I know that he and I have only seen the best sides of our natures in a holiday situation, just as Liam and I had done before pregnancy forced us to embark on marriage. Though I am excited by the idea of living in the States I wonder, how I will survive a different culture without friends or family to turn to in need? And how will Toni and I cope with the humdrum business of daily living, of finding out each other's moods and weaknesses?

"Hot love soon cools," Ma used to say. And the ghost of my marriage to Liam comes back too haunt me.

I shake these doubts from my head and make my way towards the boarding gate for Gatwick. But my heart urges me to turn around and weave my way through the throng of travellers heading towards Departures. Past boutiques displaying elegant outfits and expensive, Italian shoes, past chocolate shops and bakeries smelling of fresh bread; through pungent smells of coffee, cheeses and salamis and the tangled scents of perfumes in the Duty Free and out of the airport building to where Toni parked his car. And I wish I was about to spend a second week with him, to share seven more carefree days and seven more nights in his lofty flat on the Viale della Serenissima.

Chapter Twenty

Kenmara – Isabel

As the plane flies low over Belfast Lough, Carrickfergus, Glengormley and Kenmara are visible under a clear sky. My father said his heart used to ache each time he stood on the deck of the Liverpool or Holyhead boat and watched the Irish coast disappearing from sight. And he talked of the pleasure of picking out each familiar landmark on the homeward journey to the Dublin or Belfast docks in the early morning.

At Gatwick I left a message on Ma's voice mail and phoned my neighbour, Glynnis, to say I would be back in Brockley on Monday. As we approach City Airport, a ship glides down the Lough, its long wake flowing like a bride's frothy train. For a change my thoughts are not with Ma – my time in Italy has wrapped me in a protective cloak, thick enough to deflect her moods and indifference – but with Liam. The numbing journey to his bedside in the Royal Victoria, his silent drift from life. Air travel distorts all sense of time. At four o'clock this morning I was in bed with Toni. Nine hours later, a single woman, nobody's wife, nobody's mother, I'm waiting among couples and families inside the airport building to collect the suitcase I took to Pescara. It appears on the conveyor belt, bursting with my Rome shopping and a white pashmina for Ma's birthday. I'm braced for her reaction to it.

"Isabel, Isabel!" My sister-in-law, Rose, waves and comes towards me.

A tall lad trails behind her, a rucksack slung over his left shoulder. He peers through a curtain of hair and I recognise my nephew, Johnny, Rose's youngest son. He puts up with the kisses I aim at his unshaven cheeks, while Rose explains that he is the only one of her three sons who will be present at his granny's party. How long was it since we last met? How did the exams go? His replies to my questions are brief. Rose offers to drive me to Kenmara before taking her son home for a square meal and a good scrub, but Johnny wants to be dropped near the centre, where he's meeting a mate in twenty minutes. A look that is more hurt than anger crosses Rose's face. I expect her to protest and am amazed to see that all her fight seems to have drained from her. How gaunt and unwell she looks since I last saw her, how unlike Rose is her little-woman shrug and her sigh when she says she wishes she had a daughter like me.

She asks if she will be intruding on my reunion with my mother. I assure her that the last thing my mother and I need is quality time with each other. She will be doing both Ma and me a favour. After Johnny is deposited, Rose tells me Italy has put a spring in my step and a gleam in my eye. She asks about my holiday, what Grace and I did, where we went. Had I met anybody interesting? There is something of the old Rose in her hunger for news and in her need to extract minute details that puts me on my guard. To deflect further questions and to stop her worming out information I don't want to share with her, I tell her about the anonymous letter warning me against going to Italy. Set alongside my time in Abruzzo with Grace and in Rome with Toni, the letter is of no importance, no more than a kink to be straightened out. So why do I go on to ask Rose if she knows anything about it? To fill a twitchy silence? Because I suspect my sister-in-law? Because Rose has the knack of bringing out the nasty side of me?

"I didn't send the letter. It wasn't me."

Her quick reply and her emphasis on 'I' make me prick up my ears. "But you know who did?"

She slows down, signals, crosses the road to a restaurant and parks her car beside a terrace overlooking the Lough. "There's something I think you should know before we get to Kenmara."

"It was John. Wasn't it? But why?"

Suddenly Rose, the matriarch who ran her family and her life with terrifying efficiency, Rose who bulldozed her way through any crisis with a non-stop tirade and a hot meal, bursts into tears. Since leaving Rome, I have felt detached, an onlooker observing life from a distant height. Rose's collapse, as unexpected as it is shocking, jolts me back to earth. Heedless of the waitress who puts a teapot, milk jug and two china cups in front of us, or of the summery-dressed young women at the next table, Rose's tears overflow like pent-up water after a canal lock has been opened. Though it's a warm day by Irish standards, I shiver and goose-bumps prickle my skin. I pat Rose's tear-damp hand.

"Please don't cry, Rose. It doesn't matter. I'll have a word with John," I say, knowing full well that her grief has nothing to do with the unsigned letter that Marie made me chuck in the dustbin.

"John's left me," she sobs. "He's moved into a flat with some woman he's been seeing for ages. He says he needs to sell my lovely home to make ends meet."

Rose welcomed me to her home after Liam died, as she often did when I couldn't bear life at Kenmara. She used to hug me when I was small and it was time to leave her noisy house to return to Ma and silence. She would say she wished she could keep me and assure me that my room with 'Isabel' on a plaque on the door would always be waiting for me.

"Oh Rose, that's awful. Maybe it's just a fling. The sort of thing middle-aged men get up to. He'll come back any day now." I stroke her bare arm and mutter platitudes. Liam didn't come back. Liam would never have come back.

"He won't, Isabel. He hates me, says I get on his nerves. He can't stand the sound of my voice and the boys hardly ever come home. He says I drove them away."

"Rose, oh Rose, I'm so sorry." I hug my sister-in-law to me. She used to have a no-nonsense bosom and cushiony arms. I could weep with her. Instead I go on stroking her hair. Stroking, stroking till her sobs subside. "Would you like me to talk to John?"

I don't want to talk to John and I can't face my mother. If only it was last Friday and my week with Toni was still in the future. But already my family is taking over my life and Toni is a diminishing figure in some distant city, crowded out by the events in Rose's and my brother's lives.

In a play by Sartre I read at university, a couple meet in the ante room to eternity. They fall in love as they had been destined to before their violent and untimely deaths. Not having physical bodies they cannot touch or make love. Due to a clerical error, they have died a day too soon and are granted one day on earth to fulfil their destiny. They are immediately drawn back into the problems of their former lives and have no time to meet during their twenty-four hour reprieve.

194

With a workmanlike blow into a tissue, Rose sits up and drains her tea. I pour another cup.

"No, Isabel, no! John would go mad if he knew I told you about his goings on, but thanks for offering. And please don't tell Rita."

Unless Ma has lost her sight as well as being blinded by her first-born son's virtues, she will have sussed out the trouble in his family and will have laid the blame, fair and square, on Rose.

"Thanks for listening, Isabel. You were always a lovely wee girl and you have had your own share of troubles. We'd better go or Rita will be worried about you."

On the short journey to Kenmara I ask Rose if she would think about getting a job or doing voluntary work. I tell her she is an attractive, intelligent and well-qualified woman with huge potential who needs to start putting herself first. I say I wish I'd done just that after Liam left. At a bend on the drive she stops to comb her hair and dab powder on her face.

Ma opens the door. She seems pleased to see Rose. I'm about to tell her that her new hairstyle takes years off her, when she says, "I've been watching for you. I'm glad you came."

"I said I would, Ma."

She shivers in my embrace, which skims her back and shoulders. I think she's as nervous as I am. Minnie appears from the kitchen. We throw our arms round each other. She holds me at arm's length and says how great I look after my holiday, asks about Grace and then hurries off to make tea for Rose and me. Ma, in hotel receptionist mode, tells me I will be in my old room. There is a vase of yellow roses on the bedside table, and the picture John took of me and Daddy at my First Communion – the one which Ma had removed along with all my personal belongings – has been reinstated. I look out at the garden and my mind's eye sees my father, his foot frozen on the lug of his sunken spade, hands on the shaft, a robin pecking at freshly-turned soil. Minnie is waiting at the bottom of the stairs. In the few seconds before we carry the tea things into the sitting room, I say I've loads to tell her. She says she can't wait.

Rose is fulsome in her praise for Ma's new hairstyle. The mother I grew up with would have considered baldness, or any other blemish, a secret too shameful to share with anyone but an expert. Yet here she sits, poking fun at herself as she pours tea from her Royal Doulton teapot. She goes on to explain how Linda and

Aisling, with Una in attendance, disguised the bald spot and helped her choose a party frock. There has always been a bond between Ma and Una. She regularly spends a night with her grandmother, who has encouraged her to study and make something of herself. But over the years Ma has condemned Aisling as a loud-mouthed madam who was going to the bad. Naturally Linda was to blame for bringing her up without manners or respect for her elders. She has consistently ignored Hugh's two sons and they have returned the compliment.

My heart sinks when Rose tells us she cannot stay to sample Minnie's fish pie. She must hurry home and check the casserole she has prepared for Johnny. He knows where the key is hidden but she can't bear to think of him arriving back to an empty house.

Toni will have left his office. He may already have returned to his flat and found the moisturiser I left in the bathroom and my flip-flops at my side of the bed. My Hansel and Gretel trail leading me back to him. I beg Minnie to eat with Ma and me but she is expecting her granddaughter for her tea.

Ma and I have never sat down alone at the dining room table. I ask her about preparations for the party and am told that everything is in place. What colour is her new frock? I must wait till Sunday, she says and clams up. My throat is dry from embarking on one dead-end conversation after another and my back aches from sitting on the edge of my seat. It's a long time since I left Rome this morning,

I need to talk to you, Isabel. It is very important. Please come before the others. Please Isabel.

Did she really beg me to come early or have I misremembered? Already I'm counting the hours till Grace arrives; till I get out of here.

Ignoring my last remark about the wonderful weather, she pushes her chair back and rises to her feet. "I need to talk to you. We'll go the summerhouse while it's still warm."

I hurry upstairs to fetch a cardigan and the pashmina, which was gift-wrapped in a shop near Toni's flat. Two messages from him on my mobile raise my spirits and assure me that he really does exist. I want to reply but I can't keep Ma waiting. She approves of her birthday present, the colour, the softness of the wool and the embroidery above each fringed end. She drapes it around her, throws one end over her shoulder with the poise of a model and smiles at her full-length reflection in one of the many looking glasses in her house of mirrors. I follow her towards the summerhouse, mirroring her footsteps as a mother would her infant's faltering steps. A sudden breeze ruffles Ma's hair. It exposes the pink skin under the back-combed nest on her crown. She clutches her pashmina and pulls it tightly round her.

Rigid as a statue, she asks, "Did Grace find her father's grave?"

I stutter. I'm rambling on about the cemetery, when she interrupts.

"What did she say about him?"

"Nothing. Nothing much, except that Uncle Harry agreed to adopt her. Her mother didn't talk much about him."

"Her mother?"

I remember my promise to Grace. Sweat drips from my palms and tension paralyses me. Ma indicates a space on the bench beside her. Before sitting down, I inhale deep breaths of air heavy with the scent of night stocks.

Without any preamble, she starts to speak in short rapid bursts, "My mother knew I was pregnant before I did. I'd just turned seventeen. We were very ignorant in those days. She kept on asking who had done this filthy thing to me. She wouldn't give up, day after day she asked, even threatened to tell my father."

She has shed what my father called her Lady-of-the-Manor voice and it's as if in reminiscing, she has reverted to the language and the accent of her girlhood. I hear the emotion and the inflexions in her voice, how she pauses and stammers before starting a new sentence. I hear a rush of words but their meaning slides over me.

"I couldn't tell her it was the boy who stood in for Jemmy, the yard man. She wouldn't have believed me, wouldn't have known his name if I'd said it. Your granddad called all the yard men Jemmy. They were nobodies, not worth giving a name to, dirt poor and glad to have a job, any job."

She turns and looks straight at me, as if she expects me to blame her. Blank faced, I return her stare. I could be an eavesdropper, listening to information not meant for me, like turning on an old-fashioned radio, searching for a station and hearing people talking; trying to tune in to what's being said, but there's a lapse in understanding.

"You have to understand, Isabel. It was the forties. There was a war on. Things were very different then. It was the greatest disgrace a girl could bring on her family. A girl with a bastard child was finished."

She abandons her abrupt way of talking. Her voice becomes slow and soft.

"One day I met a lad in the street near our pub. He called my name and said he was Jemmy, the yardman. I didn't recognise him for the lad who swept the bar and carried barrels and crates up from the cellar, though I'd often watched him from my window. I'd been in bed for well over a year, and I wasn't used to the outside. He asked if I'd go for a spin on the bike with him on his half-day off. I said I would. I didn't know any boys. He was very nice looking and he had a nice way with him."

I go on listening. Occasionally, I feel I've hit the right station and what Ma's saying might be true. Again the crackling starts and I can make no sense of the confusion of sound.

She tells me she cycled to the coast road to meet Jemmy, how they went down quiet lanes away from prying eyes, how they abandoned their bikes and walked along the path that follows the sea. In no way can I reconcile the shy girl of her story with the woman I've known since I was born. I wonder if she's made the whole thing up, or if she has reached a stage where she can no longer separate fantasy from reality. Rose implied that Ma was in the early stages of dementia and needed to be looked after. But something rings true, the passion of her telling, her precise descriptions and her way of stopping as if to censor her feelings. Without fearing she'll snatch it back, I take her hand and caress the papery skin and tapering fingers. She doesn't resist, but goes on to speak of the love between herself and twenty-one-year-old Jemmy.

"I had led a very sheltered life. I was ill in bed with consumption when girls of my age were starting to go out with boys. I used to wonder if I'd ever be well enough to go out with a boy. I wondered what it would be like." She stops speaking, as if she's reminiscing, as if she's confused. "I'm not sure if I can tell you the rest, if you'll be shocked."

"I won't be shocked, Mamma."

Her shawl tightly wrapped round her, she has shrunken into an old woman, a 'shawlie' from pictures of the 1920's. Protective of the

198

woman I have just called 'Mamma' for the first time, I put my arm around her shoulder and urge her to continue.

Eyes fixed on the reddening sky, she talks of her meetings with Jemmy. She says the few months when she knew him were the happiest of her life. He had a gentleness she didn't associate with men and his love for her was tender and heart-felt. Then, one day as they walked towards Whitehead, he told her that the real Jemmy was coming back to the pub on Monday and he would be out of work.

She pauses, as if unsure whether to continue or not. I'm about to speak, when her raised hand silences me. I wait for her to continue.

Chapter Twenty One

Kenmara

Isabel waits for the rest of my story. Her face is blank. I'm not sure how much I should tell her. Not sure if she believes what she's already heard.

"…I remember the last time I saw Jemmy as clear as yesterday. There was nobody around because the wind was bitter. We lay down in a grassy hollow. Gulls shrieked, swooped and flew so low we could feel the rush of their wings above our faces. We both wept when he told me he had to go to England. With her husband long dead and her daughter in bed with bad health, his mother couldn't afford to keep an out-of-work son. His brothers sent money from England. They wrote that most of the men were away at the war and there was plenty of work in factories and on the land. We didn't have conscription in Ulster. The government didn't dare bring it in.

As the meaning of his words seeped into my head, I cried for the empty weeks until Jemmy earned enough to return, and I cried for the end of happiness. We lay in each other's arms, kissing as if we wanted to drink each other in. The smoothness of his skin under his rough shirt, his rich smell of workman's sweat, his breath warm on my cheek. His softness, his hardness. Hands touching where I'd never been touched and me desperate for him, crying out for him. Pain slicing through pleasure, pleasure through pain. Clutching every second before it slipped from my reach. And again. This time bliss such as I'd never known as we melted into each other.

'I'll think about you all day, Rita, I want to be with you, to wake up in the morning and know you're beside me. I'll never love anybody except you.'

Soft rain on our faces. Gulls' cries muted. Time galloping by. Jemmy taking from his shirt pocket the photo I'd given him, the one with *Remember me. Think about me.* written on the back.

'I'll look at it first thing in the morning and last thing at night till we're together again. Wait for me, Rita. I'll be back soon, I promise.'

The sky turning dark. Time to part. We covered each other's faces with kisses before I broke away from his arms. Half turning back, half looking ahead, I left him standing by the roadside and cycled blindly towards home and my mother's anger.

My mother took me to a doctor on the other side of town. I heard him tell her I was about four months pregnant and much more that I didn't understand. She told Pa and anyone who asked her that I had to stay in bed because the doctor was afraid my consumption was coming back. Isabel, I'd no way to let Jemmy know about the baby. All I could do was wait for news from him. I had no news. Not a letter. Not a postcard. Nothing.

Your granny must have gone to the phone box on the Antrim Road to ring my sister in England. Because Kate was married to a doctor, they had a phone in the house. Your grandmother was a clever woman, Isabel. She knew how to cover her traces. She told Pa that Kate was expecting, that she was delighted because the consultant had told her doctor she couldn't ever have children. I was to go to England with her and stay for a while to help my sister after the birth. I knew nothing about this till Kate told me years later."

The sun is setting in the sky to the west of the city and the heat has gone from the day. When she sees me hugging my new shawl tight around me, Isabel asks if I want to go inside. I shake my head. If I stop now, I may not be able to go on.

"...My mother took me to Kate's house. It was a long journey and an exhausting one, even though she'd managed to get berths for us on the Liverpool boat. Kate met us at Euston Station and your granny took the train straight back to Liverpool."

I've never told any of this to a living soul. In the last weeks I've gone over what I'd say in my head, over and over, but I never thought it would be so hard to put into words. I sound like somebody else talking. And it's as if I'm telling Isabel about a person I knew a long time ago. In a way I am. I don't mention the heaving sea and me throwing up over the side of the deck. Or the feeling of standing outside myself and Kate's questions sliding over me as I trailed behind her to another station, another train.

"...I had no idea why I was staying with Kate and her husband. He was a quiet and gentlemanly person. He said I had to rest every afternoon and to drink as much milk as they could get for me. Rationing was very strict in England. The war had hardly touched us over here. We had to sleep in the cellar during air-raids, but apart from the bomb sites and the soldiers, you'd hardly have known there was a war going on in Belfast. I think Kate and her husband did without to make sure I was well fed because of the baby. Oh, Isabel, you know that giving birth isn't easy and I was ignorant and frightened."

I say nothing about the nurses who called me a filthy, Irish slut and other terrible names, who made fun of the way I spoke and pretended they couldn't understand a word I said. I don't say how my baby girl was taken from me as soon as she was born and I was only allowed to hold her when she fed at my breast. I asked why the left side of her face looked as if it had been squashed. Forceps, a nurse snapped. I didn't know what she meant but I was afraid to ask any more questions. Isabel's daughter lived for only a few days, so I don't tell her about my baby's dainty features, her rosy skin, her navy blue eyes and the touch of ginger in the wispy hair at the nape of her neck. Her father's hair. And I don't mention the tidal wave of love that washed over me when she trapped my finger in her tiny fist and held on tight. "You're mine, wee Bridget, all mine," I whispered to her before they came and took her from me.

"...I had told Kate I wanted my baby to be called Bridget when she took her to be christened. Before I left the hospital, a middle-aged woman in uniform asked me to sign a form. Nobody told me I was agreeing to give Bridget up for adoption to Kate and her husband. I was happy to be taking her back to their house. I thought of it as the home where Bridget and I would stay till Jemmy married me. She slept in Kate's room and was only brought to me when she was hungry."

I don't think Isabel is really listening. She's humouring me because I'm old. She thinks I'm probably losing my mind. Maybe Rose has been telling her stories about me. Is she thinking I should have known what was happening? I keep making excuses. I say things were different in my day.

202

"...Every day, sometimes three or four times, your Aunt Kate tried to force me to tell her what Bridget's father was called. Said it was important for the child and I was being very selfish. She was three months old when Kate started giving her a bottle. Soon after, I was told it was time to return to Belfast without Bridget. I thought it would be for a short while till Ma sorted things out for me and the baby."

I wish I could read the look Isabel's giving me, but I daren't look at her again. I don't need her blaming me. I've blamed myself enough.

"...I was just seventeen, Isabel, and I was scared of Kate. I hardly knew her. She was ten years older than me. Your granny lost two babies before I was born. Kate had a sharp tongue and she was as severe as the nurses at the hospital. She took me to Euston Station, gave me money to buy food for the journey and said I'd done the right thing. It was best for everybody. She had to hurry home to make sure the baby had been fed. She showed me where to get the train for Heysham. Before she left, she told me my baby had been christened Grace when she was four days old.

Wind raked the platform where I walked towards a spot well beyond the front of the train. I looked down at the track, a short drop from my feet. I'd wait till the train started moving. The engine chuffed and belched. A whistle blew. I tore myself from the lure of the track and clung on to life as if it was worth living."

Isabel's hand has dropped from my shoulders. She turns to me, her face blank.

"Grace? You did say Grace?" She shakes her head, not believing, even after I nod yes. She stands up and stares at me. "Grace was *your baby*, the baby you had to give to Aunt Kate and Uncle Harry?" It's as if she has to squeeze her voice past a blockage in her throat. I nod once and wait. After what seems a long time, she says, "Grace is my sister."

"Yes." I'm shivering and my voice is no more than a croak.

"Grace is my sister," Isabel repeats. I can see the question that's taking shape behind the puckered ridges of her forehead: "Jemmy was ... he was Anthony O'Brien?"

I nod again. I haven't the strength to tell her I'd always called him Jemmy and that's how I still think of him. She turns her face from the sunset and looks to where I sit, plucking at the fringe of my new shawl, plucking as if I don't know how to stop.

"We have to go inside and get you warmed, Mamma. You've talked too much. You must be worn out."

She helps me to my feet, puts her arm round my shoulder and leads me up the path and into the warmth of the sitting-room. She opens the draught vent of the fire that Minnie has banked down.

"It's a long time since I did this." Isabel takes the poker from the brass companion set, kneels down, pokes and rakes till the embers start to glow. "Central heating is great, but you can't beat a real fire. It's one of the things I miss, living in England."

With tongs she picks a few sticks and nuggets of coal from the scuttle and criss-crosses them on the embers. Hunkering, she takes the back pages of a newspaper from the pile beside the hearth and stretches it above the grate till flames glow behind the newsprint. She fans her hands before the fire and asks if I would like tea or cocoa.

"Do you know what I'd really like? I could do with a hot toddy. And be sure you make it strong, Isabel."

I am worn out, but little by little, so gradually that I don't notice at first, I'm aware of an incredible lightness filling my lungs as the weight I've been carrying on my shoulders begins to drop away. The weight I couldn't, or wouldn't, let go even after Angela told me that I hadn't been responsible for Daisy's death. Time isn't the great healer folk say it is, though it blurs the edges of pain. I have fed off my guilt, hugged it to me, picked off its scabs for fear they would heal. Though I'm raw from remembering, from sifting and censoring what my daughter needs to know, I feel as if I've been given the all clear after a long illness and have the strength to tell Isabel the rest of the story.

She sits crossed-legged on the fireside rug as the warmth of our drinks flows into us.

"I remember you and Daddy and your hot whiskeys on winter nights. It's still a great drink for a July evening after the sun goes down."

She kicks off her sandals. She's too bright, too brittle. The knuckles on her glass are so white I'm afraid it will shatter.

"You lost a baby, Isabel, so I'm not going to talk about how I felt after I came back to Belfast on my own."

She moves towards me, leans against my chair and takes my hand.

"Grania was premature. She died because her lungs didn't have time to develop. We knew she wouldn't live almost as soon as she was born. Liam was with me most of the time. So was Grace." Her voice is lower. Calmer. "Are you able to tell me if you ever heard anything about Anthony O'Brien?"

I'm not ready for her question. Wasn't expecting it. Haven't prepared any answers.

"Years passed. He never wrote. I think he may not have known how to write. Not everybody did in those days. I was bitter at first. I thought he'd settled down with an English girl and forgotten about me, or just moved on. I got it into my head that there was something wrong with me. Maybe word had got round that I was damaged goods and no man would come within a mile of me." Isabel doesn't need to hear me *moidering* on and on. I'm saying too much. I must stick to the facts. The facts. "Your granny never once mentioned my baby and I didn't dare ask if she'd heard from Kate. My father was fed up with having a sulky daughter on his hands. He was always trying to fix me up with men he thought were good catches and he got mad when I wouldn't look at them. I suppose I was still hoping against hope that Jemmy, I mean Anthony, would return and Kate would give Bridget back to me."

It's a funny thing. I never stopped thinking about him but I couldn't really remember what he looked like and I hadn't a photo of him. Sometimes I'd think I saw him on the street, on the bus. I'd look closer until I knew for certain I'd made a mistake and my memory of him would fade or change completely.

I drink slowly, savouring the sharp bite of the last drops of whiskey.

"You haven't lost the knack of making a hot toddy."

"I had a good teacher. I remember Daddy saying it was important to leave the spoon in the glass, to stop it cracking."

I say nothing for a while, not because I've forgotten what I must say, but because I need time to remember.

"Years after the war ended, I'm not sure how long it was, a woman came up to me as I was leaving Sunday Mass. She called my name and drew me aside. She kept looking around as if she was afraid of something or somebody. I could tell from the way she spoke and the clothes she wore that she was a country woman, and she had the weather-beaten skin of somebody who worked outside." My voice is low and Isabel is straining to hear. I'm struggling for breath, but I have to go on. "She groped in the depths of a bag and handed me a letter. It was from the War Office. They regretted to tell her that her son, Private Anthony O'Brien of the London Irish Fusiliers, had been killed in action on the twenty-first of November 1943. I think there was another letter saying his remains were buried in Italy in the Sangro River Military Cemetery. Maybe it was the same one. I'm not sure."

Shock can do funny things to you. You'd think I would have said something to Jemmy's mother. Done something. I remember noticing bristly hairs growing out a mole on the woman's chin and thinking she should pull them out. I couldn't take my eyes off them. I must have felt something else. Being dizzy. My legs giving way. I can't remember. She caught me. Propped me against a wall.

"Then Jemmy's mother showed me this photo."

I open the drawer in the table beside my chair and show Isabel the black and white snap I gave Anthony before he left for England. She studies it as if she's memorising every feature of the shy girl leaning against a wall in Limestone Road; as if she's trying to find any trace of her mother in a snap taken in the spring of 1942. She reads the words I wrote on the back.

"Oh, Mamma, poor Mamma." She wants to say something, but can't find the words. She asks "Did you meet his mother after that?"

"It's a terrible thing to admit, Isabel. I was so stunned, I never thought to ask her where she lived or how I could get in touch with her. She had shown the photo to her neighbours and somebody thought that the girl might have been someone Anthony met when he worked at our pub. I'm not too sure. I think one of them recognised me. His mother had come to Saint Joseph's a couple of times and seen me, but I was always with my mother. I knew that Jemmy was from Ballycarry, up the country, a long way from where I lived. Poor woman, she must have walked all the way. I remember her shoes. Splayed and battered and down at heel."

We sit in silence for a while and I re-live my meeting with Jemmy's mother, a woman old before her time. I watched her make her way up the Antrim Road, shoulders hunched against the wind, feet walking along parallel tracks. Then I went into the park where I used to go with Angela and Daisy, trying to take in what she had told me. Trying to accept that my hopes were dead.

"From that day Bridget ceased to exist for me. She was Grace Sheridan, the baby who belonged to Kate and Harry Sheridan. I wrote to Kate telling her everything I had learned from Anthony's mother and sending the letters from the War Office. They had a right to know. I begged her to say nothing to my parents and as far as I know she respected my wishes."

Oh God, but I'm weary. I stretch my arms behind my head and close my eyes tight before looking at my daughter. "And now, Isabel, I could do with another toddy. Not as strong as the last one. Are you going to have one with me?"

It's good to sit alone for a while with an emptied mind. Isabel returns with the drinks. She says to take care. They are very hot.

"Thank you for telling me. It can't have been easy. I'm still trying to take in the news that Grace and I are sisters." She goes on as if she's talking to herself, rather than to me. "All the time I spent with her in Italy and she never said. When I think of it, she's always been like a sister to me."

We sit on either side of the hearth, gazing into the fire, sipping our drinks.

"You must be worn out, Ma. It's time you were in bed. You need to look your best for the party."

I am tired, worn out. I still need to tell her about Daisy and the far-reaching effects of her death. She tries to protest when I say I have to explain why I was such an unnatural mother to her...

"...In my generation everybody, especially women, was brought up to feel guilty. Guilty for wanting possessions, for having too much. Sex was the biggest sin, at least as serious as murder. Even thinking about it was sinful." I remember those months of sweating in bed when I wanted to die for killing Daisy and I remember the impure thoughts that consumed me and were my only source of pleasure. Neither the parish priest nor the curate came to hear my confession. Why should they? What sins could an innocent girl, stricken by consumption, commit?

"Having to give my baby away was my punishment for having sinned with Jemmy. It was my punishment for causing Daisy's death. I couldn't confess a sin for which there was no forgiveness. One thing I knew for certain. I could never again be trusted to look after any wee girl. And I couldn't believe my good fortune when my two sons were born. I never expected to be pregnant when I was forty-nine. And I was terrified the baby would be a girl."

Then, because I haven't lost my knack for passing on blame, I attempt to soften my behaviour by blaming Jack. I don't confess to begging him to put Isabel up for adoption. And there's no point in telling her how Jack threatened to apply for sole custody of his daughter and leave me. It's easier to blame the dead and wash my hands of all responsibility. Isabel loved Jack. To her he was a loving father. What she doesn't know is how much the love between him and her rankled with me. I was like the dog in the manger in my school reader. Though I didn't want anything to do with either of them, their devotion to each other was a cancer eating through me. Nowadays, they'll have a name for that sort of behaviour. Some syndrome or other. I know exactly what it was. Downright nastiness.

Dear God, don't let it be too late for me to change my ways. Don't let it be too late to convince my daughter that I have always loved her.

"Your father was a good man and I treated him badly. I treated him badly because he was my father's choice. I didn't deserve him and I didn't deserve to have you, Isabel. I think I lost my mind after you were born." There I go again, pretending I didn't know what I was doing, that my behaviour was beyond my control. "I was obsessed with the fear that I would do you harm, that you wouldn't survive in my care. I thought the only solution was to ignore your existence. And when your baby daughter died I was convinced it was my fault, that I had passed my bad blood on to you."

I wait for her to speak. She says nothing and I have no choice but to go on.

"Talking to you tonight has lifted a huge weight from my mind. You've become a lovely woman, Isabel. Any mother would be proud to have you for a daughter. Maybe… maybe in time you'll think less badly of me… Maybe one day you'll find it in your heart to forgive the wrong I've done to you."

208

"What's to forgive, Ma? Life had been hard on you and you did what you thought was best. I wish I'd known what you had been through. I wish I had been kinder, more like a daughter." She puts her arms around me. When she kisses my cheek and holds me close, her tears are damp on my face. "I'm so happy to have found you, my real mother, I...I don't know what to say."

I take her hand and lead her to the sofa where we sit, side by side, till the fire turns to ashes.

Chapter Twenty Two

Kenmara – Isabel

Curtained half-light. Seagulls squawking, pecking at the window pane. Somewhere between sleeping and waking, I identify my old bedroom – faded green curtains, fluted lampshade, the tea stain I'd tried to scrub off new wallpaper, the cigarette burn on the dressing table that I used to hide under a box for jewellery and knick-knacks. Fortunately the hot toddies made me sleep instead of spending the night mulling over Ma's revelations. Hazy memories from yesterday evening begin to filter into my mind. Her face after all her stories had been told, when we sat together beside the dying fire. Still beautiful, despite her exhaustion. Remnants of the beauty that had entranced my father. Though it was no longer the face of the shy sixteen-year-old year-old girl that Anthony O'Brien had carried with him until he died, there was a serenity in my mother which I had never seen, the peace of a woman with no more secrets to conceal. I remember Antonella telling us about that photograph. How Anthony O'Brien transferred it from his ragged shirt to the one belonging to Renzo Fronelli, the shirt Elisa made him wear the night she took him to her home. Antonella had explained that her mother wanted to make him look like an Italian labourer.

I wish I had time to absorb Ma's story, but my watch tells me it is half-past nine and there's a message from Toni on my mobile. He says his bed is a lonely place without me and asks when I am returning to London. I text him my flight times and add that my bed in Kenmara is too narrow for two. I lie back on the pillows and smile. If Ma had married Anthony O'Brien, Toni would be her step-grandson and I would be his step-aunt.

I hurry along the corridor and knock at the door of Ma's room. No answer. I brace myself for discovering my mother's body, or for her voice scolding me for barging in without permission and ordering me to my room. Her bed is made. Cool air flows through an open window. Framed photos of my father, John, Hugh and me hang on a wall beside the door.

She's sitting at the table in the kitchen, her hands clasped round a cup of tea.

"Will you have tea, or are you into coffee these days?" she asks.

"Tea will be fine, Ma."

"Would you like an egg? Bacon and egg?"

"I'll just have a slice of toast, some of that wheaten."

"Good, I made it specially for you."

"Thanks, Ma. Nobody makes wheaten bread like yours."

Does she regret telling me too much, revealing what had been hidden for so long? I put two slices of wheaten bread into the toaster and look out into the greenhouse which is empty of tomato plants, of seedlings and cuttings that used grow in trays. Stems and leaves have withered in the bone-dry compost of flowerpots and bird shit is spattered over dusty panes. I butter toast and sit opposite my mother. She passes a pot of marmalade to me and pours tea into two cups.

"We've bridges to build, Isabel. You and me."

"We'll build them, Ma." I place my hand on hers. "We'll build them together." While I'm wondering what to say next, a key turns in the lock of the front door.

"That will be John. He's taking me to the hairdresser's."

"Good. Tomorrow's a big day. You have to look your best." She looks as relieved as I feel when John comes into the kitchen.

He wraps his arms round me. "Isabel, wee Isabel. I heard you'd arrived." He holds me at arm's length. "You're looking great. Really great. Your trip to Italy has done you a power of good. Where did you go in the end?"

Ma interrupts him to say she will be ready to leave in five minutes. I pour a cup of tea for John and tell him about the places we visited in Abruzzo and in Rome, making no mention of the cemetery on the Sangro. Ma will spend at least ten minutes getting ready, so I tell him about the letter warning me against going to Italy. Because I don't know how I should phrase the question I ask him straight out if he sent it.

"What makes you think it was me?"

"Because I've ruled out everybody else," I try to cover my embarrassment with a laugh.

After much hemming and hawing, he says, "I suppose it wasn't a very clever thing to do. It was more of a shock tactic." He adopts an aggressive tone, though still managing to sound aggrieved. "You're impulsive, Isabel, and you listen to nobody. You've always been headstrong. I thought a letter might make you think before you plunged into a situation you knew nothing about."

In reasonable solicitor mode, he informs me that a few weeks previously, Rose told him some gossip she'd heard about a lad Ma had known when she was young. He'd joined the army and was killed in Italy, where he had been buried. There was some mention of a snap of Ma that was sent home with his belongings. John hadn't paid much attention. He told Rose she should get herself a job and stop listening to gossip. He'd put the incident to the back of his mind, until he witnessed Ma's reaction to the news of Grace's trip to Italy.

Ma is still in her bedroom. Enough time for John to tell me what he found out.

"You've got to remember, Isabel, finding out information is something I do. It's easier now with the Internet. I knew that if there was something fishy, it had to do with Grace. Why else would she go haring off to Italy? I knew she was born on the eighteenth of March 1943, so I checked the Registry of Births in Ulster, in the Free State and in England." He gives me a sharp look as though he's gauging my reaction to what he's said. "To cut a long story short, Grace Sheridan's birth wasn't registered, but a baby girl, named Grace Daly, had been born to Rita Mary Daly, on that day in a hospital in Hastings." He pauses and adds sharply, "I can tell from your face that none of this is news to you."

Ma will be ready in a couple of minutes.

"Why didn't you want me to find out that Grace was Ma's daughter?"

John's not used to being questioned. And certainly not by me. He listens at the door. In a half-whisper he says he also discovered Grace Sheridan's adoption details.

"Can't you see that if Ma acknowledges Grace as her daughter, her estate could be divided in four. As things are, there's little enough to go round three of us."

I stare at my brother in disbelief. I've always admired him. I would never have imagined he'd be thinking about his inheritance.

212

He's the affluent one in the family and he's always been very generous.

"Grace isn't interested in money. She has enough already. We all have. More than enough."

John has the grace to look embarrassed but he's still annoyed. He adopts a softer, though an even more patronising tone.

"Isabel, I was dealing with family squabbles over money when you were in nappies. Grace has two sons. They'll want their share. It's all very fine for you to have high ideals. You got all Daddy's money, remember? Besides, you don't have children. You haven't the faintest idea what it costs to bring up a family."

John's remarks strike a raw nerve.

"I may not have children, but I don't have two households to support."

Ma calls from the hall, "I'm ready to go, John. I mustn't be late for my appointment."

The veins on my brother's neck and temples bulge red and angry. His whisper is a growl, harsh with menace. "What's that supposed to mean? Has Rose been shooting her mouth off to you?"

I've never rowed with John. There was never any need to. In a quiet voice I tell him his affair was common knowledge the last time I was in Ireland. Then I turn to smile at Ma who appears in the doorway.

"John, you'll have plenty of time to talk to Isabel. If you don't get a move on, I'm going to be late and Tracey's doing me a favour seeing me on a Saturday."

After they leave, I mooch around the sitting room, annoyed with myself for antagonising my brother and for losing my temper. Being alone in this house where I grew up makes me uneasy. Like an interloper, I'm waiting for an alarm to sound; for someone to come and order me to leave at once. I go out by the front door and wander up to a bend in the drive, to the spot behind the hedge where I used to change into my 'streetwalker' outfits that Ma had forbidden me to wear. On the way back, I stop to admire Kenmara, strong and solid against the varying greens of beech, oak, pine and rhododendron, and I'm shocked to see how rundown the house has become since my father died. Paint is peeling on windowsills and on the front door; one of the cloakroom fanlights is cracked and a gutter hangs away from the wall. It's as though sadness is seeping through the seams of this building that was once a centre of family life in all its aspects, a building that for the past seven years has been home only to one lonely woman and her secrets.

I go over the story Ma told me yesterday evening. At first, it had felt as if I was listening to an account, told by a somewhat demented old woman. A story, half-invented, half-forgotten. But as she went on talking and the events she described in detail became more credible, I found myself interested in how they affected me; how they had affected Grace. Of course I felt sorry for Ma, and I was worried about her catching cold in the night air and being ill, or too tired to enjoy her party.

But not until this minute, sitting on the steps at the top of the garden, do I really begin to consider what it was must have been like for a naive seventeen-year-old girl to lose trace of the man she loved and to find herself pregnant in the harsh, moral climate of the 1940s.

I was nineteen when I became pregnant. Though the baby was unplanned, the prospect of giving birth to Liam's child thrilled me, together with the hope that she would bring her father and me together as we had been in the early months of our affair. Remembering my overwhelming love for Grania and the pain that tore at my heart when she died, I am overcome by raw compassion for Rita Daly. I grieve to think of her, alone and desolate on a platform at Euston Station, after learning that she had signed her baby over to her sister and her husband.

My poor mother, already burdened with the guilt of causing Daisy's death, she had no-one to turn to and had kept her daughter's birth hidden from everyone until yesterday evening. A life in which her past was shared with nobody must have been a dark and a lonely place. But those secrets had continued to echo and re-echo throughout her marriage and beyond. And they still affected the lives of those closest to her, especially Grace and me.

This morning on my way down to breakfast, I wondered how Ma and I would greet each other. There would be no hugging and kissing – we're not that sort of family – and no dissection of last night's confessions. Ma is astute. She must have been as nervous and unsure as I was. I remember too, my relief on hearing John's key in the lock.

I stand up and stroll round the garden. The apple tree my father planted for my tenth birthday hasn't been pruned for years, and branches that will be heavy with fruit are reaching for the sky.

Dandelions, daisies and clover bloom in the grassed-over patch where he used to grow most of the household vegetables. But the garden is nothing more than a backdrop for memories that come crowding thick and fast into my head – Ma's urgent plea for me to come to Kenmara before her birthday party. Visiting Anthony O'Brien's grave. There had been clues in conversations between Grace and me. At the time I had registered her desire to limit what Ma should be told about our time in Italy. As the pieces of the jigsaw begin to slot into position, the significance of her request becomes clear and I understand why I wasn't as surprised as I might have been, to discover that Grace is my half-sister.

John's Jaguar glides down the drive. I rush up to meet him and Ma. I open the door for Ma, kiss her lightly on both cheeks and admire her hairdo.

"Don't we have a beautiful mother, John?"

John agrees with me. He looks as embarrassed as I feel. Ma goes into the cloakroom to brush the straight-from-the-hairdresser look out of her hair and to admire the result. I help him carry a large box into the dining room.

"I'm sorry, John. I was out of line earlier," I say. "God knows, I'm the last person to comment on anybody's marriage."

"I was out of line too." He ruffles my hair, the way he used to. "Well out of line. We'll say no more about it and we'll all make sure Ma has a great party."

John always called me his wee sister and I loved him, especially when he used to ask Ma to let me spend a few hours with him and Rose. To civilise his rowdy sons, he'd say. He can't cope with me as a grown woman, challenging him, questioning him.

As we leave the dining room I say, "John, does anyone else in the family know about Grace?"

"Hugh does. He'd a right to know. You know Hugh. Nothing fazes him. He may have told Linda, but she'll keep it to herself."

"And Rose, what about Rose?"

"Rose has a big mouth. She'd have it all over the country before you could turn round. Look Isabel, it's time I got a move on."

He hurries past me, his face set in stone.

Minnie arrives as John leaves. She has made one of my favourite dishes for tonight's supper – ham marinated overnight in red Martini, coated with mustard and honey and baked at a low temperature until it's 'ready'. Minnie has a slight figure and a gentle face that hardly seems to have aged over the years. When I was small, I used to plait her hair and tell her I wished mine was snow-white like hers. I ask her about her three clever children and her seven grandchildren.

Then I say, "How's Ma been? Rose says she's a bit forgetful and very moody."

"Your mammy has her wee ways, Isabel. She always had. *You* know that. The trouble is, she's on her own too much. That's when she gets notions. Thinks everybody's got it in for her." Minnie fetches a bag of potatoes from the pantry and passes the peeler to me. She stands beside me at the sink, her chin cupped in her right hand. "She really misses your daddy. They didn't always get on. I don't have to tell you that, but he was always there." We both laugh when she adds, "Except when he wasn't. Typical man! You remember the way he'd take himself off, without a word to anybody?"

As I help Minnie peel potatoes and slice onions, she asks me how my holiday was. I tell her about Toni, whispering to her to say nothing to Ma, or to anyone in the family. I haven't spent a full day in Kenmara and I'm falling back into the old 'Best not let your Mammy know,' and 'Don't tell your Daddy/Rose/Linda,' routine.

This is where I grew up, a place of nods and winks and sidelong glances, where information is funnelled down cupped hands on street pavements, behind shelves in supermarkets, at wakes and in the muttering silence of churches. A place where secrets are revealed to a chosen few; where censored versions of the same secrets are drip-fed to others, where certain folk – and we all know who they are – must be kept in ignorance at all costs.

Ma and I sit in the back of the taxi taking us to City Airport. I squeeze her left hand when she shows me the park where she and her cousin used to take Daisy and to the spire of the church where she met Anthony O'Brien's mother. She tells me how the lower part of the Antrim Road near her father's pub had been razed during the Troubles of the early seventies. Though this is a journey I have travelled dozens and dozens of times, it is the first time I've made it with Ma, mother and daughter, at ease with each other and looking forward to meeting Grace and Simon.

216

We're surprised to see Johnny at the entrance to the airport, a more spruced-up version of the lad I met yesterday. Rose has asked him to take care of Simon for the rest of the day.

Grace embraces Ma and introduces Simon.

She holds out both hands to me. "Isabel, I've missed you." There's an unspoken acknowledgment of our new relationship in the pressure of her fingers on mine, in our ear-to-ear smiles.

Ma submits graciously to the embrace of her eldest grandson, who may, or may not know that he is her grandson. I watch her eyes flit from Simon who is blond, clean-shaven and wearing a smart, though casual shirt and jeans, to Johnny, in a sloppy, checked shirt and trousers that hang loose on his hips.

Simon and Johnny carry luggage to a taxi and say goodbye to Ma, Grace and me. Johnny promises to phone later in the evening.

In the mirror above the passenger seat of the taxi I see that Grace is holding Ma's hand, chatting, giving her an update on her family. Though I know how to be a friend and a lover, I have yet to learn the role of a daughter. I brush away a tinge of envy at Grace's long established relationship with my mother. I'm a fast learner and Ma and I have made a good start.

The afternoon passes in a flurry of callers. Last minute details are checked with the caterers, phone calls answered, guests added to and struck off the checklist. Hugh and Linda arrive with Una and their sons, Fergus, who is a mechanic, and Jack, a paramedic, who is still on duty and wearing his green uniform. They are fitting an extension for music to be relayed to the patio. Linda and Una decorate the hall, sitting-room and patio with balloons and streamers. Interflora brings bouquets for Ma, which Grace and I, under her supervision, arrange in vases. Rose arrives with the birthday cake. She explains that it is a light fruitcake, covered with real almond marzipan. She talks us through the two layers of royal icing, the pink hearts, rosebuds, gold *dragees* and the 'Happy Birthday Rita' written in gold letters. Ma thanks her for the trouble she has taken, says nobody makes a better Christmas cake than Rose and the icing is so perfect, it could have been shop-made.

"But Mrs McGlade, everything Rose does is always perfect. She's a perfectionist," Linda says, gazing with admiring eyes at the cake.

"Perfectionist? Hey, Linda, where d'you learn big words like that? Mind you don't get too clever, or I won't be smart enough for you."

Rose presses her fingers hard to her lips, as if trying to force back the tears welling in her eyes.

Grace rushes to gloss over Hugh's remark. "I can't wait to taste your beautiful cake, Rose. Now that I've retired, I'm enrolling in a cookery class in September."

Over tea and Minnie's butterfly buns, Grace and I give an edited version of our holiday, concentrating on the sunshine and scenery of the Adriatic and the sights of Rome. In reply to Rose's questions, we talk about Marilena and the Cellucci family and say how much at home we were at the Aragosta.

After supper, Ma says she's going to have an early night and goes upstairs. I suggest to Grace that we should sit on the patio and enjoy the long, northern evening where it is still light at half past ten.

"Good idea," Grace says. "I'll pop upstairs first and say goodnight to Rita. Are you coming?"

"You go on up. It must be ages since you and Ma spent time together."

The envy I felt in the taxi returns to rile me. I cannot enter Ma's bedroom, her ivory tower which had always been out of bounds to me, my father and my brothers. I don't have the confidence to go up by myself, or to tag along beside Grace. I start to text Toni, but there's no room for him among the grievances that swirl through my head, like clothes whirling round in a washing machine. I picture Ma and Grace chatting, laughing together and making plans for tomorrow. If my mother lives to be a hundred, I'll never feel like a daughter of the house. In the mirror above the fireplace, I catch sight of a woman's face, eyes slits of discontent, lips a thin scowl.

What's got into me? Last night my mother wore herself out baring her soul to me, and here I am, erecting barriers, imagining slights, needing to be a victim.

"You are a nasty, self-obsessed bitch," I tell the face in the mirror. It nods in agreement.

I hurry up to Ma's room and stand in the doorway.

"Isabel, come in, Isabel," Ma says.

I go to my mother and bury my face in the pillow beside her. As she strokes my hair I smell on her skin the sharp-sweet scent that used to warn me of her presence and the oily richness of her night cream. I lie beside her, while Grace describes Scerni, the scene of the battle in which Anthony O'Brien lost his life and his grave in the military cemetery. As soon as she starts to talk about our time in Rome, Ma says she must get her beauty sleep and asks us to leave. We go downstairs with the wordless agreement to tell Ma nothing more about the man she knew as Jemmy. As we sit on the patio, we reminisce about our stay in Abruzzo and the party on our last night at the Aragosta.

"How did you get on after I left Rome?" Grace leans forward, a smile stretched over her face.

"Well, Toni took me to Castel Gandolfo. It was great being out in the hills and it's a lovely spot. Oh, and I went to…"

"And Toni? How did you get on with him?"

"Toni's lovely. We got on really well together. We went to…"

Grace's smile can stretch no further. She bursts out laughing and I laugh with her. Then I say, "I'd been drifting aimlessly since Liam and I parted. After he died I felt rootless, with nothing to tie me to anybody or to any place. But during these past weeks I seem to have found my bearing, to know where I'm going." I stop speaking, at a loss how to continue. "I'm not explaining this very well."

Grace looks towards the Lough and says, "I know what you mean. I can understand you losing your bearings. For weeks after Andy died I felt as if I was groping in the dark. Having to look after the boys kept me grounded. And I had my parents." She turns to me and asks, "Do you remember Fred telling us that when he was in the desert and on the Sangro, he got his bearings by looking at the moon?" We both smile at the memory and Grace says, "Isabel, could Toni have anything to do with how you feel? You still haven't told me how you got on with him."

I don't tell her how beautiful our bodies are together. I don't tell her that I long to taste his mouth, to breathe the scent of his skin, to feel his long body stretched over me. I don't say that in the few, unfilled moments of these days at Kenmara, my thoughts are with him. Grace's expression tells me I don't need to.

Chapter Twenty Three

Kenmara

Three quarters of an hour before the guests are expected, Aisling and Una take Ma upstairs. There should have been a fanfare to herald her descent, flanked by her two granddaughters. Aisling and Una are lovely teenagers who are wearing bright, short-skirted dresses that show off cleavages any woman could envy. But the star of the day is their grandmother in a cerise dress, a matching jacket draped round her shoulders. With the confidence of an Oscar winner, she pauses on the half landing, bows and smiles to applause from her family and friends. Hugh whispers to me that she should have been on the stage. His son Jack says she thinks she's the Queen and somebody should have got her a crown. Grace and I are wearing outfits we bought in Rome which have been much admired. Linda, in a wide-skirted floral dress, would pass for thirty and Rose has abandoned her mumsy look for a slim-fitting suit in blue silk, chosen for her by Aisling. But Ma outshines us all. She has waited seventy-eight years for this moment and she is milking every second of it. An image of seventeen-year-old Rita at Euston Station flashes before my eyes and I dab them with a tissue.

No sooner has Ma made her entrance, welcomed everybody and ushered us all into the sitting room or the garden for champagne and *canapes,* than the caterers set up tables in the hall and lay out the buffet. I catch up with the latest news from my nieces and nephews and their partners and lap up compliments from Ma's friends, some accompanied by elderly husbands, others in brightly-coloured widowhood. All of Ma's bridge friends have survived, despite the needles I used to stick through the hearts of their plasticine effigies. A little bird-like woman, whose face is a pallid mask with a gash of scarlet lipstick, says I was a lovely wee girl, but awful quiet, and would you just look at me now. Another, who walks with the help of two sticks, says I'm gorgeous, and wasn't it awful me losing my husband and all, but it won't be long before I get another one.

Ma's friends are seated in the dining room and the younger guests eat in groups on the patio or in the summerhouse. Grace, Linda, Rose and I see that everyone is catered for while Ma circulates. With her Lady-of-the-Manor smile, she asks her guests to excuse her for five minutes. She's going to have a very brief conference with her family and explains that she doesn't know when they will all be together again.

John and Rose have been avoiding each other since they arrived separately. On occasions such as this, my elder brother enjoys taking control as the jovial head of the family. Today he hovers in the background, talking to Simon, overseeing events and signalling to waitresses when glasses need refilling. For someone with a new and probably much younger lover, he does not seem very happy. I wish I could break through the barrier he has put up between himself and the other members of the family. At a nod from Ma, he ushers Hugh, Linda, Rose, Grace and me into an east-facing room, which Ma calls the morning room. It is now used mainly for storage. John tells us she has several announcements to make.

We are seated round a small table, John on Ma's right, Grace on her left. She takes Grace's hand.

In a faltering voice, she says, "I...I thought this would be as good a day as any... to tell you all that Grace is not my niece. She is my daughter."

Her eyes travel over each of us, weighing up the effect of her revelation. Rose's mouth hangs ajar. Linda studies her white-edged nails. Hugh fidgets in a let's-get-on-with-it sort of way. I stare at a pile of boxes behind Linda's head. Out of the corner of my eye, I see that Grace and John are looking intently at Ma whose hands are trembling. We strain to hear the words she spells out.

"I was seventeen when Grace was born. It was 1943 and I wasn't married." Gone is the confident woman who posed on the stairs a few hours previously. Eyes downcast, she swallows hard and clutches at Grace's hand before continuing. "My sister Kate and her husband adopted my baby when she was four days old... They said it was for the best." She tries to speak, but no words come. She leans against Grace, who puts an arm around her shoulders.

John pats Ma's back gently, stands up and says, "Isabel, Hugh and I have known Grace all our lives as our cousin, and a much loved and valued member of our family."

What has made John change his tune since yesterday? Is he putting on an act for Ma's sake or has she promised to leave Grace very little in her will? I'm still wondering when he adds, "It's only a short step for us to know her as our sister, our big sister, and to welcome her into the McGlade family."

Rose's mouth slams shut. We bring our hands together in muffled applause and mutter our agreement. I can tell from her face that it will be a much longer step for Rose.

John gestures for silence. "Our mother has asked me to tell you that Grace has, on her own behalf and on behalf of her sons, waived all rights to her estate. She insisted on doing this in writing." He shows us a piece of paper.

Grace says, "My parents, your Aunt Kate and Uncle Harry, left me and my sons well provided for. We have no need and no wish to share in Rita's estate."

John bows in acknowledgment and asks Ma if she would like him to continue.

She shakes her head from side to side, composes herself and says, "My will is with Peter Kavanagh. I've decided to leave Kenmara to Hugh and Linda because I'd like the house to remain for as long as possible in the McGlade name." Linda gasps. Her hand shoots to her mouth. Hugh, as if he has misheard, wrinkles his brow and exchanges puzzled glances with her. Waves of hurt and astonishment sweep over Rose. John betrays no hint of his feelings. Ma must have discussed her will with him when he took her to the hairdresser's. "I think their children are more likely to stay in Ireland than John's."

Ma puts on her reading glasses and continues, speaking from notes, "I value both my sons equally. Thanks to their own hard work, John and Rose already have a large, family home. I'm telling you this now, so there will be no disputes when I'm dead and gone. The rest of my estate will be divided between my sons, their wives and my daughter, Isabel, taking into account that Hugh and Linda will have inherited Kenmara." She peers at each of us over her glasses. "I wish especially to thank Rose for her kindness and her tolerance over many years – and God knows how often I tested her tolerance. My gratitude will be reflected in the share of my estate which she and John will receive jointly." She turns to Rose. "I hope you will forgive me my nastiness and be certain that I value you for all your qualities and appreciate you not only as my daughter-in-law but as my friend."

Having delivered her bombshell to a silenced audience, Ma fixes each one of us with a stare that dares anyone to challenge her. She glances at her gold watch and says it is time to return to her guests. She takes a compact from her cerise clutch bag, powders her face, pats her hair and makes her exit, serene as a swan gliding over a lake.

Simon has caught the first plane to London and Grace has decided to stay for a week at Kenmara. Ma looks as if she could sleep for a week. She says she will spend the afternoon in bed while Grace goes shopping with Rose. She is delighted with the success of her party, where music played and many of her guests stayed till nearly midnight. Over breakfast and umpteen post-breakfast cups of tea, we analyse the evening. Who wore what, who was the chap with Aisling, was that Johnny's girlfriend, the one with the English accent and four-inch heels? Which of Ma's chums has aged out of all recognition, and doesn't Ma look miles better than any of them? And that the man in the evening suit, who sang *My Lagan Love* and *The Green Hills of Antrim* to Ma, didn't he have the voice of Pavarotti? And the figure?

Grace and I say that Rose's new image takes years off her and we agree with Ma that John was a first class Master of Ceremonies. Not a word is spoken about their marital problems.

Last night after all the guests had left, I walked with John to his car.

"Come and stay with me in London if you need a break, John. Any time, for as long as you like." I talk over his interruption. "You've done so much for me over the years. Please let me do something for you for a change. Please."

"Thanks, I might just take up your offer. Besides, I haven't had a chance to talk to you with all the commotion here." He puts his arms round me. I hold him tight. "Isabel, you're not my wee sister any more. You've grown up."

John was the rock of the family, the person we all admired and looked up to. I'd never known him vulnerable or insecure.

"It was time I did."

He holds me at arm's length. "Take good care of yourself and I'll see you soon."

He starts up his car, lowers the window and waves goodbye.

A taxi arrives to take me to the airport. Each previous leave-taking was a rollercoaster of relief, guilt and regret for what might have been. And sadness at leaving my home and my father, wondering how would he cope without me as a buffer between him and Ma, would he survive until my next visit?

Ma has shed her society hostess guise. She stands by the taxi, an elderly and exhausted woman. She is not dishevelled. My mother would rise from her deathbed to adjust her hair, apply a discreet amount of make-up and put on a high-necked, freshly laundered-nightdress. Today she relaxes in a Paisley dress she has had for many years and flat sandals. Despite the shadows under her eyes and the weariness in her every step, she seems at ease with herself. When I hug her and promise to come back soon, there are no nameless, but almost tangible, obstacles to be avoided. And there is no resistance in the thin body I hold against me.

"You say that every time you leave and I see neither hilt nor hair of you for years."

That's my mother! I take her hands in mine.

"I know that, Mamma. This time I really mean it. I do."

I carry in my mind the picture of her and Grace waving until the taxi turns a bend in the drive and goes along familiar streets, past the Riverside Theatre, past the twin cranes, Sampson and Goliath, and over the estuary to the airport.

How much time will Ma and I have to make up for the years we have wasted? I will come back soon to Kenmara. Weekends will be long enough to start with. I will take her to Belfast Castle for lunch and afterwards we will walk along part of the Blackhead path towards the lighthouse at Whitehead; the path she walked with Jemmy. From rocks close to the shore, grey seals will size us up and gulls will squack and swoop around us. We will look across the Irish Sea to Aran and the Mull of Kintyre and we will stop at the Old Quarry where the peregrine falcon is said to nest. Ma will search for the place where Jemmy made love to her the last time they were together. Neither of us will speak, but I will know when she has found it.

She and I will not unlearn overnight the habits and hurts that were part of our life together. When, and if, we have become comfortable

224

in each other's presence, she will stay with me in London. From the window of a Tour Bus, she will see the sights of the city. Along the Thames I will point out the Houses of Parliament, the Tower of London and Tower Bridge. She may well tell me that she is not blind and knows from films and the television what London looks like. Neither of us will mention the times she passed through London to give birth to her baby and returned without her.

Grace and I have very different histories with our mother. Grace, the much-grieved-for daughter of her girlhood, who was taken from her. And me, Isabel, the unwanted infant inflicted on her when she thought her child-bearing days were long over. Maybe one day, Grace and I will take her to Jemmy's grave at the Sangro, and to the hillside village of Scerni, where we will sift and censor how much she needs to know about his time in Italy. We will go in early spring before the green hills and the rich countryside of Abruzzo are scorched by the summer heat. In my dream, the three of us will stay in my little house, rebuilt on a lawn in the middle of an olive grove, somewhere between the foothills of the Apennines and a quiet bay on the Adriatic.

A text from Toni as I am about to board the plane. He's coming to Birmingham for a three-day health and safety conference. Can he stay with me next weekend, if I'm free? And maybe on Tuesday night?

"Yes, yes," I text. "Stay as long as you can. Can't wait. Will ring from London. Love Isabel."

Liam used to say I could be quite clever if I learned to concentrate, but I flitted like a butterfly from one topic to another. I sit back, planning meals and outings. Dreaming about nights with him in my double bed. How well does Toni know London? Has he been to Canary Wharf? To Greenwich? During my action packed time in Kenmara he had become a figure seen through the wrong end of a telescope. Now he is back with me again as he was in Vieste, on the beach near the Aragosta and in his Spartan apartment in Rome, our bodies drinking in the summer heat. I see myself after showering, wrapped in his dressing gown, on a rug beside the sofa. I lean back into the cradle of his knees while his fingers make patterns in my wet hair.

But Toni is not just someone I hope to spend my life with. He is Anthony O'Brien's grandson. In this age of finding out about our ancestors, doesn't he have a right to know of the direct link between Anthony and my mother? Though the past is often edited and rewritten, it does not change and Anthony O'Brien cannot be air-brushed away like some out-of-favour character from history. I remind myself that Toni lives in the twenty-first century. His eyes are fixed on a future in the United States, not on events that occurred over sixty years ago.

Though my mother succeeded in shutting off her past from the rest of the world, she had never escaped it and lived under the long shadow it cast. Consumption had left a shadow on her lung and stolen eighteen months of her girlhood. I pray that no other shadow will dim her newfound peace and serenity.

As we approach Gatwick, I ask myself who owns the past. Is it the person who lived it, or those whose lives have been darkened by the same shadow? I am not sure of the answer. I go over the events of Friday evening when my mother revealed to me secrets she had guarded since her childhood and I know for certain that for as long as she lives, I will respect those confidences and share them with no one. Not even with Toni.

~ End ~

226

Also by Monica Tracey...

**_Don't you think lack of forgiveness
is what's wrong with this country?_**

Here, forgiveness and how to deal with enormously powerful
tragedies from the past, is expressed explicitly for the first
time. – _Jill Dawson, Myslexia_

Novel on Ulster life tipped for the top

_...received rave reviews on C4's
Richard & Judy Show.
...unforgettable characters and a
shattering tragedy...beautifully
written and filled with a gentle
humour._
   - _Grania Mc Fadden,
      Belfast Telegraph_

Very funny and moving ... a distinctive voice
   - _Hilary Mantel_

As **Unweaving The Thread** progresses, Mary Ann's childhood
and adolescence are brought vividly to life. Idyllic summers in
Donegal with her father's relatives, a wartime exile to her
mother's homestead in Co Monaghan, complete with crude
sexual assault by a casual farm labourer.

Memories constantly bubble to the surface. Did her maternal
grandmother really commit murder? And if she did, is it
possible to commit murder in a good cause?
   - _Irish Times_

More fiction from Circaidy Gregory Press...

Small Poisons

Catherine Edmunds

A contemporary novel for Midsummer Night's Dreamers

With charm, wit and magical style
Catherine Edmunds conjures a
fairy tale for grown ups, in a place
where dreams and stark reality
meet.

- Neil Marr, BeWrite Books

Small Poisons by Catherine Edmunds UK £9.50
Pub Circaidy Gregory Press ISBN 978 1 906451 16 5

Charity's Child

Rosalie Warren

Dark deed or virgin birth?

Who is the father of Charity's Child? 16-year-old Charity Baker has her own crazy ideas but even her loyal friend Joanne finds them hard to believe.

As the story reaches its disturbing climax, darkness is revealed in unexpected places and we learn with Joanne that many things in Charity's life are not as they seem.

This powerful tale of teenage sexuality, religious fanaticism, self-harm and other highly topical issues has proved a popular reading group choice, shedding a much-needed light on the experience of the younger generation in modern Britain.

Charity's Child by Rosalie Warren UK £9.50
Pub Circaidy Gregory Press ISBN 978 1 906451 07 3